A FATAL BRAGG

AN IAN BRAGG THRILLER: BOOK 4

CRAIG MARTELLE

CRAIG MARTELLE SOCIAL

Website & Newsletter: https://craigmartelle.com
Facebook:
https://www.facebook.com/AuthorCraigMartelle/
Amazon:
https://www.amazon.com/Craig-Martelle/e/B01AQVF3ZY

Ian Bragg 1—The Operator
Ian Bragg 2—A Clean Kill
Ian Bragg 3—The Replacement
Ian Bragg 4—A Fatal Bragg

This book is a work of fiction.
All of the characters, organizations, and events portrayed in this novel are either products of the author's imagination or are used fictitiously. Sometimes both.

A Fatal Bragg and *Ian Bragg Thrillers* (and what happens within / characters / situations / worlds) are Copyright © 2021 by Craig Martelle

All rights reserved. No part of this publication may be reproduced, stored in a retrieval system, or transmitted in any form or by any means, electronic, mechanical, recording or otherwise, without the prior written permission of Craig Martelle

Version 1.0

Cover by Stuart Bache
Editing by Lynne Stiegler

Published by Craig Martelle, Inc
PO Box 10235, Fairbanks, AK 99710
United States of America

To those who support any author by buying and reading their books, I salute you. I couldn't keep telling these stories if it weren't for you and for the support team surrounding me. No one works alone in this business.

The Ian Bragg Thrillers team Includes

BETA / EDITOR BOOK

Beta Readers and Proofreaders - with my deepest gratitude!
Micky Cocker
James Caplan
Kelly O'Donnell
John Ashmore
Chris Abernathy

CHAPTER ONE

"Nobody was born a master; amateurs become experts because they did not give up on learning." –Israelmore Ayivor

The fog of a cool morning floated across the Potomac toward the Jefferson Memorial. I wrapped an arm around Jenny's shoulders. She nestled her head into the crook of my neck. We were nothing more than lovers enjoying a morning before the rush of people and traffic.

Into the cesspool of humanity that was Washington, DC.

Maybe that was changing. For the first time in my life, I worked *with* politicians and not at their whim. Damn Jimmy Tripplethorn. A good politician.

It was inconceivable until it wasn't. Then he became the apple of the party's eye. Now he was the vice president.

I didn't kill him when I had the contract. I ended up taking out three others instead—the one who paid for my time and the two who tried to cover it up. It was also where I met Jenny. She became embroiled in my complicated life of invisibility and secrets. She's been with me ever since. I wouldn't have it any other way.

"We'll need to hit the gym when we get out of here. I'm feeling weak," I said.

"Weakness is only in one's mind," she replied without looking at me. "Tough it up, Marine."

"I knew I married you for a reason. We are not skipping leg day."

"We never skip leg day or any day except when we're on a contract."

A contract to terminate a target. I'm an operator. I kill people for money, and Jenny is my partner. She's the contract acquisitions manager because we aren't just operators, we run the Peace Archive, our organization. We did a quarter of a billion dollars in business last year because Jenny is a shrewd negotiator.

For those who want their neighbor to disappear, it's going to cost them, but it also has to matter. We have to live with ourselves afterward.

That means we only kill bad people, those who the world is better without. That's my role in the business. I call myself the ethical compliance officer. I can give myself whatever title I want. It's good to be in charge.

Until we're working for a client like the United States government. That work was off the books, and Jimmy had a tendency to request that I do his jobs myself.

I wished he wouldn't do that, but there was no reasoning with the vice president. I liked our big house in Chicago on the golf course, with the Club a short golf cart ride away. We owned the Club because it was important to have a legitimate business. That was how all criminals worked, but then again, we don't see ourselves as criminals. We provide justice when the system is destined to fail.

Rich people avoided jail, no matter how bad their

crimes were. We rectified that shortcoming in the legal system.

"What do you think Jimmy has for us this time?" I wondered.

Jenny raised her head and pointed with her chin at a black SUV with darkened windows. "We'll find out soon enough."

The vehicle stopped in front of us. An arm reached out the passenger side window and stabbed a thumb toward the back door.

"You guys used to hold the door for us," I joked. "Where did our relationship go wrong? I'm calling my mother!"

Jenny chuckled and climbed in first. I followed and shut the door. The vehicle smelled new. They always did. I wondered why when the government was always running out of money. No need to buy a new fleet every year. Then again, it was a way to satisfy corporate donors. Pay them back for their support.

Using other people's money, and here I was, taking that same money.

I reasoned that it was cheaper than a trial, and I wasn't a contributor. I never donated money to politicians or political parties. That grated on my soul. We sent lots of money to animal shelters because we could. Also, politicians were out of bounds for contracts. I didn't want to get involved in any of that or have any of my people mixed up in politics gone bad.

"You guys catch yesterday's game?" I asked the two men up front, wearing dark suits and sunglasses. I had no idea if there was a game. I always tried to get them to talk. It was part of the other game, a deadly game where the losers died at the hands of those who had more information. Those who had found the leverage points.

They didn't reply. They rarely did. Must have been on the Secret Service job application that a sense of humor wouldn't be tolerated. Or maybe it was just us. They didn't like watching Jenny and me make out in the back seat of their ride.

"Where are we going?" Jenny asked when they drove past the Lincoln Memorial and turned toward the Roosevelt Bridge.

Once again, they didn't answer.

"Hearing aids not turned on?" I quipped, but they weren't biting. I leaned back and ground my teeth. I hated working for the government. I was okay working for Jimmy Tripplethorn, which created a certain irony. He also paid double our usual fee, which took the edge off any unease I may have felt.

And it was tax-free since we only accepted payments through our bank in the Caymans.

The government-special SUV pulled over at a Starbucks.

"Get out," the driver said.

"You strike me as an unhappy person. You probably shouldn't say anything at all." We stepped out and slammed the door. The Escalade sped off.

"I'm about ready to walk." I wasn't happy.

"This is not the usual, and I don't like it," Jenny agreed.

We both took half of what was before us to do a risk assessment. They had dropped us off at that point for a reason. We had to figure it out.

"Ten o'clock. A single man in a sports coat with executive gray at his temples." He had not taken his eyes off us from the second I spotted him. I turned and gave Jenny a long hug.

She looked over my shoulder to give our voyeur a chance to stop watching.

"Coming this way," Jenny said. I let go, and we faced him together.

Quick assessment. No bulges. Dad bod. He was an

executive type, not a front-line guy. He also wasn't the vice president.

"I was told to meet a couple from Seattle," he said when he was still ten feet away. "Is that you?"

I didn't smile. We hadn't been told any of this. Surprises in our line of work were never a good thing.

"We're from Seattle. What else were you told?"

He looked around before leaning close. "That the coffee here is exceptional because they get the new bean deliveries before anyone else."

"We're not interested in coffee," I replied.

"I'm buying," the man replied. I had thought he was taller when he approached, but he was about an inch shorter than me. Maybe it was the age and the extra few pounds. He had probably been in shape once, before middle age and a desk job did him in.

"Not interested."

Jenny took a step back.

"Wait, please. My name is Rick Banik, and I'm head of an anti-terrorism tiger team. We have a unique problem, and I was told that you would be able to provide a unique solution. I was sent here by the DCI. How about you stop playing coy and join me for a steaming-hot cup of java?"

I cooled at the name-dropping approach. DCI. Director of Central Intelligence. I'd hated those guys when I did my time in the Sandbox. They showed up looking like agents, never blended in, and created chaos for those left to clean up their messes. They didn't seem to answer to anyone.

But they were the CIA, not the FBI. That meant the target was international and not domestic. The Peace Archive was not yet equipped for international missions, but soon. That was in our growth strategy. Jenny and I would discuss it at the next board meeting.

It would only be us there, but it sounded official. It was

the least we could do for a company with gross revenue of nine figures a year.

"We're listening if you're still buying, but don't ask us any questions. You don't have the clearance for the answers," I said, figuring it would get under his skin.

"I have clearance for everything," Rick replied.

It worked like a charm. He was a bureaucrat. My dislike for him was growing by the second.

"What did they tell you my clearance was?"

"They didn't, but I was told to share everything related to Project Rose Petal. I'll need you to sign these forms first, so you can be read into the program."

I laughed out loud before reining it in. Rick wasn't smiling. "You're serious? It's been nice, Mr. Banik, but you can kiss my ass."

He stuffed his forms back into the inside pocket of his sport coat while chuckling. "I've been doing this too long. Look what I've become. I'm a total dork. *Here. Sign this form.* I can't even hear the stupid come out of my mouth anymore. You don't need to sign anything. You don't need to tell me anything. I'm supposed to tell you. Will you stay for that? And I'm jonesing for a java. If you don't want one, that's on you, but I'm getting one. In the Marines, I would have never let a form stand in the way of my next cuppa."

"You did your time?" He piqued my curiosity. We followed him into line.

"A long time ago. The Sandbox."

"Not so long ago. The Sandbox." I held out my hand, and he took it. "You've been skipping the gym."

"You haven't," he replied. "I didn't get your name."

"I might tell you later. Remember? You don't have the clearance."

"You were a grunt, weren't you?"

"That's a leap. I'm a corporate executive." I waited. He raised an eyebrow. "How'd you know?"

"Clearances. There are only three: confidential, secret, and top secret. That's it. But there are a million different accesses. You get read into and out of programs. Generally, we tell our fellow intel weenies that they don't have the need to know, not that they don't have clearance."

"Have you taken one of those lie detector tests?" I wondered. Jenny watched us, observing Rick Banik from a third-party perspective. She watched for a weakness we could leverage if we needed to. She watched for subterfuge. We had to maintain a certain level of paranoia. This meeting was already beyond the typical ones that happened in the Club in an electronically protected booth to prevent the recording or transmission of the conversations.

"I have. They suck. But you have to be a total clown not to pass one or an unprofessional liar. Pathological liars tend to pass with flying colors."

"An unprofessional liar puts their job at risk by only lying on weekdays and not all the time. They really need to up their game if they want to continue suckling at the government teat."

"You really don't like the government, do you?"

"Bureaucrats. Weenies. Butt-smackers. Ne'er-do-wells. And all of them with a modicum of power because they walk the halls of power. They give me the willies, Mr. Banik. I despise every fiber of their being."

"For not telling me anything, you're telling me everything. Maybe you should have stuck to land wars in Asia," Rick quipped. He gripped my shoulder like an old friend. I stared at his hand until he moved it.

"In my mind, you're still one of them. You have the time it takes me to choke down my venti café mocha to convince me otherwise."

Our turn came. Rick ordered his Pikes Peak, and I stood aside for Jenny to order. Rick stuck a silver credit card with nothing showing into the machine and waited. An expense account. Maybe he *was* somebody.

"I'd like a small dark roast, please." I wondered why she held back. I'd ask later if I remembered. Our contact, although not the vice president, was starting to be interesting. The cashier wrote our names. Rick, Ian, and Jenny. I had to throw the guy a bone.

When we received our cups, I looked at mine. "They spelled Ian wrong. It's with an E and an O."

Rick rolled his eyes, dumped half and half into his cup until it licked the rim, and replaced the lid. He wiped the side of his cup, then ran the napkin over the counter's surface before tossing it.

We took a table in the corner, one of the few with three chairs. The traffic was loud outside, even though it wasn't heavy. The noise echoed between the buildings. How anyone could work in this environment their entire lives without going crazy befuddled me.

Then again, maybe they were mad to work there in the first place. Sane folk need not apply.

I took a sip and waited.

"You two look like a power couple," Rick said. We didn't answer. We knew we didn't just look like one; we *were* a power couple. Banik didn't need to know that. "Fine. Operation Rose Petal. There is a terrorist financier operating out of the United States but funding terrorism abroad. American money going straight to the bad guys."

"If you know this, what do you need us for?"

"We don't have proof, even though we know it's him."

"Plant the evidence and move on."

"Don't get me wrong. I would do that because it is the right thing to do, but he moves in the kind of circles where there would be too many questions that we wouldn't want to answer."

"You're the government. It's your business to not answer questions."

"Showing your hatred of bureaucrats again, Ian. May I call you Ian? I feel like this won't be our last meeting."

"I feel like it is if you don't get to the point pretty soon."

"We need Maksim Odenkirk to disappear and in a way where any of his powerful friends won't ask questions. And this is why the DCI arranged for us to meet."

"Mr. Odenkirk. Is that his real name?"

"Astute. The name he used to immigrate to America was Abayev, but his parents divorced, and his mother remarried. His formative years were spent in New York City. That's where he lives—off Wall Street in the lap of luxury, riding a seat of power."

"How do you think we're going to help you with this problem?" I asked, wondering what he'd been told.

He leaned close. "You are a strike team for active sanctions within the US but outside of the government. A contractor that no one has ever heard of or would ever admit to knowing."

"If you think I'm going to admit to any of that, you're smoking crack."

"I don't need you to admit anything except that puts us at an impasse. If you can help us, I need a figure to take to my boss. If you can't, I wish you well for the rest of your day."

"Eight," Jenny said softly.

"Eight what?"

"Million dollars," she mouthed without saying.

"That's a big number. I was thinking more like a mil. Are prices that high nowadays?"

I rubbed my temples in a sign of waning patience, but the government lackey's naïveté was refreshing.

"The nice lady told you the number."

"I don't know what to do with it since I don't want to

insult my boss."

I removed the untraceable satellite phone from my pocket and dialed a number from memory since the phone wiped all numbers. It was a special piece of technology built for the exclusive use of Peace Archive executives.

The line was picked up almost immediately. "Jimmy, it's Ian. I'm here with Rick Banik. Can we deal with him?"

"Yes. Put him on."

I handed the phone over. "It's the vice president."

Rick looked at me sideways but put the phone to his ear. "Mr. Vice President?"

"Agree to his terms, give him the details, and let him resolve your problem." The voice was unmistakable.

"Is he that good?" Rick asked before remembering who he was talking to.

"Yes. Put Ian back on." Rick returned the clunky phone to me. "I'll miss you this time around, but when this is over, Trish and I will have you and Jenny up to the house for a quiet and private dinner."

"We look forward to it. Thank you, Jimmy. See you on the flip side." I looked at Jenny and whispered, "We need to fulfill this contract if we want dinner with Jimmy and Trish. I don't trust his steaks, so maybe we can ask for gourmet burgers?"

Jenny smiled at me. That always made me feel good. We'd been together for less than two years but hadn't missed a day since we'd eloped. We had been running for our lives, but getting married made sense at the time in order to change our names. I became Mr. Lawless, taking Jenny's maiden name until we took care of those chasing us. Then she took my name. We had identification for both. All of it legitimate, Nevada state government-issued.

Banik cleared his throat. When we turned back to him, he started talking. "I guess we agree to eight mil." Rick produced a thumb drive from within his sleeve.

Jenny and I looked at it skeptically. "Is there a Rush song that might apply in this situation?" she asked.

I didn't need to think about it. "*Vital Signs*, of course."

Rick nodded. "Obscure. I would have to agree."

"You're a believer?" I asked.

"I may feel like a lesser human at times, but I assure you that I'm not. Yes. I can't get enough of Rush, ever."

Once again, I shook Rick's hand. "My name is Ian Bragg, and this is my wife Jenny. We will resolve your problem with Mr. Odenkirk. Do not force us into a constrained timeline as these types of targets are less than congenial when it comes to failing in their personal security." I leaned toward Miss Jenny. "Now would have been a great time to employ Jack Palance's unique talents."

"Jack Palance?" Rick looked confused.

"A female operator with an allure that gave her access to powerful men."

"That sounds right up Max's alley."

"She's not with us anymore," I evaded.

"Did you have to fire her or something? How does that even work? Sorry, you can't kill people anymore. Don't go away mad, just go away?"

"What are you talking about? No one said anything about killing people. We solve *problems*." I took the thumb drive and tucked it into the front pocket of my pants, where I'd keep my hand on it.

"I'm sorry, that's what I meant. You can't get her back?"

"No. Necromancy isn't one of my skills." I finished my mocha. It was time to go.

"I understand. How do I get in touch with you for status reports?"

"Bureaucrats gotta bureaucrat. The answer is, you don't. If you need to get in touch with me, ask the vice president for a favor. He knows how."

"I'm not going to ask the vice president to call you on my behalf."

"You *do* understand. Give me a card with your personal cell. I'll call you if I have any issues or need information that you might be uniquely suited in getting for me."

"I'm not going to access classified databases to give you information without any controls."

"Bureaucrats gotta bureaucrat."

Jenny wrote a series of numbers on a Starbucks napkin. "Put the money in this account. Half up front. Half upon completion. We'll start when we see you've paid. Until then, it's been nice meeting you." She held her hand out and shook his with a firm grip. I was proud to see Rick's fingers turn white.

"Like I surmised. A power couple." Rick looked at his hand as if it had betrayed him.

"If this memory stick has a virus or tracking software or anything besides data, I'll drop a contract on you, Mr. Banik, and use the money you just paid me to have an operator ruin your day."

"I don't respond well to threats, Mr. Bragg," Rick replied.

"Once again, we understand each other. We need our complete freedom to do what we do. Can't have bureaucrats trying to get into our business. We will continue to fly below the radar. And I know you're going to return to your office and start building a dossier on us. I ask that you not do that so the vice president's office doesn't have to come down on you like a ton of bricks. I don't need that information on any server. As far as the world knows, Ian and Jenny Bragg are owners of the Club, an exclusive establishment with an attached golf course in the high rent district of North Chicago. That is what you'll find out. Do not speculate. Do not try to read between the lines. Do not torpedo our working relationship. This could be extremely beneficial for both of us."

"It doesn't surprise me that the senior level of the government has—what did you call them?—*operators* on call, but I thought they'd be ex-Special Forces without a wife in tow."

"Don't those guys stick out? Like the knothead agents who dropped us off. If you're an intelligence analyst, you know the deal. Who can you never find? The one who hides in plain sight."

"Funny you mention that. I did find a terrorist who was hiding in plain sight right here in DC. It was a close one. Once this is over, maybe we can have a real chat about how the real world works over some barbecue. I may not be a pro, but it gives me a chance to build a fire and drink a beer. I think you might be more like me than you know."

"You ever break the law, Mr. Banik?"

"Not that I'll ever admit to, Mr. Bragg." Rick stood, nodded, and walked out, tossing his empty cup in the garbage on the way.

I kissed Jenny on the cheek. "Where'd you come up with that number?"

"Rectal defilade," she replied, using my term for pulling something out of one's butt. "We've never had a contract for that much. The way he talked around it, I suspect this won't be easy. We'll need all the resources we can muster."

"Which means we need to call the eastern director and see if someone is available in the Big Apple."

We looked for the signs to the metro station and found it was nearby. We used our WMATA passes to hop onto the train headed into the city, where we would get off at the Smithsonian and walk. It was a nice spring day. The cherry blossoms had not yet arrived, so we were ahead of the festival crowds. But not for long.

We needed to leave DC as soon as possible.

CHAPTER TWO

"It's going to be hard, but hard does not mean impossible."
–Chuck Palahniuk

Toulon, France was a majestic port city, a vacationer's paradise, and a bustling urban center supporting the headquarters of numerous major corporations.

The convoy of buses left the port where Wasp-class amphibious assault ship LHD-3 *Kearsarge* had docked. A flat top, a Navy helicopter carrier with a well-deck that could submerge to launch and recover landing craft. With seventeen hundred Marines embarked, it was a single-ship solution to a landing operation, providing maximum flexibility when the United States needed to project power overseas.

The joint US-France exercise was taking place inland, designed for light infantry—Marines without their vehicles. It would be a different exercise, but good training. Sometimes the front lines relied on their lift assets when they shouldn't have. Vehicles broke down at inopportune times, often leaving Marines on foot.

They were going to run through a three-day exercise, carrying everything they needed. Their packs with seventy pounds of gear were stored in the luggage compartments under the bus. All weapons were in the vehicle with the Marines.

At least they didn't have ammunition. Blanks and exercise explosives would be issued at the training site.

The Marines stared out the windows, taking in this small slice of France. For many, it was their first time in-country. They tried to read the French signs while looking for the supermodels they expected to see on every street corner.

In the internet age, the younger Marines had a misplaced sense of reality.

The buses twisted through narrow city streets on their way north to a mountainous area leased for Exercise *Forêt Alpine*—Alpine Forest.

The company commander sat in the front with the first sergeant, looking at the GPS to get their bearings.

"Doesn't look like rain. We could use the rain to do this right," the first sergeant quipped.

"It'll suck plenty without trying to make it suck more. Are the corpsmen ready with splints? I bet you a steak tartare dinner that we break two limbs and twist five ankles during this," the newly promoted captain replied.

"I hope not. Once they walk in, they have to walk out." A sharp turn ahead signaled the move to a road that left the small homes behind. The first bus scraped tree branches on either side of the road while the wheels rode the outer edges of the pavement. "Good driver."

From the side of the road, a puff of smoke sent an object upward. Other puffs followed. When the first dark ball reached window-level, a rocket motor ignited, trailing a fountain of flame and sending the device crashing through the window. The others followed, exploding within to shred metal and blow out the windows on the three remaining sides of the bus. Black smoke billowed skyward as the bus ground to a halt.

The captain jumped up and screamed at his Marines. "GET DOWN!" an instant before six devices shattered the windows and blasted the inside of his bus with explosions so violent they launched him through the front window.

The plane landed at John F. Kennedy international airport with a gentle bump and quickly taxied to a spot beyond the terminal where they waited for a plane to clear before pulling in. Jenny and I waited in our business class seats, ready to be the first ones off the plane.

I hated waiting, and there was never any need. We had the money to be first in line for everything. The Peace Archive issued its senior people a gold card not unlike Banik's silver card, except it had an unlimited credit line and no identifying criteria. It showed as an overseas company with no ties to anything.

Nondescript, and any trace would hit a roadblock at the bank in the Caymans.

"We're spoiled," Jenny said.

We always flew the best class we could get. We'd grown accustomed to it, even opting for different flights if first class wasn't available on our first choice. "I don't know how to respond to that because it's true."

The plane nudged forward, and the engines spun down. We grabbed our small carry-ons and prepared to bolt. We'd opted not to get a rental car since parking in the City was painful on the best of days, plus driving in the City was painful.

For me, everything about being in big cities was painful, but they were the places we worked most often.

"You should see the look on your face," Jenny said as we walked hand in hand, following the signs to Baggage Claim. "It's like you ate a sourball."

"It's just…big cities. Taxi is for the best. I'm not up for driving in this place."

"I might be."

I slowed. I always drove except when we were power-driving over a long distance or I was injured. After the snake bite, Jenny had driven us from Tucson to Vegas, but that had been a lifetime ago. We lived in the 'burbs of Chicago, where the worst threat was getting hit by a stray golf ball.

"Do you want to drive?" I asked, positive I should have asked earlier.

"Of course not. What idiot tourist drives in a big city?"

"Indeed, my love. Maybe we can rent a thirty-foot motorhome and head downtown." She had put me on notice without challenging my miscue.

"We could be *those* people." The mood lightened. We had a great deal of preparation to do before attempting anything. Straight to the Loneham on Fifth Avenue.

We checked in to find our suite was not yet available. We checked our bags with the concierge. I dropped him a twenty-dollar bill just because. I had no idea what tips were in this part of town, but in the land of the big spenders, one didn't want to stand out by not tossing cash around for personal well-being.

Hiding in plain sight by being flashy. It didn't make sense, but it did. We were the nice couple, always with a kind word for the staff. Because we were. We also were there to kill a man, but that wouldn't affect them.

It never did.

"The concrete jungle." We took in our surroundings. It had been hard to realize the full magnitude during the cab ride, which had been like driving through a tunnel of lights and people. The crowds morphed from a mass of humanity to individuals, from tourists to business professionals to a mob waiting for a light.

We looked for a place to eat an early dinner. I held Jenny's hand and kept the other on my custom phone. Jenny had the thumb drive in her pocket with her fingers clasped tightly around it.

The two things we wouldn't let out of our sight. Every other thing we owned was replaceable.

We bought a new laptop every few months and never stored any research thereon. It meant memorized websites and passwords. It meant downloading new software every three months. It was about taking care of our personal security and not leaving a footprint for an investigator to follow. We had to stay low-profile while working a high-profile job.

We turned down a side street toward Korea Town. Three steps later, two young men with their hoods pulled up rushed at us from an alcove. Jenny was on their side because I always walked with the street between her and me.

She dropped my hand and jumped backward, twisting as she went to land on the balls of her feet and face this new threat. He didn't take the hint, thinking he was bigger.

And she was a woman. He reached for her purse, which only contained a private cell phone, a wallet with cash, and a replaceable ID card. But there was no sense handing it over.

She blocked the arm reaching for her purse, trapped it, and twisted it sideways. She pushed him onto his heels and followed with an elbow strike to his eye socket and temple. He went down hard.

The second denizen of the seedy underworld came at me, not to rob me but to keep me from intervening with his crime buddy. He hadn't seen how quickly the first young man had gone down. I lunged without telegraphing the move and powered a heel of my palm into his chin. His jaw slammed shut on his tongue, which had been sticking out. He howled and clutched his face. I stepped back.

Jenny bounced toward him, and once the distance between them was right, she rotated at the waist to increase the power behind her right cross. His head jerked to the side and he fell, blood running freely from his lacerated tongue.

I held out my arm, and she took it while carefully stepping over her victims.

"Hang on, you two," a loud voice called from close by.

We looked for the voice, but he wasn't hard to spot, walking toward us in his uniform. NYPD.

"Were these two bothering you?" he asked.

"Tried to snatch my purse. We've been in town five minutes. We can't spend money in your wonderful city if it gets stolen."

He looked both ways before leaning close. "I wish more tourists would defend themselves from scumbags like this. My hands are tied. Our mayor caters to their type over decent folk like you and me."

"I don't know anything about that," I replied. "All I know is that we won't be robbed by street thugs."

"What if they had guns?"

"We won't be robbed."

"Let 'em get within arm's length and put them down. I'll wait for them to wake up before giving them a stern warning."

"You're not going to arrest them?"

"No. It'd be a complete waste. City won't do anything. Best I can do is laugh at them for getting their asses kicked. Maybe they'll leave their lives of crime behind."

"We are on the same page, my man. Have a nice day."

"Hang on," the officer said before we could escape. "I

need your name, where you're staying in the City, and home address."

"Can't we just leave, especially since you're not going to arrest them? What does it matter who we are?"

"What if you're vigilantes using the streets as your personal training ground? Thugs, so no repercussions. You guys were good, too good. Those two never had a chance, did they?"

"We won't be robbed," I reiterated.

"Names," the officer insisted. I produced my Illinois driver's license.

"There you go, wild man. We're staying at the Loneham. Like I said, we've been here for five whole minutes. Any good places to eat around here?"

He talked while writing down the information from my license. "Are you kidding me? Korean, Chinese, five-star steak, kosher—you name it, and you'll find it within two blocks. You are in the eating capital of the world."

"We've spent a lot of time in Vegas. They would contest your claim, but we'll see for ourselves. Thanks for being there for us in case things turned bad."

"I'm just here to make sure no one gets killed, and even then, it doesn't always go as it's supposed to." He nudged one of the bodies on the sidewalk. The young man groaned. "Get up. You act like you were punched by George Foreman."

"She goes by George. How funny is that?"

"Your ID, ma'am." The officer didn't smile.

She handed her license to him, and he recorded the information.

"A husband-wife team. Good for you guys. The family that fights together stays together."

"I think I can smell kimchi," I said, trying to hurry the process along. Every single person who walked by gave us a good look.

"Officer Grant!" a voice called, and a young woman wearing obscenely tall high heels hurried up. Her tight skirt and blouse showed too much. She also carried a microphone.

The press.

I started inching backward while a cameraman with a unit that was smaller than a shoebox moved in, getting close-up footage of Jenny and me.

"Hey, Babs," the officer said without looking up. I would have liked to leave, but he had a death grip on Jenny's license. We stood our ground and waited. I tried to look bored. The cameraman stepped back to get footage of the two on the sidewalk as they started to move.

"I expect these two ran into someone unexpectedly, and it knocked them down," Babs suggested.

"Something like that," the officer replied. He handed the license back, keeping the face and name turned away from the camera. Jenny stuffed it into a pocket rather than risk opening her purse.

"Can I get your names, please?" Babs stuffed the microphone in my face.

"Are we free to go?" I asked over the top of her head. Given her heels, she must have been shorter than short.

"On your way. Let peace return to this great city," he announced in a loud voice.

"We have footage of the attack. I'd love to do a spot on you, Miss…I didn't get your name."

"No, you didn't," Jenny replied. I put the press far behind politicians in their overall uselessness, but a story on reducing crime had merit. Maybe she wasn't that bad. And it didn't look like she was going away.

The cameraman was wearing running shoes in case we tried to hot-foot it.

"Ma'am. You were wonderful. We have a lot of young girls who watch our show," the reporter pressed.

A sticker on the side of the camera suggested it belonged to a news channel.

"How many young girls watch the news? You want us starry-eyed about being on TV when you're lying? No relationship based on lies can survive, as your ex-boyfriends will tell you, so now if you'll leave us alone, we'd appreciate it. You might want to help the guy who's trying to look up your skirt or bury your heel in his chest, whichever you think will get you the most viewers. Be the powerful woman you know you can be."

I didn't even have to coax Jenny. We bolted at a half-run to get in front of a crowd and hunched while walking quickly ahead. We crossed at the first corner.

When I was finally able to look back, I found the reporter trying to get away from the young man who had his arms wrapped around her legs with his head between her ankles. The cameraman captured it all. The officer was nowhere to be seen. The second thug was pulling himself upright using a parked car for leverage.

"We should help her," Jenny said.

I wanted to be angry about trying to help people whose purpose in life was to harm us by shining bright lights in our direction. "We can't." I held Jenny back, but she slapped my hand away and ran before the light turned red. I ran after her. By the time we reached the reporter, she was beating the man's head with her microphone but not hard enough to get him to let go.

Jenny gripped one of his hands and twisted it until he let go with a scream of pain. He started yelling that he couldn't breathe.

I grabbed the woman around the waist and lifted her away from the man. When the cameraman raised his lens and pointed it at me, Jenny kicked him in the head. The second thug was running in the other direction. I put Babs down and grabbed the camera that had been thrust in my face.

"Next time, how about you help instead of just recording?" I snarled at the cameraman.

"Not my job. They tell me that every time we go out." He followed his claim with a shrug. "Why, when good-guy Samaritans like you are nearby? This will make leading footage. Vigilantes loose in Manhattan. I can see the spot right now."

I tossed his camera in front of a truck driving past. The front tire missed it, but the dualies in the rear did not.

"Oops."

He started an F-bomb-heavy tirade that ended when he leaned too close and got himself kneed in the groin. He staggered away, coughing.

"If you'll excuse us," Jenny told Babs, icicles hanging from her words. Jenny was a head taller than the woman.

"We'll get your names from the official police report, and then you can standby for all the attention you never wanted."

We hurried away, this time, not crossing the street. I was angry. "In New York City, you mind your own business. They prey on anyone who comes from out of town. And now we've got bullseyes on our backs. That's great," I grumbled.

Jenny stared at the ground. I pulled her to the wall of a building where I could hug her to me away from the mass of humanity. "Please don't do that again."

"Everything we've done has been to protect the little guy from scumbags like those two. I can't just turn it on and off. I'm sorry. I don't think she was in as much danger as it appeared."

I blew out a breath, probably too loud and too hard since it moved Jenny's hair. "Yeah. Cameraman could have stepped in at any time. You see how no one else helped?"

"What a city, huh?" Jenny lamented. "I don't think the policeman is going to file a report. He didn't even take down the information from those two on the ground."

I stared at the wall behind my wife's head. "He didn't. There won't be a police report, but they are going to start a file on us in case any more local bad guys get face-slammed into the concrete."

"It's kind of what we're here for." Jenny smiled.

"Of course, but we don't want anyone knowing that. Now, please…I'll try to keep you from being the good guy, and you stop me. No press is good press."

"I'm sorry, Ian. I've put our business at risk, and everyone who works for us and who we work for."

"Like you said, it's what we do. We'll get over it. Since we're here looking for a possible site to expand the Club to, it's all good."

"We are?" Jenny smiled. "Next time, we should probably start with that."

"The tourist angle wasn't working. What do you say we eat in the hotel? The allure of the big city has already soured in my stomach. We can hit the workout room. Eat. Secure a little private time in the nice suite…"

Jenny smiled. "Incorrigible."

"What can I say? It's our honeymoon."

"It's been our honeymoon for two years," she replied.

"And don't you forget it. By the way, how's your hand?"

Jenny showed her unblemished fist. "I have the knuckles of a boxer. Not very feminine."

"Nobody cares about your knuckles except those two punks. Nice work. Like I told them, we won't be robbed."

We walked around the block to get to the Loneham in our desire to steer clear of the press and a police officer with our information.

CHAPTER THREE

"The camera can be the most deadly weapon since the assassin's bullet. Or it can be the lotion of the heart." –Norman Parkinson

The data on the thumb drive contained original classification markings up to top secret with added codewords. Since Mr. Odenkirk was a person of interest in an ongoing terrorism investigation, his file contained material from both the FBI and the CIA.

Their efforts to compartmentalize the information boggled my mind. I was certain the FBI did not have the CIA's information. Since the CIA had given us the data, they had it all but wouldn't necessarily be able to act within US borders. Jurisdiction and such things didn't interest me except in knowing how I could use those boundaries to my benefit, like to avoid the authorities.

While Rush's *Hold Your Fire* played in the background, I built a target profile behind the firewall of the Peace Archive's system buried in the underbelly of the dark web. It wasn't something any search engine would find. It took five separate passwords and accesses to get to where any data was stored. Operators could bid on available contracts on the third level.

We had forty-one active operators, the same number as a year prior. No new hires, no one retired from the game. We tried not to overwhelm any of our team, and we paid extremely well. The average payout for a hit was one million dollars. The average price to take out a contract with the Archive was one-point-five million.

The operators liked the money because it bought a certain lifestyle they found agreeable. Many made two to four hits a year. Others were happy with just one. There was enough work to go around, which was the hardest part of running the company. We couldn't take out ads, so everything was word of mouth by trusted players.

Now the government was using our services. That kept me on edge, but we checked bidders thoroughly to make sure it wasn't a sting or so high-profile as to shout to the world that it was a paid hit and not an accident of circumstances. The people we had contracts on were the kind of people who were constantly at risk of being on the wrong end of a gun barrel anyway.

"He has an office two blocks down. We'll need to check that out," I mumbled to myself. "Philanthropy. Hedge fund executive. Those offices are in the finance district, but he doesn't go there much. He only enjoys the power of the company's success. OdaFuture Asset Management has eighty-four billion under management. It's mind-boggling."

Jenny sat next to me, taking in the information without comment. "Odenkirk runs OdaFuture. Cute. But look at his charity. He disburses a billion a year to a broad range of charities. Lots to children, animals, and," she pointed at the screen, "even veterans. Maybe you should apply for some health-improving cash."

"Maybe. He employs veterans. I wonder if I could go undercover and work the phone lines for him."

"How much of that could you take? A billion dollars? You would never see him."

"But as a donor willing to drop two million into his charity, he might see *me*. Sometimes, I like meeting my contract names. Other times, not so much. This time, I do want to see what we're up against."

I closed down the computer and looked at the thumb drive. There was a time when I would have hidden it inside a light switch. Given the police and media encounter a few hours ago, those days looked to have returned. We had to assume that if someone could enter the room, they could open the safe.

As I always did, I had checked the room thoroughly before we said a word. Jenny had showered while I looked in the vents, inside lamps, underneath the furniture, and more. I was able to join her before she finished.

No sense going out on the town looking a mess, even though we had returned quickly.

I pulled a small multi-tool from my pocket and undid the switch plate in the bathroom, placed the thumb drive within, and screwed the plate back on. I took one last look and joined Jenny at the door. Leaving was never as easy as just opening the door and walking out. We needed to make sure that if we never came back, we wouldn't leave evidence behind.

There was nothing on the computer except a minimum number of programs downloaded recently. The volatile memory had been scrubbed; it was part of the shutdown routine.

We took almost nothing with us. The gold card, our driver's licenses, and the custom phones were the few items we carried with us at all times. I had a burner phone with a data plan, and so did Jenny. We had each other's numbers because we changed phones often. We mostly used them to browse for local restaurants or watch videos on YouTube. The casual investigator would probably consider us the most boring people on the planet.

Exactly how we wanted to appear.

The hotel's restaurant was Italian but five-star, like everything else related to the boutique experience. We arrived at the beginning of the dinner hour and were able to get a table after listening to the host's recommendation that for a future optimal dining experience, we should make reservations.

We were given a table by the window, through which we could look into another building with more buildings surrounding it. "They call it the beating heart of civilization, city center."

"What's the plan?" Jenny asked in a low voice. No one was near us. It was early. We were acting like old people, showing up when the doors opened to get in and out before the crowd.

"We visit the nonprofit and start a conversation. Then we refine his schedule, locations, routes, and methods. Then we get what we need to make it happen. Depending on his availability, this could be a three-day or three-month op."

"I hope not three months. I'll go crazy watching you go crazy." Jenny gave me her best side-eye.

"I don't like big cities." I threw my hands up as if I were powerless against the feeling.

"Vulnerabilities. I saw one right away. He wants to be liked."

I mulled it over, and it made sense. "That might be key in the big picture. Friends everywhere. He's made tens of millions of dollars for people through a sound investment strategy, and now he's all about the charities. Where does the other funding fall? Does he skim from the first to pay the second? How does he manage those relationships, and with who? The packet we got from Rick had nebulous connections at best."

"Maybe he has more. You should give him a call. You guys are birds of a feather."

"He's weenie! A bureaucrat. 'I'll need you to sign this!' That was pretty funny."

Jenny chuckled. "It was. I'm surprised you didn't take it, throw it in the trash, and then pour coffee on it."

"That was next. 'Sign this!' The guy's a hoot." I amused myself. Bureaucrats. If anything made a big city look good, it was spending time with a bureaucrat. They made my skin crawl as if I were getting a rash of the worst sort.

But, eight million dollars.

A target who was popular in all the right circles. The public information about Maksim Odenkirk seemed too good to be true. Maybe it would be better to destroy him by cutting him off from his money.

"You're right," I said. "I need to give Rick a call, but tomorrow, after we've seen the nonprofit."

"I don't feel like I'm getting inside this guy's business. This one feels different from the others."

"Bid it out. Let one of the locals handle it," Jenny replied.

"When the vice president gives us a job, he expects you and me to do it. The other governmental gigs come via the out-of-date bulletin board, which I find apropos in an odd way." I scratched my head. Jenny smoothed my hair afterward.

"I know. Just checking to see if you were going to reconsider."

"Maybe we pull a local for a surveillance-only part of the mission for a few hundred grand. It's low risk."

She shook her head. "Who's going to do the time-consuming work and not seal the deal? They'll want the full Monty."

I dove into the computer and twisted sideways through my VPN to get into the dark web, and two minutes of logins and passwords later, I was into the back end of the Peace Archive's bidding area. I typed in the information without revealing Maksim's name. I made it a locked bid of three hundred thousand and two weeks to compile a dossier. I gave them nothing besides my need for a dossier.

They would have no preconceived notions.

Jenny tapped me on the shoulder. "I'll say I'm sorry yet again before you see this." She put her phone in front of the computer screen and tapped play on a video. The reporter was front and center for a moment to introduce a crime-fighting diva, then the view cut to Jenny dropping the first assailant. The camera zoomed in on me. A car in the way blocked the view of my knee to his choice bits, but Jenny's sucker punch filled the entire frame.

"You gave him what he deserved. Good form."

"Wait for it…"

The reporter came back on, and our names appeared over the picture of us trying to get away. *Ian and Jenny Bragg.*

"Great," I mumbled.

The video stopped, and the reporter cropped in a shot from the studio.

"But then I was attacked and sexually assaulted. No one came to my aid except for Jenny Bragg."

More action video. Jenny flying into the picture and freeing Babs from her self-induced predicament.

"Let there be no doubt that there are heroes in this world. And sometimes they appear when you need them most, and they look like they just walked the red carpet. I welcome the Club's owners to New York City. I hope you're looking to expand here. We could do no better. Barbara Jaekel, reporting."

Jenny removed the phone.

"I'm sorry," she tried a second time.

I held up my hand and went back to typing. I added to the bid that it might include the full job, to be negotiated after a successful surveillance, and pressed Post.

"We'll check out the nonprofit and work that angle, but then we have to leave. We cannot run this job out of here. As the cops might say, our cover is blown."

"I'm sorry," she repeated. Now it was my turn to say what she wanted to hear.

"We were set up. Why would the news crew be recording that particular spot? Freeze the first part of the video. Where's that policeman?"

She stopped it and blew it up. He was behind an old couple, watching us before the attack.

"What if he wasn't a cop?"

"You'll see he wasn't in any of the other shots when he should have been. Him taking our information while managing the thugs. I think it was these four creating the news and not reporting it. You gave them an angle—a high roller with mad combat skills. Gotham yearns for people like you. And you're not paper-thin like their usual runway models."

"I'm not a model."

"No. You only look like one, but with curves in all the right places."

"You are incorrigible!"

"Have I said today how much I detest reporters? If I haven't, now seems to be a good time. And I forgive you. Please don't do it again."

"How did they get the footage?"

"Must have been a live link where everything was recorded elsewhere. That was still gratifying. Don't point your cameras at us or guns. Don't point anything at us, just to be safe."

"How were we to know?"

"We weren't. We never would have known if we let them take your purse. That faux policeman would have melted into the background, and the footage of yet another violent attack would have been archived. You saw that the perps' mugs were fuzzed out. They're accomplices. I guess we look like lackeys. Too rich and not smart enough. Perfect targets."

"Makes me want to punch a reporter in the face," Jenny stated.

"I always feel that way. We'll have a conversation with her when we return. Not now. We'll kill the rest of the day and be out of here back to O'Hare first thing in the morning. And by first thing, I mean noon."

"I like how you think," Jenny told me.

It was time to go. We'd grab a light breakfast on our way, not because I needed more coffee but because I wanted more coffee.

We had done some light sparring in the room before getting cleaned up just to keep our eyes sharp. We found that wrapping our hands in towels limited the bruising. Black eyes and split lips were no way to present a professional appearance, but we tried to spar every day when not in a dojo.

In our line of work, one could never lose the edge. I called it "the game." We were players without extra lives. We had to get it right the first time every time when we engaged someone under contract.

Yesterday had been business as usual. Someone always wanted to test us. We could never let them win. Maybe that was my ego. Maybe it would be easier to blend in as a victim sometimes. I still couldn't go that route. I was used to dealing with strong people in a profession where physical and mental strength carried equal weight.

What would a client say if we showed any weaknesses? Two mil for a contract might become one, or worse, nothing at all. I felt we needed to exude confidence and strength even when undercover.

As a power couple. I liked that moniker.

We headed toward the lobby to grab something from a cart, along with a designer coffee. There were plenty of seats available to relax while eating a piece of fruit. It would be enough to hold us over. We had no idea how long the engagement with the nonprofit would take. I expected we'd get chased away quickly.

When we left the hotel, a young girl screamed, "There she is, Queen Jenny!"

My face fell while we froze in place. A dozen young girls ran up to us. "All you, babe," I told her and drifted to the wall to lean against it with my arms crossed. I needed a ball cap. The sun reflecting off the windows of the tall buildings was blinding.

"Can I get your autograph?" a girl shouted over the others.

Jenny smiled and accommodated them. She didn't have a pen, but one of the girls did.

Then it struck me. I scanned the area until I saw her—the creator of the news herself, Babs Jaekel. I made a beeline for her at a full run. It was New York City, so people ran with some frequency. Others would look, but no one would get in the way. She tried to backpedal and thought better of it. She straightened her once again too-revealing outfit and looked at me.

"Well, hello, Ian Bragg."

"Well, hell, Barbara, creator of the news."

"You aren't owners of the Club?"

"You show up with rent-a-thugs and a phony police officer and make the magic happen, camera ready to roll. Are you getting this? There he is. Good to see the newsroom provided another camera after yesterday's unfortunate accident."

"He's a real police officer, but he was off-duty at the time. And the young men, misled by society? They earned a little extra to keep them out of jail for at least one more day, and the beat down put on them by Miss Jenny might encourage them to leave their life of crime altogether. You see, there are no losers with this story."

I didn't like her or her logic, but I couldn't see who would be hurt by this except us. And with this kind of publicity, *would* we be hurt? Opportunity. It solidified from the random thoughts I'd had in the shower. We could use the publicity to leverage our way into Odenkirk's philanthropical organization, OdaPresent Charities, made possible by the success of his commercial venture, OdaFuture Asset Management.

Our leverage made possible by a couple of million dollars, compliments of the CIA.

"I guess we'll let you go this time," I replied. "Jenny deserves the limelight. She's better than I deserve."

"You strike me as a good provider. What's your backstory?"

"Marine, layabout, fell in with the right people, did the right things in the right way, and here we are. Not just catering to the rich and famous, but we have our own place among them. Working out keeps us grounded. This is all off the record, of course."

"Who do you think you're talking to?" Babs replied, which made me laugh.

"On the record, yes, we are scoping properties for a possible expansion of the Club. But that cat is out of the bag thanks to you, which means any realtors will jack up the prices."

"This is New York. Prices are already jacked up."

"You're okay when you're not making up the news, but the focus needs to be on Miss Jenny. She's the star of the show."

"Curvy girl power."

"All the power." She was talking with the teen girls and had them mesmerized. Teaching skills sprinkled with a superhero aura. Once again, Jenny might have to take the lead on a contract. She could go where I could not and disarm the mark.

When I turned back, I found the cameraman recording me. "Get away from me, you toad."

He laughed and sauntered toward Jenny and her fans to get some shots from different angles.

"The viewers will eat up the look of adoration. Thank you for your time, Mr. Bragg. And good luck bringing the Club to the City." Babs followed her cameraman, swinging her microphone like a stage performer building excitement for the next lines. I returned to the wall and waited for Jenny to disengage.

Eventually, she convinced them that she had to visit a charity. They bought the excuse. A real cover. So much easier to lie when it was eighty percent truth. She was getting good.

She found me and waved to the girls before taking my arm and urging me forward.

"I have a plan," I told her.

"I'm all ears because I'm fresh out of motivating things to say."

"You have fans, Miss Jenny." She didn't smile. "We use your new celebrity status to get inside OdaPresent. Who wouldn't want you at one of their parties? We can expand the business while," I looked around to make sure no one was too close, "scoping the contract."

"The contract is all yours. I don't want to do that again, Ian." She frowned with the memory.

"I don't blame you. I'll take care of that if it's called for. We have a lot of info to gather before we make a decision. Damn! I forgot to check if that bureaucrat made the payment. I better check before I give him a call."

Jenny glanced over her shoulder.

"Don't look now, but we have a tail."

"Your admirers?" I didn't look to confirm.

"The reporter."

"Looks like we're her personal mission. We need to cross the street, so let's wait until there's about three seconds left on the crossing light, and then we run for it." We slowed at the light and waited at the red while watching the countdown. When it hit three, we ran for our lives. It turned red while Babs and her cameraman were on the other side. We crossed the side street and they followed, but from across Fifth Avenue. Another block and we hurried into the high rise where OdaPresent Charities had half a floor.

"Must be a hundred different businesses in here," Jenny noted while we waited for the elevator.

"All with that coveted Fifth Avenue address. I wonder what kind of clout that has? Can you see the Club with one of those? Can you imagine coming down here every day? Not relaxing at all."

"For you, maybe, but a nice spa and casual drinks in a soundproofed bar and darkened dining and sitting areas. I could see it."

I tried to visualize it, but it didn't work for me. Parking would be a challenge unless we hired a valet service, and then there were the high taxes and clientele who were already members elsewhere. In Chicago, we had the advantage of old money. They had already been members when we took over. We had no such advantage here.

No. We'd keep it as a cover, but I would not waste too much time or effort exploring it.

We took the elevator to the twenty-fifth floor and stepped out. Glass doors showed the stylish OdaPresent Charities logo. We went through. The reception area didn't have any seats. When we stepped up to the desk, the receptionist held up a finger and took a call. As soon as he hung up, he took another but only needed to reroute it.

When he looked up, recognition danced across his face. "You're Ian and Jenny Bragg."

Being recognized was an uncomfortable twist I felt I needed to get used to.

"We are," I replied. "We are looking at donating a couple million to Mr. Odenkirk's charity, but we'd like to talk with him first. We don't toss that kind of money around without being completely comfortable with the organization first."

"Of course. We have donors who regularly make those kinds of contributions. Would you like a list of our donors? We are a registered 501(c)3 charity, and as such, all donations become public information. Are you still comfortable with your commitment?"

"Writing it off the taxes is a good thing. On the face of it, this charity is a worthwhile endeavor, and I feel we should be associated with it."

"We can help you with any wire transfer details you need."

"Once we're comfortable and since you know who we are, you know that we're legitimate and not just trying to bag time with someone of Mr. Odenkirk's stature. When might we be able to get an appointment?"

"Mr. Odenkirk is a very busy man whose time is at a premium."

I stared at him until he relented.

"He is currently out of the country and won't be back until next week, but he has meetings already scheduled for his return. How about the week after?"

"Pencil us in to the first available slot." He added us to the computer and handed us a business card with a time and date. We had three weeks to kill. "We're going back to Chicago. We'll be back for the appointment."

The phone rang, and he waved as he took the call. We headed for the door. He finished before we reached it.

"Mr. and Mrs. Bragg, it was nice to see you in person. You are as intimidating as you appeared to be on television."

"Intimidating?" That wasn't what we were going for. "Only to the bad guys."

Jenny smiled at the young man. "Everyone should be able to protect themselves."

He made a sour face. "Violence is so twentieth century."

I clenched my jaw to keep from laughing before I delivered a hearty dose of reality. "Seems like it's twenty-first century, too. If we surrender to the violent, then violence is all we'll know."

Jenny waved as we walked out. "Profound, Mr. Bragg."

"No wonder street thugs operate with impunity. If 'civilized' means being a victim, I'll have no part of it. The Marines taught me to always fight back."

"And New York legend Yogi Berra said it ain't over until it's over."

I put on my best confused face before turning back to the business at hand. "What did you take away from the office?"

"Only mildly interested in two million dollars," Jenny observed.

"That and the artwork on the walls. Looked expensive but out of place. I would have expected a collage of people they've helped or causes they've funded like other charities do. Go to any of their homepages and take a look. This charity is about *the man*, Max Odenkirk. I see why certain people are bothered."

"Did you hear any of the other conversations?"

I shook my head. "The receptionist kept us from hearing anything going on in the rest of the office. His job was to hold people off. Not even a deputy or someone else. You'd think they would have an executive type in the office. The receptionist didn't even try to pawn us off on someone else."

"Back to Chicago, my dear?"

"Sounds like it. We have a company to run. Need those contracts."

CHAPTER FOUR

"Our purses shall be proud, our garments poor; for 'tis the mind that makes the body rich." –William Shakespeare

We drove our Jeep Grand Cherokee home to Lake Forest, a kinder and gentler section of urban sprawl north of Chicago. It almost had a country town feel to it. We liked that part.

It took the edge off brokering the demise of our fellow humans.

After a good night's rest in the mansion, we headed to the Club for breakfast and business. We showed the flag, meeting and greeting our members as they strolled the hallways. It was a good crowd already, but the golf course was in good shape, and many members were looking to play.

"Mr. Allsice, how are you today?" He'd given us work in the past. The way he approached me suggested he was interested in talking about a new contract.

"Join me for nine?" he asked, looking at both of us.

My clubs were in the shack as they always were, like most of the members. "Of course."

Jenny waved me off. "I have another appointment, unfortunately, with Mr. Smythe." She looked at me. I wouldn't be there to hold him off since he always hit on Jenny. Then again, he was eighty, and he'd hit on Jenny whether I was there or not.

"Looks like a twosome. I'll see when I can get us on the tee."

I hugged Jenny quickly before we went to our separate engagements.

Albert Allsice, the oldest heir to Allsice Industries, makers of heavy construction equipment with fingers in a number of supplier chains beyond the one they dominated. Not just money, but Allsice had influence as the main subcontractor on most of the nation's infrastructure projects.

And powerful friends with powerful enemies. He wasn't a good golfer and didn't like playing. That meant he wanted two hours of my time to talk through his problem. I expected something spectacular.

We were given the next tee, squeezed between two foursomes. I took an easy swing because staying in play was more important than hitting a long drive. I'd let loose later when no one was watching.

"I'll play from your ball," Albert said, not bothering to take the cover off his driver. Once away from the tee box, he started talking. "I have a problem, and Vinny helped me in the past with other problems. He told me I could trust you. So here we are."

He waited.

"I have taken on all of Vinny's duties since he retired. I'd like to hear about your problem, and then we'll go from there."

"It's my wife," he started.

I held my breath. I wasn't keen on accepting a gig to off someone's spouse, but I didn't want to lose his business. The age-old ethics question and tradeoffs politicians made every day until they had no ethics left.

"She's seeing a spiritual advisor who is costing her a fortune, and he's advising her to leave me. I think he's a scammer who wants whatever she might get in a divorce. She knows too much about the backroom deals for me to fight her publicly. It would cost me billions and destroy the company. I can't put those good people out of work because her mind is getting twisted by this *opportunist*."

"What's his name?" Steer the conversation clear of any actions against his wife.

"The Reverend Gil Twain."

I blew out a breath between my teeth. "Isn't he the spiritual advisor to the ex-president?"

"The same."

"He moves in elite circles."

"He does," Albert admitted.

"What is it worth to you to make him disappear?"

"Now you're talking. Five mil. I'll pay it all upfront. I need this nightmare to end. And then I'll take my wife on a private yacht cruise of the Mediterranean. We don't spend enough time seeing the sights. I'll take care of that part. You take care of the problem. I'll have the reservations set up for two weeks from today. I'd like to see him out of the picture shortly thereafter."

"Won't she fight you about going on vacation?"

"I can be persuasive when I need to be. It's been a long time since we've vacationed together."

"Maybe you can fix this without having to spend the money?"

"Vinny would have never turned down a contract," Albert replied coldly.

"It's not that. The business would love your money, but

when targets are too high-profile, it exposes us rather significantly. That is what I'm worried about."

"Ten million. The cost of failure is billions. Ten mil. My final offer."

I had no choice. "We'll take it. You want the problem resolved in two to three weeks." I held out my hand, and he shook it. "I believe you have the account information to make the transfer."

He nodded. The green cleared of the group in front, and I lined up a five iron. I probably could have gotten a shorter club there, but I was trying to keep myself from overswinging. A smooth swing, a mis-hit, and a hundred yards later, I'd get the opportunity to hit another approach shot.

Albert climbed out of the cart and waved. "I'll walk back to the clubhouse. If you can have my clubs put up when you finish, I'd appreciate it."

He left me standing in the middle of the fairway, where I tried to look inconspicuous after my poor shot. I was still learning the game. I wasn't sure I had enough life left to master it.

And we had a new contract for the largest amount ever paid. Target complexity was increasing.

If we wanted to be the best, we had to pull off the hardest jobs. I didn't have two hours to invest in my golf game. I finished the first hole with a double bogey and declared victory, then drove back down the cart path to the clubhouse.

I dropped a hundred-dollar bill with the head caddie for taking care of the clubs and getting us into the rotation. It had been well worth the price.

"You are the best, Mr. Bragg," he replied.

"We are nothing without the good people surrounding us. Thanks, Leon. You help make my life exceptional."

"I saw your drive," he muttered.

"It's now less exceptional. Thanks for that," I joked. He chuckled with me.

"Pro is free at three. Maybe you can get a few minutes of his time to help your attitude."

I hesitated. "It's not my swing?"

"You could be the physically strongest member of the Club. It's not your physical abilities. Once you embrace what the game is about, you will see a significant change. Mathematics. Physics. And focus. You should be driving that first green off the old-man tees, and that's when you know it's time to move back to the big-boy tees. You could be great in a matter of weeks. A good golf game is life's allegory."

"That's deep, Leon. Pencil me in for three. I better get after this crushing workload, which helps pay for all this." I spread my arms wide.

"A good golf game will take the edge off. You have a great day, Mr. Bragg." Leon took my and Albert's bags off the cart and headed into the storeroom.

I hurried upstairs toward our office suite and found Gladys in the outer reception area. She intercepted me. "You have a few messages you may want to check," she said cryptically.

"Phone?"

She shook her head. The dark web. Responses to the request for bids.

"Thanks, Gladys. I'll be in the office."

"You won't be alone. You better not be making out in there."

"So what if we are?" I gave her my best inquisitive look.

"Don't make me call the bouncer to kick you out of your own club."

"I love you, too, Gladys. No making out. *This time.*"

I found Jenny upstairs in the main office at the big desk.

She was on the computer with three windows open as she worked on new contracts.

"Three of them?" I asked after shutting the door to secure our privacy.

"Mr. Smythe has been beating the bushes hard. Los Angeles, Portland, and Boise."

"Boise?"

"Drug dealer moving into paradise and trying to bring MS-13 with him."

"As long as those facts are true, yes, he needs to go, and his lackeys with him." I dug a scrubbed laptop out of the safe and started downloading the software I needed to use the VPN, a system for hiding where the internet is accessed from. And then special software for maneuvering through the dark web.

"Are you going to call Rick?"

"Oh, snagged a new contract from right here in Chicago. South Side for ten mil."

"It isn't a competition," Jenny shot back, a sour look on her face. "All three of mine came to eight."

"Twenty-six million in new work. Not a bad week." I tapped to get into the deepest recesses of the Peace Archive's system to review the information I had on OdaScumbag, the nickname I had given Maksim Odenkirk. I did that with every one of my targets because it made it more palatable than letting them retain their humanity.

I pulled out Rick's card and called his personal phone. It went to voicemail without ringing. I checked the time—one in the afternoon in DC. He probably had his phone off while suffering through a meeting with his peers. "Rick, Ian. Call me at this number." I listed the digits twice. "Call me from a secure phone and then destroy that number by eating it, filling out a form to attest to the destruction with an accompanying witness attestation, filed in triplicate. Later, bureaucrat."

"You're going to make him mad," Jenny said without looking up.

"He loves being needled. I better check that he paid." I tapped on the keyboard, accessing the bank using memorized streams of numbers. There was no option to write anything down. Data had to be stored in the most volatile of all memories.

"Why, that sorry sack of…" The ten million was already there, along with three million from someone else, but no payment of four million as the first half deposit from the CIA. "I don't feel so bad about being in Chicago, then."

I frowned at the screen while I moved the money from the transfer account to the main account before heading in to see if there were any bids on the surveillance.

My untraceable phone rang.

"Morgue. You kill 'em, we chill 'em," I answered.

"Nice, Ian. Rick here."

"I see that you haven't paid yet." I stared out the window at the well-maintained golf course beyond.

"We've been up to our ass in alligators here. Haven't you seen the news?"

My stomach dropped. "I haven't had time to check the news for two days. What happened?"

"Terrorist attack in France. Seventy-eight Marines killed by extremely sophisticated devices, similar to a bouncing Betty but designed specifically for buses. They shredded the insides with a one hundred percent kill on one bus. Thanks to the sacrifice of the company commander, only lost twelve on the second bus, even though most are in critical condition. We think it was your boy's money paid for those things."

"*Semper fi*," I whispered. "What do you have that would suggest it was him?"

"A transfer from a couple years ago. It's a tenuous link, but it went to the ones who did this."

"They do charity work too, don't they?"

"How'd you know?"

"Hide in plain sight. Day job, night job. Same money. It's, like, the ultimate in money laundering. Nobody crawls up a charity's skirt when they are in public doing great things, but the bigger they are, the harder they fall."

"And he needs to fall soon."

"We're in Chicago."

The long pause suggested he thought we were elsewhere, like in New York City. "Is that where you need to be on this contract?"

"I appreciate altruistic souls like yourself who give body and soul to keep the wheels of the big green machine turning, but we have our wheels to turn out here. We're doing a significant favor for the US government at extreme risk to ourselves, and now you want us to do that for free. You're not coming to our rescue if it goes south. No one is. Not doing it for free. Plus, our boy is out of the country until next week. We have an appointment to meet with him in two weeks."

"Why are you meeting with him? Is that how you always do it?"

"We *do it* every way we can," I joked. "But that sucks about the Marines. We've done all we could so far, seen his office in the big city and started a surveillance." Well, almost. Rick didn't need the details. "I wanted to talk to you about timing, but I guess that has become OBE."

Overcome by events. It was a three-letter acronym I used fairly often.

"Yeah. The sooner, the better." Rick sounded tired.

"Can you get us the latest information?"

"Probably not unless you want to meet me for coffee."

"I don't think we'll be available. We've got a business to

run in Chicago, and if you want this job done right, we can't be taking side trips looking for information that probably will have no bearing on what we'll end up doing."

"He's a bad dude wearing an angel's mask," Rick stated.

"I'm counting on you to be right, Rick, because we won't be able to find the smoking gun when we're not looking for it. We're watching for something else in entirety." I didn't say it out loud, but Rick had to know. We were looking for a vulnerability to exploit where he would step into the crosshairs.

We rarely used guns. There were far more elegant ways to kill people without drawing so much attention.

Same with the good pastor. What was their routine? Where were they out of sight of those who would protect them, as well as the prying eyes of cameras? It was part of the deadly game of being an operator. It was best the targets didn't know they were playing, but the more important they were, the more they embraced a certain level of paranoia.

Paranoia was bad for our line of work. Just because they think someone is out to get them doesn't mean they're wrong, but arrogance and hubris came with the territory, and that usually led to their demise.

"I understand," Rick finally replied. "I'll get on the budget weenies to expedite that payment. And let me know if there is anything else I can do to speed things up."

"I'd say cancel his passport, but that might let him know the big green machine is onto him because his travel will remain a challenge. I have yet to find his schedule. For a public dude, he is low-profile."

"Because he's a scumbag at heart, maintaining a death grip on his secrets. We might never break through the veneer."

"Not what I wanted to hear, but I'll work with it. Your company is betting big that this is the right call. Who am I to argue with that? I'll call you if I have more. I'm sure you have some papers to push and underlings to mismanage."

"Same to you, Ian. Take care of that uber-hot wife of yours."

"You know I will, Rick. Get some rest, man. You sound dogged. You have my number. Call if you feel lonely."

"It's been a long two days. *Semper fi*, man." Rick hung up. I checked the charge before stuffing the phone into my pocket. It scraped against the cheap throwaway I was using as an internet phone. I continued looking out the window as I replayed our conversation. "Can you turn on the TV, please? The news."

Jenny punched the button on the remote. Since the television was always set to the news, that popped up first. Local stuff. We cycled through the channels, but nothing was showing. Jenny went to the news channels online and showed me the lead articles.

The buses had been destroyed. "Most of the passengers made it out of that second one alive, but they're in rough shape. No one survived in the first bus."

"Our boy?" Jenny asked.

"Supposedly. I didn't need to see that because it makes me want to strangle him with my bare hands."

"Me, too." Pictures showed rows of body bags with the gendarmerie standing around the site. They were helpless in the aftermath, just like the Marines with their M4 carbines, helping to secure their own after the damage had already been done.

Explosive Ordnance Disposal dug through the bushes at the side of the road, looking for evidence.

What they initially found was like nothing they'd seen before. It was far more ominous—smart bombs that found their way inside vehicles.

In France, where the Marines should have been safe.

Jenny and I watched with our jaws clamped tight.

Anger rose. A charity that funded attacks on our people on friendly soil.

"We better get back to work. I have to bid out this contract on Reverend Gil Twain. We need to end *his* influence, too."

"Gil Twain? Pastor to the president?"

"Ex-president, but yes, same guy. He's leading our Mr. Allsice's wife astray and at great cost. He doesn't want to join the billion-dollar divorce club, and he doesn't want his wife out of the picture—I would not have accepted that contract—but he thinks Gil Pickle is leading a lot of people astray. So, let's take a closer look and see if we can show Señor Pickle the errors of his ways."

Jenny nodded and kept jamming on the proposals she had. I turned my full attention to the one in my hand, diving into the back corridors of the dark web to look for dirt. In this case, there was almost more than I could document. Lawsuits buried in red tape. Complainants disappearing. Gil Twain had the earmarks of a cult leader. His public face was tightly controlled and always positive. He had power, the kind of visceral power the average Joe couldn't stand up to.

Or even try.

I put enough information into the request for bids to let our operators know this would be high-profile and high risk. I also put it to bid to the entire country. No sense limiting it to just the central region. This one was too important.

Not that they all weren't important, but this one could break the entire organization if done poorly.

I rolled over to check on the surveillance bids. I had two.

CHAPTER FIVE

"Learning is not attained by chance. It must be sought for with ardor and diligence." –Abigail Adams

A light rain fell over Washington, DC. The locals were unenamored of spring rain. The cool and the bite on the skin were fodder for talk in the local coffee shops. On the street, a man walked…no, marched in his smart blue uniform and wheel cap, the brim keeping the rain out of his eyes.

A swarthy man with dark hair ambled close and bumped into the Air Force officer. With apologies from both, they went their own ways. The dark-haired man disappeared around the corner.

The officer kept walking straight ahead, jaw clenched as if he were on a mission. A block later, he started to meander, his steps no longer sure. He caught a fence railing and used it to hold himself upright, then his eyes rolled back and he fell.

Strangers hurried to help. They found his breathing

labored and his skin turning hot. One of them called an ambulance.

A second officer ran up to the mob. He worked his way to the front to find the man on the sidewalk. "Lieutenant Colonel!" He lifted the officer's head, but the man was unresponsive.

"Already called 911," a faceless name said.

On cue, an ambulance siren screamed in the distance.

The back of the unconscious man's hand had an ugly scratch, half purple. It was new since it would have been obvious wherever the officer came from. The man wearing a major's insignia stepped away and through the crowd. He pulled his cell out and dialed a number from memory, not one stored on the phone.

"Colonel Sykes, please." A moment later, a new voice came on the line. "Colonel Hamblin is down, sir. Arlington. I believe he's been poisoned. Just happened. Ambulance on the way. Roger. I'll go with him." He put the phone back into his pocket and waited for the ambulance while the gawkers drifted away.

The emergency medical services vehicle drove straight to the scene. It was impossible to miss.

They checked the man quickly before lifting him onto the gurney and sliding him into the back of the ambulance.

The major tried to climb in. "No passengers."

"No choice. He is the business of the US Air Force, and I've been instructed not to let him out of my sight."

"What's his claim to fame?" the attendant asked, blocking the way into the ambulance with his body.

"He's in charge of a counterterrorism unit working with those three-letter guys. I have to make sure he doesn't say anything untoward while delirious. I expect not, but just in case..."

"Counterterrorism? Doesn't look like he was very good at it," the man quipped and made room for the major. They closed the doors, and the ambulance rolled away.

From the shadow of a nearby building, the swarthy man watched.

I slept for garbage. I rose early after running my fingers down Jenny's naked back. I dressed and headed downstairs for a cup of coffee.

I dispensed with the Keurig and went straight for the French press, using one hundred percent Kona beans I'd picked up the day before. After a quick grind and basket fill, I poured boiling water over it and let it sit with the plunger raised, ready to squeeze the grounds out of my righteous cup of java.

It always put grounds in my cup, but I couldn't complain. It wasn't a packet of MRE coffee from my time in the Corps. Or from the Italian rations when we worked with them. A single twenty-four-hour Italian food ration contained seven packets of espresso. They understood the needs of their people.

MRE coffee was like the stuff rejected from the black-label generic brand. The Italian stuff was dreamy by comparison.

I jumped on my computer while sipping my coffee. Three minutes later, I stared at the unposted bid for the reverend. I wanted to take care of it myself because it was so high risk, but if I was caught, the whole company would go under. There was no backup in place. It was challenging enough to accept the special projects from the vice president, but the benefit there was the amount of future work. I posted the gig and moved to the surveillance bids.

One was from the northeast regional director, Lou Marconi. The other was from a newer operator with three successful contracts under his belt. For the same reason I bid out the Gil Twain contract, I accepted the operator's bid over the regional director with a requirement for the first report to be uploaded a day prior to our return for the appointment with OdaScumbag.

I looked at my phone. It was still too early to call New York, although it was an hour later there than where I sat. I expected the regional director to be snug in his bed for another couple of hours. I made a note on a pad by my computer—Call Lou. I didn't write more, like his phone number. I'd pull that up when I needed it and not before. The phone would erase it after the call.

I shut down the computer and headed to the modest workout room we maintained at the house. I would have taken space in the garage, but there was no need. The basement had been finished with a layout to entertain up to fifty people at a time with a pool table, a full wet bar, and seating where twenty guests could recline to watch a wall-sized high-definition television. I don't think I ever turned it on. I reminded myself to check the batteries and promptly forgot. The basement was for working out, weights and machines for muscle building and maintenance. I didn't do any cardio work down here. That was upstairs where we could look outside while watching the twin brother to the downstairs screen.

I hadn't bought any of that stuff. It was compliments of the Peace Archive, but not from there because that company didn't exist. My predecessor had left it all in the house. He and his wife had bequeathed it to us when they retired from the business and relocated to Grand Cayman. It was every hitman's dream: retire to a tropical island and swim in a pool filled with cash.

I didn't know if Vinny had a pool. He hadn't left a forwarding address and hadn't been in touch since he left. That was also part of the game. One never just walked away. It had been a long road with an immense amount of planning.

"Go, Vinny," I cheered through my final set. I figured a couple more years in the game, and Jenny and I would be ready to move on. Our personal wealth was already enough to set us up for life, but it was the other considerations. Forty-one operators counted on us for their livelihood, and we had no successor. I hadn't considered anyone yet.

I needed to get on that, but the world's scumbags… There were many who needed to meet their Maker. I was there to arrange the introduction, and I was surrounded by a company of professionals to help make that happen.

It kept me in the game.

Which brought me back to Gil Twain. I had never been a fan of televangelists who bilked their donors out of millions with promises of redemption in the afterlife. How would they know? But they were riding in a Rolls Royce in the meantime. Or a fleet of them. Gil did not live in the low-rent district.

Despite the blaring whistle from the Gil Twain positive public relations train, I knew I'd follow that contract with the greatest attention. I took people like that personally, and that was one of the reasons I had gotten into the game—a chance to right the wrongs of the world.

Mr. Allsice would benefit from a world without the Gil Pickle. What did he have on the people in power? Leverage usually came in the form of sex or money, as in dirty money. Men in power.

I wiped away the sweat with a towel I had used too often and opened my computer. I pulled up the request for bids and added a short statement.

Minimum bid is $2,000,000.

I updated the listing, made sure it stuck, and shut the computer down once more. That would draw extra eyeballs. We never listed minimums, but this one called for it.

I heard the dull thump of bare feet.

Jenny appeared. Her feet weren't the only part of her that was bare.

"Can I interest you in a cup of coffee?" I asked while peeling off my shirt.

"I'll just drink yours while you shower."

"Join me?" I hoped.

"Maybe." Her green eyes drew me in as they always did. They sparkled with emerald fire. Being on the receiving end of those looks had mesmerized me from day one. I knew we'd get our private time before getting back to work. We had a retreat to help plan and contracts to bid out. The two weeks would go by quickly.

"This is one step above useless," I complained. The interim surveillance report had arrived. I crossed my arms as I stared at the screen. "Not sure I've ever paid more to get less."

"Remember when you paid a hundred and twenty grand to call Chaz?" Jenny reminded me. She raised one eyebrow.

"Yes, but…" I paused because she didn't like it when I provided that kind of counterargument, but she didn't bite. Her patience was better than mine. "I did get something important out of that phone call. It set the wheels in motion that delivered us to this point. I'm glad we're here, but I had hoped there would be less hands-on with the move to the top."

"I'm plenty hands-on. You can't believe what I have to do to get a contract." She flicked her hair.

I scowled.

She smiled and walked away with an extra swing of her hips.

"Did you just troll me?"

"Players gotta play," she replied.

"Right in the X ring." A shooting target had a bullseye. That was the X ring, the direct center of a target. "Which reminds me, when are we going to go shooting again? I'm jonesing for it."

"We have to go to Wisconsin for that," Jenny reminded me from the hallway.

"I need to shoot to clear my head. Gil Pickle is distracting me from OdaScumbag."

"When we get back." We had to leave for the airport.

"Thanks. I'll deal with the info here, as well as start digging again on my own. This is my responsibility. Trying to sub it out was a bad idea."

"You didn't know until you tried." Jenny ran up the stairs to get changed before we left.

We had not yet received a bid on the good reverend. I was starting to lose faith. There had to be someone with the chops to pull it off, and it needed to be done soon. Albert Allsice would be at the Club and give me the hairy eyeball until I updated him. Telling him it hasn't even started might result in him yanking back his ten million. Worse than that would be the loss of future work.

Look at what I had become—a corporate weenie. We wouldn't stop by the Club on the way out of town. That was the ultimate in avoidance.

I checked the boards one last time before shutting down and found a bid on the Twain contract. An operator out of LA. Five successful contract completions. He wanted six mil. I accepted and jumped over to the bank to send him three million to get him started.

"Get here and get on it, big dog," I said to encourage the faceless operator.

After the money was transferred, I pulled the bid down and deleted it scorched earth-style. When we removed old contracts, we removed everything, scrubbing that part of the server to make sure nothing remained. We couldn't leave records like that lying around for just anyone to find. What had happened last year or last month was no one's business.

I powered down the computer, stuffed it and the power cord into a small backpack, and ran upstairs to pack the few clothes I thought I might need.

Jenny had laid my suit on the bed.

"You want to act bigwig, you gotta look the part," she said. She had also set out the bigger suitcase. The suit took up most of it once I included the shoes. Jenny had a business suit as well but tailored for her shape. "It'll be nice to dress up."

I finished loading the suitcase and closed it. After Jenny finished with her bag, I carried them both downstairs and to the garage. With one last quick look at the house, I set the alarm, and we left. Next stop, the Big Apple.

CHAPTER SIX

"There can be no peace without war." –Ancient Chinese Proverb

We arrived at JFK International Airport in the early evening hours. Waiting for us at the end of the jet bridge was none other than Rick Banik. He used a badge to exit through a door leading to the SIDA, the secure area of the airport. Under the terminal, he stopped in a busy area free of casual listeners.

"There's been a development." That was all he said.

"You have to give me more, man. I'm not good at guessing what bureaucrats think is important."

Rick rolled his eyes and sighed. Jenny nudged me in the ribs. I wouldn't guess what was next.

"We had an officer murdered in Arlington. And yes, the DC area can be a dangerous place, but he wasn't just murdered; he was poisoned with ricin, weaponized ricin. Back in the seventies, the Soviet Union carried out a hit in London on a journalist using the pointy tip of an umbrella modified to inject the toxin. This time, it was far more potent. He died in a matter of hours."

"The Soviets are still around?"

Rick shook his head. "How would you come up with that from what I said? Never mind. Grunts gotta grunt, I guess. This guy wasn't just your run-of-the-mill officer, which are a dime a dozen anywhere near the Pentagon. He was the head of a counterterrorism unit working with us on the Odenkirk case."

"That makes things interesting. Why are you here? Because it doesn't change anything. We are still on track with the contract. I won't let the vice president down, and by extension, that means I won't let you down either. How did you know what flight we were on?"

"We're the good guys, remember? We know all kinds of stuff."

"Which means you were searching our names when I asked you not to."

"I didn't agree not to. Listen, Ian. This isn't easy for me because," he looked around before leaning close, "you're a hitman. You are going to execute Maksim Odenkirk. He's an American, but he won't get a trial or any chance to defend himself. He'll be gone. That was the CIA that was hated by the public. We've reformed a lot since then, but we still have people like you on the payroll. This is something that could get us put in jail for the rest of our lives."

"That's why you hired me. So we take care of your problem, not admitting to anything related to a conspiracy to commit murder. That is simply deplorable and unfounded. And no one will get in trouble. The exit strategy is more important than the engagement itself. To keep everything aboveboard."

"These are very bad people, Ian," Rick replied. "If they

get an idea you're coming after Max, you will be hard-pressed to save your own life."

"Then let me do my job, Rick. We'll make your problem go away. We can't be rushed. You know what they say. If you want it bad, you get it bad."

Rick nodded while looking at the ground. "Right in DC. His people know we're on to him."

"Then it'll make my job that much harder, but hard does not mean impossible. We have checked bags and would like to get to them before the vagrants. We'll be in the City for a while, looking at properties to possibly expand the Club."

"Put a Club in DC. There's an endless amount of work you'd contract there. Endless."

"Maybe we will. No, wait a minute. I don't like it here." I offered my hand, and we shook. He showed us back into the terminal while he returned to the secure area and jumped into a car not far from where we had talked.

"He's spooked," I said.

"Just a lot. Should we be afraid?" Jenny wondered.

"Probably. Can't be worse than the Gomez cartel." We walked quickly to get to Baggage Claim before they shut the conveyor down.

The good news was that it was still running, and the better news was that both our bags were on it. We snagged them and headed out while a few passengers waited with hopeless expressions on their faces.

Straight to the taxi stand and back to the Loneham. They didn't have the suite we stayed in before, but the desk help remembered us and upgraded us to a better one.

It reinforced my attitude toward life. Always be kind to the people who are helping you, even if they can't.

We moved into our suite and spent the next twenty minutes looking for bugs, cameras, or other ways outsiders could intrude on our business. We unplugged the phone and smart television, pulled the curtains, and started running through our engagement for tomorrow's meeting with Mr. Odenkirk.

Babs Jaekel was nowhere to be seen, which made for an uneventful walk to OdaPresent Charities. We entered the lobby dressed to kill and were rewarded with a significantly different attitude. "Look at that. People *do* judge a book by its cover."

"When dealing with a place like this, of course they do," Jenny whispered while the ever-present receptionist took a call with a look of apology. "As you said before, everything is about the charity's figurehead."

I nodded, watching the receptionist watch us while he talked. When he hung up, he punched a couple of buttons on his phone before standing up to greet us properly. "Please follow me, Mr. and Mrs. Bragg."

He bowed his head slightly and strolled to the interior of the office complex. This wasn't an open floor plan but a maze of metal and frosted glass. Most of the office doors were closed. We heard voices but saw no faces. Around corners and through a common area with an oversized printer and office supplies, we found another corridor of wood and panels—the executive suites. We were ushered into another outer office, where an executive assistant took the handoff from the receptionist. He faded away without a word.

"Mimosa?" she asked.

"Of course. We're here to share our success, and that deserves a toast."

"Well said!" She even clapped in her feigned

enthusiasm. She lost her smile instantly on her short walk to the wet bar, where she opened a new bottle of champagne and two single-serve bottles of orange juice. She made them with well-practiced movements.

In no time, we had our champagne flutes. We toasted each other and took a small sip. I knew I wouldn't finish mine. I needed to stay sharp. Jenny probably wouldn't finish hers either.

"Reminds me of a thunderbolt special."

"A different kind of mimosa?" the assistant asked.

"A Shirley Temple with a more manly name. It's what he was drinking when we met," Jenny explained. Innocuous. No details. Enough personal information to disarm the listener.

"Where was that?"

I stepped up as we had choreographed the dance. The game was on. "I'm less than proud to admit that it was in a bar out west." It was New York. Ninety-nine percent of the country was to the west. "A bar! But we've been together ever since. One of us didn't have beer goggles on; otherwise, I would have never stood a chance." I shifted gears. "Have you lived in the City a long time?"

"My whole life. Once it's in your blood, you have no choice. I tried moving upstate but couldn't stand it. I need a certain amount of noise, background sounds to tell me the world is still turning. I feel connected and alive here." She smiled and gestured toward a plush couch before she sat and returned her attention to her computer screen.

Jenny and I took the offered seats, barely sitting before the inner door opened and Maksim Odenkirk stepped out. He was dressed in a double-breasted suit, a shirt with a button-down collar, and no tie. Made me want to take mine off.

"Mr. and Mrs. Bragg, I presume." He strode briskly

across the office. He was far shorter than I'd thought, at least six inches shorter than me. I didn't crush his hand when we shook but let him have his power without being patronizing. He dove past Jenny's hand for a quick hug. "Please." He gestured toward his office.

He led us into a dark-wood-paneled executive suite, immaculately decorated, with art on the walls and pedestals holding small statues. The desk was massive. Mahogany. There was a side seating area with a couch and a chair. Once again, we were offered seats on the couch. He took the chair and sat across a small table with neatly arranged literature, along with a couple of forms.

"I hear you are looking at possibly expanding the Club into the City," he said.

"Worst kept secret ever," I replied. "We have hit our limit on memberships and services in our Chicago branch and thought it was time to grow the business. You've checked on us and have seen that our revenue has reached a magical point of fifty million dollars a year. We think it should be a quarter of a billion, but that will take expansion. And coming to New York City to offer an elite club will require moving in the right circles. We are wealthy in our own right, so moving in those circles isn't solely for the Club."

I added the last part so we didn't come across as being there only to get something.

"Our donation would be private, not something we would tout through marketing materials, even though we understand that any monies transferred are a matter of public record as this is a recognized *and tax-deductible* charity."

"What would we be without that?" Odenkirk replied with a broad smile.

"Those are details best left to accountants. I believe in your mission, Mr. Odenkirk. Delivering money where it can best be used to shape world events in ways that matter." I let the ambiguity hang in the air while holding his gaze without coming across as a pandering fool. Maybe he would read more into that.

After a short hesitation, he replied noncommittally, "We do our best."

"Who will we help for two million dollars? Maybe we can nudge the money toward animal care."

"We have a number of great charities that we work with, but these are local, limited to New York because the need worldwide is so great. We prefer helping people, and in that, our money—your money—has a much greater reach. We have charities in all twenty-four time zones. If you were to choose human recipients, where would they be?"

"I like the home front. Right here in America. Homelessness and hunger seem out of place in this country."

"I agree completely." He was losing interest. It was time to take the conversation to the next level.

"I think the country spends far too much on national defense. If there were any way we could help cut that back, we would all benefit."

His ears perked up like a dog's on hearing the word "treat."

"An interesting perspective, Mr. Bragg. Do you agree, Mrs. Bragg?"

"I do. So much pain without need. So much presence without a goal. So much money wasted." Jenny sounded philosophical. We'd repeated our approach until it felt natural. We didn't have to agree with it. We needed OdaScumbag to *think* we believed it.

He studied us closely, me far more than Miss Jenny. "You carry yourself like a military man," he pressed.

"Nah. The old man was a cop, and that's how he

insisted his boys carry themselves. I never changed because I like the look. I like being in shape, better than any soldier." I tried to look disgusted but ended up looking over our host's shoulder and out the window. I wasn't yet ready to share that I had served in the Marine Corps.

"I play golf three times a week because I must get out of the office. Can you join me tomorrow, Blackledge at eleven?"

"I don't have my clubs with me but expect a private club like Blackledge will rent the latest Callaways to me."

"You will get what you want. We can continue our conversation without the time limitations. I know we had no time today, but this was a first meeting of what I hope will be many." He turned to Jenny. "I'm sorry, Mrs. Bragg. Would you like to join us tomorrow, too?"

"I have clubs, but golf is not for me. I will entertain myself in some of the finer shops on Fifth Avenue."

"Ah, yes. You will find *all* the finer shops on this street. Enjoy yourself. Where are you staying? I can send around a car about ten."

"The Loneham. It was the closest and, might I say, the nicest hotel in this area."

Odenkirk stood and bowed his head. He ushered us out. "Until tomorrow, Mr. Bragg."

"See you on the course. I hadn't planned on playing, so I'll need to pick up a few things from the pro shop. I'll look like I just took up the game, except I have improved my tee recently to keep the ball in play."

"No one will judge you at Blackledge, while everyone will judge you at Blackledge."

"As expected. Until tomorrow." We strolled out. The executive assistant deposited our fingerprint-smudged champagne flutes on the wet bar before escorting us to the front desk.

"I hope your meeting was productive." She handed us a small packet of papers.

"Very. You'll be seeing us again, and thank you."

We hurried out. There was nothing else to be gained from being inside the offices of OdaPresent Charities.

And there was much to mull over from the short conversation, barely five minutes' worth.

CHAPTER SEVEN

"Keep your friends close and enemies closer." –*The Godfather* Part II

Although the sidewalks were busy, some people simply stand out—like the guy who appeared behind us once we left the office building. We stopped in a number of shops, even a café to get a coffee. When we emerged, he stood at the edge of sight.

We'd faced him enough times that he had to know that we spotted him.

I had to wonder if that was the message. We were now under surveillance as persons of interest. I wanted to double back within a building and come up behind him, confront him. Let him know that we didn't like to be followed, which would probably not bode well for our relationship with OdaScumbag. I settled on something a little more congenial.

Jenny bought him a coffee. We headed straight for him. He made believe he was on his phone. Maybe he was.

"We went with black, medium roast, but here are a

couple packets of sugar and creamer if you swing that way." I forced it into his hand, and he almost dropped his phone. Once he had the cup, I walked away.

It was good to make my point. *We know you're following us, and we don't care.* It was a powerful message. Sometimes it was better to have allies than enemies.

It was always better to have allies. We didn't need this guy hating on us. He was only trying to do his job. Whatever job that was. If he was muscle, he wasn't very good at being intimidating as he stood there clutching his phone with two fingers while cradling a hot coffee with the lid off. One bump would ruin his day.

Simple but effective. A real pro wouldn't have taken it and probably wouldn't have been spotted at all.

Like the second person, a woman in New York business attire. She blended in well, but she was following, too.

I caught a glance. Twice. And that was enough to convince me the first guy was for show, and the second was the real tail.

"Straight to the hotel, my dear?"

"Since I'll be browsing shops tomorrow, I think you are obligated to see what lies before me."

I schooled my expression and cleared my throat before speaking. "Of course. I'll carry your bags."

"I know how hard that was for you. You hate shopping."

"Have mercy!" I cried, falling to my knees and begging her, creating a scene. People stopped to watch.

"Make him pay!" someone shouted at Jenny.

"Cheating scum," another grumbled.

"Not cheating," Jenny called back. "He doesn't want to go shopping with me. I think he should be happy carrying my bags."

"Carry her bags. Carry her bags," the crowd chanted.

That backfired. I stood and waved to the crowd before

bowing deeply. "I shall do just that. Jenny is not a princess or a queen. She is Merlin!"

The women in the crowd cheered.

"That's Jenny Bragg!" someone shouted through the cheering.

"Oh, crap," I mumbled.

Jenny waved again and took my hand to make a beeline for the hotel. "Nice."

She never meant nice when she said it. "I think we're going to have to move out of the country."

"Undoubtedly," Jenny replied. "Did we lose him?"

"Yes, but I think she's still following."

"She?"

"A tail for the tail. A double-switch. Plain gray, your height and build. Brown hair. Sunglasses. That's what stands out. It's not that sunny."

"Maybe she's simply photosensitive," Jenny quipped. We turned abruptly and headed down a side street that was no less busy than the main road.

We dodged into a deli that smelled of sauerkraut and pastrami. "I can taste lunch," I said.

"It's barely past breakfast," Jenny replied, glancing out the door.

"Perfect to kill some time before hitting the gym for a monster workout. We'll explore the shops later after rubbing our sweaty bodies all over each other."

"You remain incorrigible," Jenny said. "And I love you for it. Get your sandwich."

"Reuben with mustard, not thousand island. This is an important distinction." I bellied up to the counter and ordered, happy to find they carried a spicy brown mustard, although the counter person seemed less than amused with my order. "It's an acquired taste."

"Reuben with brown mustard for Mr. No Taste," she shouted toward the kitchen in her heavy accent. "Next."

I started laughing. It was the most New York thing we'd experienced in our two trips to the City. All the while, we watched for the woman watching us but didn't see her. She was the pro.

"Why?" Jenny whispered.

"We have piqued his interest. That's both good and bad. If we had any doubts about this gig, those are gone now. We'll have to see it through to the end. If, or I should say, when something happens to OdaScumbag, then his minions could retaliate. People don't like it when the money train leaves the station and never comes back."

"I remember what you did after Chaz was murdered."

"They shouldn't have killed him," I said in a low voice.

"No, they shouldn't have. Maybe the minions will feel the same way about our boy."

"That would require an extended effort, one that would need additional preparation. We'll have to move hotels, someplace out of the spotlight."

"That's what I was thinking," Jenny replied. She'd had enough of unwanted attention from Fifth Avenue.

"But you're a vigilante hero."

She didn't look amused at first, but then she lightened up. "Maybe I've always been that person. Others finally recognize it." She stopped me before I could protest. "Besides you. You always believed." Her smile disappeared. "Our tail just strolled past without looking in. She must have some peripheral vision."

"It's a learned skill," I replied.

They called the number for my sandwich. I hurried to the counter to retrieve it. The smell of the warm rye overflowing with sauerkraut and pastrami with the brown mustard on the side almost overwhelmed me. "This smells like heaven."

"Maybe that's what we should rename it. Reuben is so last year."

I dropped a five-dollar bill on the counter for her even though I'd already tipped with the first payment.

Jenny was shaking her head when I arrived, cradling my plate as if carrying a crystal treasure. "You should see your face. Just like a kid at Christmas."

"What can I say? I like to eat. Maybe the City has some redeeming qualities after all. Or, cheaper and easier, we can send one of the Club's chefs here to learn some of these recipes." I kept my back to the window and trusted Jenny to keep an eye out. The tail didn't return, but we knew she was out there where she could see us while we had no eyes on her. We didn't need to watch her because she was going to be there. We'd have to play her at the right time, but that time was not yet. It would be later tonight when we took multiple cabs to a new hotel.

Until then, I was going to enjoy my sandwich.

A little slice of heaven.

"I don't see her," I whispered to Jenny. The driver threw our suitcases into the trunk, and we directed him to the 33rd Street Train Station, which was only a few blocks away. We tipped the driver well as we carried our luggage down the stairs to the metro, where we used our passes to snag the subway to Grand Central Station. We transferred to the train that took us to Times Square.

We strolled out two stops later to catch a waiting cab to take us north to our new hotel. In the evening traffic, the drive took an hour and the meter kept running, almost like a power meter at the height of air conditioning season.

We ended at the Royal Plaza Yonkers, another boutique hotel. Chains shared their information where boutiques kept it to themselves. It would take a more concerted effort by hackers to find us in a one-off business.

We paid the taxi driver in cash and helped ourselves into the hotel.

"If anyone can follow us through all that, good on them." We had already checked our luggage for bugs, but I hadn't thought they'd been tampered with. When we'd left the room at the Loneham, we had put them in a dark closet with a hair balanced across the back. Anyone pulling them out to look would disturb the hair. It was low-cost and effective. The simpler the device, the easier it was to implement and for bad guys to overlook.

We settled into our new hotel and headed out for dinner. A five-star steakhouse was nearby, and we availed ourselves of it even though we knew it wouldn't rival the options we had in Vegas.

The entire evening was dedicated to thinking about what was next—conversations in the cart during our golf game. How much would I divulge? Only the Club's business. If he searched, he would find that Ian Bragg didn't exist earlier than three years ago. I was ready for that inevitable question.

I counted on it.

I showed up at the golf course in slacks and a golf shirt, newly purchased. I planned on buying soft spikes from the clubhouse, along with balls and tees. I carried a five-dollar gold piece to use as a ball mark.

With an hour to go before our tee time, I finished my outfitting, rented clubs, and headed to the small range and putting green for a few minutes of prep, which meant watching the world while swinging the clubs.

I focused on my game only so much as the doorway into the world of those who fancied themselves as players in both golf and the real world. Watching how someone played gave me a great deal of insight into how they lived their lives.

I preferred not to keep score and simply enjoyed hitting the ball around. This was unfathomable to many of my so-called colleagues at the Club. They used scores as a measure of their performance, which would have been fine, except they cheated. They adjusted the lie of their ball or took mulligans. In life, one gets a limited number of do-overs. One shouldn't waste them.

Not on a good drive that ended up in a bush. Take the penalty and move it out. A free-kick isn't in the rules.

Golf. A single game played a thousand different ways.

Maksim Odenkirk showed up fifteen minutes before our tee. The professional caddie team picked up our clubs, two bags per caddie. I thought we'd be riding in a cart together. I was perfectly happy walking.

"I appreciate you carrying my clubs and helping guide me through the course. What's your name?"

"Tommy D, sir. I'm happy to be of service. Been here for two years now. There are no surprises left on these greens for me. I'll help get you in the hole."

"I can ask for no more, Tommy D." I clapped him on his shoulder and headed out to meet the man I called OdaScumbag.

"Maksim. So much better being out here in the fresh air than in the filtered air of the big city."

"So much better, Ian. How are you today? I trust breakfast at the Loneham was gratifying?"

"We moved hotels. Fifth Avenue was a little busy for us. We're in Yonkers now, and yes, breakfast was magnificent."

Max wasn't surprised as he had sent a car for me. I was sure he knew that we had left the Loneham, just as I was sure he didn't know where we had gone.

"You'll have to share where because I also enjoy a magnificent breakfast."

He didn't know. Moving had been a test, and we had passed. Building his trust while keeping our motivations secret. Could I do that? I dropped two balls on the putting green and lined the first one up on the nearest hole while I answered.

"We're at the Royal Plaza. It's a nice location. Their suites are worth the price of admission. Also, I like the open environment more than the hustle and bustle of the big city. If we're going to bring the Club to New York, it has to work for me. Lake Forest looks like a small town. The old money of the city has a hold on it, much like the Hamptons. Maybe that's where we need to go. We're still exploring. The legal wrangling alone will take twelve to eighteen months."

"I might be able to expedite that for you. I know a few people who can be had for a good steak."

"Hell, *I* can be had for a good steak." I smiled and stroked the putt. It rimmed the cup since it broke more than I expected it to. I stepped back to study the line. "I didn't see the break."

"Not everything will be as you see it," Max said.

"And that's why we need good people like Tommy D, to help us see what we might not otherwise," I replied, tipping my new Blackledge ball cap to the caddy.

"Shall we?" Max gestured toward the walking path to get to the first tee. I picked up my Titleist balls and followed. He had carried his putter to the green but hadn't taken any swings. But he played three times a week.

We met two others on the tee, who introduced themselves as Ace and Clutch. I wanted to ask if they were made-up names but didn't press it. If that was how they wanted to be called, then so be it.

"Twenty-dollar skins?" Max asked. The other two nodded.

"Ringers?" I asked, expecting they'd take my remaining

cash, but the good thing about skins was that the hole winner took all. Three good players would compete against each other and save me the embarrassment of not winning any holes. They just looked at me. "It's all good. I got four hundred dollars that isn't doing anything productive."

Ace snorted. "Newcomer's tee." They stepped aside to let me up. I looked at the hole.

"Tommy D, up," I called. "I have a slight draw on my drive, maybe two fifty, two seventy. Where's my aim point?"

He selected a towering tree on the right. "Just left of that in case you catch it clean. You don't want to hit a great shot and start tree-knocking."

"I like your style." I took two practice swings while the others waited. I focused on the ball to the exclusion of everything else. I let my body do the work and hit it easy, closer to two hundred and fifty yards, but with the slight draw, it ended up in the center of the fairway.

"Who's the ringer?" Max said with a smile. "Right on the sprinkler heads."

The other three hit their shots, outdriving me by a solid fifty yards each, but two were in the rough on the right and one on the left. I walked with Max since he was on the left side.

"Do you like it here?" I asked.

"This is a great course. You haven't seen anything yet."

Not what I was looking for, and he knew it. "The city. I'm still up in the air about coming here. I'm not sure this is the place for me."

"Depends on how deep you are. For instance, according to my people, you are three years old. Ian Bragg did not exist before that moment."

It was the first hole. I'd thought he would wait until the back nine so we didn't have to walk uncomfortably in each other's presence for four hours. But he made the first big move.

"That. I didn't exist before three years ago. That was a different person and a different life. I'm not running from something if that's what you are wondering about. I'm running *to* something, as evidenced by the success of the Club. Our clients are happy with the unrivaled opportunity to network."

"What do you do, Mr. Bragg?"

"Not wasting any time, are you?" I studied him while the caddy walked a discreet distance away.

"I want to know what it will be like doing business with someone. If I didn't know better, I would think you are a plant."

"What's there to see behind the curtain, Mr. Odenkirk?" I asked.

"I asked first," he replied.

At my ball, I was given a brief respite from the interrogation. "What club, my man?" I asked Tommy D.

He shook his head and waved his hand. "I never club players. You determine what club, based on the distance and other factors. Right now, you're at one hundred eighty-five yards to the pin. It's slightly uphill, so you'll want to add a club. A one-ninety-five stroke will put you within tap-in distance for a birdie."

"That works. Looks like a five iron." He handed it to me. I dug a deep divot with my practice swing. I started to walk out to retrieve it.

Tommy called me off. "That's my job, sir. I have to earn that monster tip you're going to give me at the end."

"I shouldn't be digging trenches like that. Punishment is my due." I took another smoother swing and then lined up, taking my draw into account. I tried to swing as smoothly as I could. I caught the ball with more left spin than I wanted and ended up in the sand trap off the side of the green.

"Not bad at all. You'll get it up and down," Max said from behind me.

"You haven't seen my sand game. It's about as good as if I were standing in the middle of a pond trying to hit the ball out."

He chuckled. Tommy D ran after the divot while Max and I resumed our walk.

"What do you do, Ian?" he pressed.

"You mean, besides run the Club?" He didn't bother answering. "I work with powerful people to help them realize greater levels of success."

"How?"

"If I said by helping them leverage core competencies, would you think less of me?"

"I'd invite you to leave the group before we reach the first green."

"Appropriate. I make introductions in a way that synergies are created, filling gaps that powerful people don't know they have. The whole is greater than the sum of the individual parts. In a way, I see myself as a lesser version of you. You've built massive wealth through bringing out the best in companies or by realizing the greatest value a company has to offer before it declines. After you achieved a personal net worth of over a billion dollars, you turned to philanthropy to build your personal brand as a do-gooder, and you leveraged that to build even greater personal wealth since you were able to draw down the amount of money you sunk into OdaPresent. There are very wealthy people out there with gaps in their businesses, and they don't see them."

Max stood over his ball, seemingly ignoring what I said. He called for a nine iron. With a smooth stroke, he put his ball in the middle of the green.

"Nice shot."

He handed the club to the caddie, and we started to walk. Tommy D left the divot since it was in the rough.

"Gaps." He said the word as if trying it on for size. "What do you see as gaps in my business?"

"Your gap is that you should just stay the course. You own your core competencies. You don't need someone like me. I work with old-money people. They have money but aren't sure how they got to where they are. A minor issue ten years ago could be nothing now, or it could be a big deal. Having money creates its own problems."

"So you help that money go away?" Max quipped.

"I help that money work toward the greater business and build. Always building unless they are past the point of no return, then we put a nice layer of lipstick and face paint on that pig and put it on the auction block. Better that than being left with nothing. I help people realize the most value for what they have. It is lucrative when the wealthy see their money grow instead of having to liquidate. It's surprising how many people choose liquidation as one of their first options."

"I made the bulk of my money from those types of people. An established business retains a great deal of value when put in proper hands. Maybe we are alike, Mr. Bragg. More than you know. Here's a tip. Think of your ball in the sand as George Washington on a dollar bill. Take a bill-sized swipe with a three-quarters swing. That'll put you back into play."

With a sand wedge in hand, I tried to visualize the shot. I set my feet in the sand, ball at the low point of my natural swing. I took the club's head back three-quarters of a full swing and rotated through, keeping my head down and my eye on the ball. I muscled the club through the sand, and when I looked up, a wave of sand with the ball at the front was arcing its way toward the green. The ball hit and rolled softly to within two feet.

"That's good," Ace said. I waved him off. "I'll play it all the way if you don't mind."

"As you wish. I guess we will, too." He looked purposely at Max's five-foot birdie putt.

Max stopped me before I reached the green. "I may have some business for you outside of the Club if you would indulge me. A friend is struggling…" He left it hanging.

Oh, crap…

CHAPTER EIGHT

"Research is seeing what everybody else has seen and thinking what nobody else has thought." –Albert Szent-Györgyi

We finished the round without further business talk. I have to say that the birdie on the par three with an eight-hole carryover put me in the green. I won two hundred and forty dollars. I felt like I should buy them drinks, but Ace and Clutch said they had to go. We shook hands, and they left while Max and I headed for the bar. The host greeted Odenkirk by name and ushered us to a private table away from the others. A server was there instantly. He ordered Perrier. I went with a Shirley Temple.

Max thought it amusing that a grown man would drink something like that.

"It's what I like," I explained.

"My friend," Max started. "He runs a shipping company, and there are regulators standing in his way."

"Didn't pass the sniff test, huh? Is there a problem with the ships, or are the regulators providing unnecessary scrutiny?"

"Yes," Max replied.

"I see. Leverage. How do we remove the pressure so your friend can get on with his work?"

"Exactly."

"I'll have to see them and check out what is workable. I might know some people who can help with that gap."

"If you could get it done within a week, my friend would greatly appreciate your help. He would owe you a big favor, and in this town, a favor from Mark Gadsden is worth its weight in gold."

The server brought our drinks. I dropped her a twenty and told her to keep the change. She stood there with the money in the palm of her hand. "You're not from around here, are you?" she asked.

There had been no check. I had no idea what the price was. "It's that obvious? You couldn't tell from the clothes I purchased today, like the Blackledge hat? How much are the drinks?"

"Thirty dollars."

I dropped another twenty into her hand. "My apologies. I'm not old enough to complain about the prices, but if you want, I can yell 'Get off my lawn' for you."

"I'm good," she replied and walked away.

"Where were we?" I asked.

"A week. He needs it done in a week. He wants to launch next Friday. That last bit of paperwork is holding him back."

"We need a signature from a man unwilling to give it? Is that the issue?"

"The bottom line, in more ways than one. Inspector is Rennie Gannon with the Department of Safety and Health."

I nodded and took a sip of my drink. I preferred the version made with orange juice rather than 7-Up as the mixer with grenadine. I had forgotten to tell them and was being punished for my lack of attention.

"Your wife is very photogenic," Max casually dropped.

"Why, Mr. Odenkirk, that could be taken as a threat."

He raised his hands in defense. "I've seen the video from our local huckster, Babs Jaekel. Jenny has some good moves. And so do you, by the way. You're not a corporate executive."

"But I am. I just believe in fitness. I can't just stop staying in shape, and if your sparring partner looked like Miss Jenny, you'd practice a lot, too."

He bowed his head. "What did you do that required such fitness?"

"In another life, I was a Marine, a combat Marine. Corporate life is little different, without the risk of real bullets. It's like the kindergarten of combat."

Max leaned back and crossed his arms, not defensively but with great interest. "You said you weren't military."

"I wasn't ready to share. Now I am."

"Kindergarten of combat. Is that how you see it?"

I shrugged. "Hard not to. I've seen both. I've seen the corporate wars. Business tycoons think they are gladiators fighting in the coliseum to roaring fans when they are verbally sparring a mile up the road in the Senate. It's important, but their risk is limited to hurtful words and maybe losing their money. Those worth their salt know how to make more."

"I like how you think, Ian. I also like how you play golf. Very measured, step by step. Tactical. You have the strength to drive the ball three hundred plus, but you settle for two fifty to keep it in the best playing position. You can tell a lot about a man by the way he plays golf."

"My sentiments exactly. I'm glad you didn't play the foot wedge or a mulligan. Life gives you one shot. You have to make the best of it."

He laughed and finished his drink, then stood and offered his hand. "See you here on Friday, Ian. I look forward to hearing about your progress."

"Friday it is. Same time?"

He nodded before taking a circuitous route through the bar to say kind words to the bartender and staff on his way out. I took a sip of my drink and watched players warming up on the practice green.

I couldn't do this alone since I couldn't risk exposing any Peace Archive assets, but I knew a guy who wanted to help. I drained my glass and headed outside. My clubs were gone, with my stuff inside. I hunted down Tommy D, who told me that they were stored with Mr. Odenkirk's clubs. I had already given the caddie a hundred-dollar tip but handed him a second C-note. "Thanks again for your help today, Tommy D."

"My pleasure, Mr. B."

"Where can I have a private phone conversation?"

"There's a bench in the trees off the parking lot. Sometimes the caddies hide there when they don't want to carry for a beauty, but everyone's working right now. You'll have it all to yourself."

"Who wouldn't want to caddie for a beauty?"

"BT, as in bad tipper. Twenty bucks for four hours of hauling a bag? I don't think so. We give them to the new guys. Let the young fellas earn their wings."

"You are the man, Tommy D." I pointed at him and nodded.

I found the bench behind a weeping willow, just as Tommy described. It was hard to see in or out. I checked around to see if there were any electronics but didn't find anything. It didn't mean there weren't, but I'd keep my voice down.

I dialed the number I knew. Rick Banik answered on the first ring. "I need you to spin up that machinery of yours and tell Rennie Gannon from the Department of Safety and Health to stand down on his paperwork for Gadsden Shipping something or other, and he needs to do it right-freaking-now."

"Why does this need to happen, Ian?"

"I'm close to getting into Max Odenkirk's inner circle. We'll see where that takes me. I need to show that I can play dirty if he's going to come clean on his other activities. Don't you want to know for sure that he's the one behind the funding?"

Rick blew out a breath, audibly rasping in my ear. "I do want to know for sure. How likely is it that you'll get inside?"

"You take care of that safety paperwork, and my chances improve vastly. If you take care of it before Friday, I'll look like a god. I'll rent a place in the Hamptons and see if I can get him to come up for the weekend. What would that be worth?"

"Having someone inside an organization like that has value beyond measure. And helps us deliver payback for the lives we've already lost. I'll take care of the inspector. Be careful, Ian. This guy's dangerous."

"So am I."

I recounted my golf game in the most minute detail for my lovely bride. I'm not sure I could have bored her more, but that was part of the game spouses played. See who could be less thrilling to the other.

She finally had enough. "Ian. If you say one more word about golf, I'm going to kick you in the face."

"Is this what our relationship has degenerated into?" I cried, falling to my knees.

"How did it work out the last time you tried that?" She motioned for me to get up.

"Not well at all. I need to get a new playbook." I hugged her and nibbled her neck.

"Please do, and make sure it does not contain the words golf, wedge, draw, hook, sprinklers, or smash. Golf is boring! There. I said it out loud."

I leaned back so I could look horribly offended. "I heard you sending subliminal messages through eye daggers. But I won two hundred and forty bucks. Not often a target pays me to do bad things to him. Not often at all."

"Do you think he's dirty?"

"He's way dirty, but is he a terrorist? That I don't know. I don't feel it, though. He doesn't strike me as a crusader for anything other than the almighty dollar. Funding scumbags is all risk and no reward unless he's got a deep dark secret."

"Another Jimmy?" Jenny wondered.

"I'm starting to think he's not our man."

"Me, too," Jenny agreed. "Are you thinking what I'm thinking?"

I knew. "We talk to him." In this business, we couldn't make mistakes.

"Is Rick good with that?" Jenny asked.

"He's warming to the idea," I lied, even though I wanted to believe it. "I'd like to rent a place in the Hamptons for a week. Nice, on the water. You know. Whatever costs the most."

Jenny shook her head. "I've been at the spa all day, and now you expect me to work? I just had my nails done!"

She hadn't. Her nails were short because of how much we sparred. Neither of us wanted to get scratched more than we already were. Although she *had* gotten a mani-pedi.

"You look gorgeous as always," I told her. "Now. The Hamptons."

She opened her laptop and, using the VPN, started searching. Airbnb showed a luxury home with a heated pool and a hot tub and a backyard set up to accommodate a party with twenty guests. "Booking for Saturday through next Sunday. Southampton. Thirty thousand total. There's a five-hundred-dollar cleaning fee and a service fee of over three grand. What's that about?"

"It's about getting more money from someone willing to spend three thousand a night for a place to stay. I'll bill it back and see if Rick pays."

"There's no way," Jenny said.

"If he pays, you come play golf with me once a week for a month, and you fake like you enjoy it. If you win, I'll get you the best full-body massage you've ever had."

"Where would I get such magnificent pampering?" she asked.

"I'm thinking Bali, but if you know of an alternative, I'm listening. Although, you're not going to win this bet."

She pulled away from me and walked around our hotel suite. "Since when did we get into the international intrigue business? This whole thing is making me uncomfortable. It's a different world, dealing with people who are willing to die for their cause. It changes everything we know about a contract. Everyone we've dealt with has been in it exclusively for themselves, and in that, they were predictable."

"Rick has our back."

"The government?" Jenny sounded skeptical and dismissive.

"I guess we'll have to see. I want to trust him, even though I know I shouldn't. Would he go down to save us?"

"He seemed straight-up, but he's a bureaucrat, and

we're supposed to hate them." Jenny cocked her head as she looked at me. "Aren't we?"

"Sometimes the right answer is 'yes, dear.' In this case, we'll see what he can do with a day and a half. It would be nice to have good news. Rent that place in the Hamptons, and I'll spin up some invites."

"Who are you going to invite?"

"Well, OdaScumbag to start with. Do we know anyone else up here?"

"Lenny, but I'm pretty sure we're not inviting any of our own people."

"No. I'm still bummed about the surveillance report. He told me nothing. But maybe there's another report. Let me take a look."

I dug through the dark web to get to the front end on the way to the back end. When I got there, a new report waited. I opened it to find a picture of me with Max. The short paragraph suggested I was the shady character with a dark past and probably the one who was funneling money out of the agency.

I didn't need even more people scouring the web, lighting up the analytics with my name.

That was me, your boss's boss. Cease and desist all research into me immediately since I'm positive I'm not the one we're looking for. Follow him from the charity to meetings in third-party locations. Those are the ones I'm interested in. And while you're at it, look up Ace and Clutch, the other two members of that foursome. I'd like to know their story. I'll be with him at the course on Friday, so you don't need to follow him there again.

Jenny read over my shoulder. "Good picture. Shady character? Can you say that he's wrong? No, you can't."

"I'm a different shady. I'm the bright and sparkly side of shady."

Jenny didn't look convinced. She pointed at her swimsuit. "Beach or pool?"

"I'm partial to staying in, so pool."

"I knew you'd say that." She stripped in front of me, and I watched shamelessly. I did the same for her. The little things kept our relationship vibrant. We had enough stress without adding to it on the home front. That always made me reconsider getting out of the game, even though we had just taken over the company. What was the lifespan of someone who manages a company filled with hitmen? Vinny and Chaz had run the company for more than ten years, building it into a powerhouse while staying out of the law's harsh light. That was the hardest part, flying under the radar while being visible.

Maybe that was the thrill we were still young enough to enjoy. A trip to Bali after this sounded like just the medicine, but I didn't think I was wrong. If we didn't kill anyone, just destroyed their ability to continue doing what they were doing, wasn't that every bit as effective without the guillotine of the law ready to drop on our necks?

A hitman with a conscience. That was how I thought of myself. Maybe I wasn't looking for the thrill but for justice.

It had always been about justice.

And Maksim Odenkirk was on the wrong side of it.

CHAPTER NINE

"Though some may see their shortcomings as the greatest evil from the pit of hell, while some throw invectives at God for bringing them into a cruel, problematic world." –Michael Bassey Johnson

I once again arrived early, same trousers, same hat, but different golf shirt. I putted for half an hour to sharpen that part of my game, but I was waiting for a call from Rick. I hadn't heard from him since I dropped my request.

In the caddie shack, I saw Tommy D maneuvering to avoid those in front of us. I thought I'd make it easy on him. I got the head caddie's attention. "Tommy D for me, please." I didn't wait for a reply as I walked back to the putting green. Two minutes later, Tommy D appeared with Max's bag and mine.

"Thank you, sir," he told me.

"What am I doing wrong here, Tommy D?"

He left the bags at the side of the green before joining me. "You aren't following through toward the hole. You're imparting spin on the ball, and that's why it always seems to break more than you expect or less if the break is to your left."

"I'll be damned. Why didn't you tell me this last time?"

"I had to sleep on it. Then it hit me, just like an errant curveball."

I adjusted things and tried it out from both sides of a hole on a slope. "I'll be. Maybe today I'll take more of Max's money."

Tommy looked around before speaking in a near whisper. "Maybe today, you should consider that they let you win. Expect hundred-dollar skins this time."

"It was still a good birdie." I winked. I hadn't played poorly, but a couple of good holes shouldn't carry the day.

"That it was, sir."

When Max arrived, we headed straight for the tee, where a couple of others were waiting. I had seen them but thought they were ahead of us. One looked to be in his sixties and was maybe a hundred pounds overweight. The other looked to be his son, also overweight. The older man was already sweating.

"Max, my friend. I'm feeling a little under the weather, so I'll probably only play nine and lament the opportunity to take your money on the back nine."

I didn't see it. Maybe Max sandbagged to earn favors.

"Let me introduce you to my friend Ian Bragg," he told the rest of our foursome. "Mark Gadsden and his son Bryan."

The instant I reached for the elder Gadsden's hand, my phone started ringing. We shook quickly. I nodded toward the group and excused myself. "I have to take this."

I hurried a few steps away and answered. "Ian here."

"It's done," Rick replied and hung up.

That was all I needed.

My companions stood in a circle, and Max tossed a spinning tee. After three tosses, the first tee's order was confirmed: Mark, Bryan, Max, and me. I pulled Max to the side while the Gadsdens took a couple of practice swings.

"Hundred-dollar skins. I hope you don't mind," Max said. I tried not to smile.

"Yes, no problem. Mr. Gadsden's problem has been resolved. He'll be able to launch on time."

"Already?" Max looked skeptical. "But how?"

I looked down my nose at him. "Doing what I do is lucrative because no one else can do it, which means I can't be sharing my secrets. I'm sorry, man."

"You could be a fed."

I snorted. "That's pretty funny, Max. What are the chances of the feds funding my lifestyle? And the Club? Zero, because I hate all bureaucrats. If I could figure out a way to run my Chicago business without sharing two cents of it with the state of Illinois, I'd do that. And hold the IRS at bay, too. Double bonus, but no. They all take a generous cut, but my accountant has done right by me, limiting my exposure. I'm sure my denial sounds defensive, but I got nothing else. Not a fed. Those guys are my enemy too. Which begs the question, why are they yours?"

We quieted as the elder Gadsden stroked the ball to about where I'd hit mine last time.

"He's much better than he looks," Max said softly.

"I figured the second you upped the skin game. You're better than you let on, too. I'm going to get taken to the cleaners today, aren't I?"

"Probably." Max smiled. He hadn't answered my question, but he had relaxed. He showed no tension. I felt comfortable around him. Too bad I was going to have to kill him.

The younger Gadsden drove the ball a solid three hundred yards right down the middle of the fairway. Max hit his close to that.

I took the tee. "I feel like I should give you all my

money right now rather than suffer the indignity of losing it one bill at a time."

I swung harder than my usual, which brought the club around quicker and threw the ball into the left rough—the heavy stuff.

"So it begins," I intoned.

Tommy D took my club and whispered, "You have a better approach to the green from there, and you got good distance. You're probably a smooth seven away."

"What happened to not clubbing the players?"

"You need to win this because you aren't the type to be played. And you tipped me better than anyone else this year. That has value in my book."

"I appreciate it, Tommy D. Don't undermine the others. Help them just as much. I want to win but fair and square."

"Of course. I do my best with each player." He stepped away at a look from Max. The group in front of us was still on the green. That gave us time.

"You should let Mark know the good news. The favor will then be yours. It is not mine to take."

"It would not have happened without you, though."

"I've earned my favors, and hopefully, one day I'll earn a favor from you."

"Maybe. We have a place in the Hamptons for the next week. Any chance you can make it up this weekend? We'll have a little get-together. I don't even know if there's a Mrs. Max or a girlfriend, but I don't recommend bringing both at the same time."

"There is a Mrs. O. I don't share that much because someone of my status is always a target for predators. We can do Sunday around lunch."

"I'll write the address for you once I get it from Miss Jenny."

"You don't know your own address?" Max quipped. "I know, renting, but maybe someday soon you'll buy. An office on Fifth Avenue? Nice address on the business card, but a place in the Hamptons? That is where the real business is conducted."

"Or on Blackledge?"

"It has its moments," Max admitted. "Looks like you're up."

I held out my hand. "Seven, please."

Tommy D hooked me up. The rough wasn't as bad as it looked from the tee. A smooth stroke, keeping my wrists firm to power through, and the ball sailed out to land on the front of the green and roll toward the back, following the slope of the green to deliver the ball beside the hole.

"Well, now, Mr. Bragg. Seems like we weren't the only ones sandbagging the first round."

"Lucky shot," I replied.

The others followed with approach shots that had all four of us putting for birdie. Caddies went out of their way to make sure we were handed our putters as early as possible. It was a badge of honor to carry the flat blade from a ways out on the fairway to the green. We walked four abreast, all headed to the same place. "Mark," I started. "Max told me about your issues with a safety inspector that would hold up your launch in a week." He looked at me without saying anything. "That phone call I received was about that. It appears that your paperwork has been signed, and you have been cleared to launch on time."

He looked at Max.

"Ian Bragg is an expediter of sorts. He runs his own high-end club in Chicago, but he does things for his members that leave him in good stead."

"Cryptic, but I'll take it. I'll have to double-check to make sure, but if this is true, then I shall be forever in your debt." He gestured to his son, who recovered his phone from his bag and flicked a finger at his ball.

Pick it up. He was done for the hole.

We approached our putts less comfortable than we'd been a few seconds earlier. We could hear Bryan Gadsden talking in the background.

"I'm away," Max noted and putted first. Tommy D tended the pin while the other caddie fixed the ball marks on the green. Max hit it close and tapped in for par. Mark did the same. No matter what, I wasn't going to lose money yet.

Live to fight another day. Tommy D pointed at a spot with his toe. "Your aim point." Then he moved to the other side of the cup to avoid giving me an artificial aiming point, which would have been against the rules.

With his alignment and my new follow-through, I was able to make the putt. I started the round at one under par and three hundred dollars richer.

For the moment.

When we reached the second tee, Bryan gave his father the news. "We've been given a thirty-day approval."

Mark stared at me.

"You wanted to launch on time. You can now do that. I had one day to work. I now have thirty more if you want me to continue. Time is a businessman's friend if I'm not mistaken. The more of it you have, the better your result will be."

He nodded tersely. "I can launch on time, and that was my greatest concern. We have a lot of wheels in motion that count on the new line to launch. The first three container ships are ready, but we couldn't load without the safety approval. Thirty days? They'll have already traveled across the ocean and back. Yes, Mr. Bragg. Thirty days works, and you have done me a great favor, one that I was incapable of doing myself."

"Let's call it the gap that friends can help you fill. Just like if I need anything shipped, I know where to turn."

"Indeed." We shook like business partners. Max looked like a proud parent.

Sunday in the Hamptons. "If there's anyone else you want to join us, ask them to come. It's short notice, so I'm good if nobody comes. I'll have to settle for chasing my naked wife around. *Settle*, that's what I'll do."

"How many can you accommodate?"

"Twenty, I think she said." I knew it was twenty.

"Plan for all twenty, vegan and carnivore alike."

The discomfort evaporated as Mark Gadsden and Max Odenkirk relaxed and accepted me as one of their own. I refused to talk more about business, and they liked that.

I played the best round of my life and ended up only losing twelve hundred dollars.

"We had to pay double for the caterers because of the short notice," Jenny said from the front door, where she waited for the catering van to show up with the crew and the food.

I shrugged, not because I was indifferent, but because that was the price of admission. I wondered what kind of individuals we'd get introduced to.

My phone rang. I expected it was Rick. I stepped outside by the pool to take the call. I punched the green button but didn't say anything.

"Ian?"

"Rick?"

"Is that how you answer the phone now?"

"It's how I answered the phone before you entered my life. Whoever calls me is the one who needs to identify himself. You know, in case the feds are listening." I dipped my toe into the pool. It said it was heated. It didn't feel like it. I wasn't going in.

"You're a funny guy, Ian. I'll kill you last."

"And now you're stealing my best lines. Hey, while you're here, we have company coming soon to the place we rented in the Hamptons that you're paying for. Our boy and at least nine power players. This is spinning higher and higher. I don't know what kind of things we'll talk about, but I'm pretty sure it's not of the type that you're concerned about. I just don't see it, but I'll keep digging. Thirty days on the Gadsden Shipping deal. Nice touch. I want this to be settled and you out of my life in thirty days. Then you can do whatever the hell you want. In the interim, I'm going to have to off someone just to maintain my sanity."

"Just make sure it's the right someone," Rick replied softly.

"Why did you call?"

"Just checking in because it's what bureaucrats do."

"I have an F-bomb and a middle finger, just for you."

"Play it again, Sam," Rick said before hanging up.

"I'm either hating that guy or loving him." I hurried toward the house, glaring at the pool as if the cold water had betrayed me. "Talking about play it again, put on *Dreamline*! Play our song, hot mama!" I shouted as I entered a kitchen teeming with bodies carrying trays and supplies in from a panel van in front of the house.

Jenny was outside directing traffic. An elderly lady looked at me. "It wasn't meant for me, but I'll take it. I haven't been called 'hot mama' in decades." She winked at me.

"Thanks for taking care of us on short notice," I replied after a too-long hesitation.

"You bet, babycakes." She pinched my butt on her way past.

I retired to the pool area, far away from our catering service's business end. I chose to play with my phone instead, reading the news while lounging in the sun. I had peace for all of two minutes before Jenny blocked my rays.

"I got my butt pinched," I told her.

"I don't even want to know. They're almost done setting up. It's like they've done this before."

"Can we put on some music?"

"By music, you mean Rush."

I held my hands up in surrender. That was always what I meant.

"I'll put on something generic."

"You mean, like Hemispheres?"

"I mean the radio." She put her sunglasses on so I couldn't see her beautiful eyes.

"I already don't want this afternoon so we can spend time alone in the hot tub."

"We have an army of people here already and a separate army coming. I'm not used to doing this stuff, so stop hiding, come in here, and do the stuff I'm not doing."

"I'm visualizing my tasks right now and coming up with nothing. I could harangue the talent, but you seem to already have that covered."

"I'm not haranguing myself so that one must still be available." She headed for the house. The sliding doors to the dining area were open. The table was filled, and the food display was getting prepped. They carried a long table through and into the pool area, where they set it up off to the side. In two minutes, it became a wet bar.

I stayed near Jenny and finally whispered into her ear, "I'm not sure what I'm supposed to do."

"I'll let you in on a secret. Neither am I."

"We need to welcome the guests, show them through where they can choose, something to eat first or something to drink. Then we'll stand around the pool and eat with our hands like barbarians while spilling drinks in the crooks of our arms."

"You're not much help." Jenny giggled. "There's no training for this. I've never had a party like this before."

"Neither have I. Gladys would have made quick work of all of this. We probably should have called her."

"Now that you mention it, we do know a wedding planner."

"You never called your sister?"

"No. She doesn't need to know that we're in New York. They might have invited themselves up."

We moved away from the workers putting the final details on the presentation for the guests.

"We can't have them anywhere near here. Anyone links them to us, their lives will be at risk."

"I know," Jenny replied while caressing my arm. "We chose this life, and that means I don't get to call my sister when I have a catering problem. I don't want to lie. Well, any more than I do already."

I kissed her on the cheek. "Our first guest."

"Who comes to a party early? We're still in New York, aren't we?"

"Looks like Max." I went outside to meet him. Not only was he accompanied by a stunningly beautiful woman, but two small children also jumped out of the car and ran in circles around their parents. Max corralled one and the woman snagged the other, swinging the young girl onto her hip with a well-practiced motion.

"I assume there will be no pictures taken today," Max said before introductions.

"None. That's not my thing. This is Jenny, my partner in life."

"I'm Clarice," the woman said with a faint French accent. "This is Anneliese, and that hellion is Maurice."

Max shrugged. "Chip off the old block."

"I fear the pool is one step above frigid."

"They're kids. They don't care. We have water wings in the bag."

"Then they are more than welcome to take a swim," Jenny told him.

I motioned for them to follow me into the house, where Maurice grabbed a pastry on our way by. He got his hand slapped, but the sweet had already disappeared into his mouth. His mother looked at his father, who lifted him to carry him out of the house.

"We all have our place. I met Clarice on a trip to Paris a long time ago, on a high school exchange. I was smitten and remain so to this day," Max said smoothly. Clarice smiled, showing slight wrinkles around her eyes. She had looked younger but was probably Max's age, mid to late thirties.

It didn't immediately register why that mattered, but I thought it should. I would talk to Jenny about it later.

"If I could get a moment of your time, Ian," Max said before kissing his wife on the cheek. I caressed Jenny's hand before letting go. We ordered non-alcoholic drinks from the bar and strolled into the grass, away from the pool and the house. "Good work on Mark Gadsden's stuff. I have to know. How did you pull it off?"

"I called a friend in the FBI who owed me a favor. They promoted the inspector and had another one sign off on the temporary approval. If there are no issues, then final approval will be a shoo-in."

"You have friends in the FBI with that kind of power?"

It was time to play the trump card. "When the FBI wants to avoid going to court, what do you think happens?"

"Private contractors make their problems go away. I believe you called them gaps."

"Gaps in a streamlined and smooth-running system. We get to remove bad guys and help make the world a better place. And they pay us a lot of money. No mud sticks to anyone. Clean is how we get paid to do what we do."

Max nodded. "Why did you get sent after me?"

"I wasn't sent after you. I'm searching for the one who has subverted the purpose of your charity. If that was you, then yes, I was sent after you."

"Subvert? What the hell do you mean? That charity is important. We do work that matters. I take money from people with too much of it and help them feel better about themselves. And one of those people is me. I feel better about how I built my wealth by giving a healthy chunk away. Dale Carnegie? Not an icon in how he managed his business but a shining star of how to cleanse your soul after the deeds are done."

"Someone in the charity is sending tens of millions of dollars to terrorist groups. Is that you, Max?"

"Screw yourself."

He raised his hand, and I grabbed his wrist. "Don't make a scene, Max. I will kill you in front of your wife and kids. And then what do you think will happen to them? The family that drowns together stays together."

He tried to pull away, but my grip was too strong. Max turned pasty-white.

CHAPTER TEN

"The problem is not the problem. The problem is your attitude about the problem. Savvy?" –Captain Jack Sparrow

I let go and gestured for Max to sit. "Talk to me like an adult. If it's not you, then it has to be somebody with access to the funds who can move significant sums."

Max flopped onto a stone bench. "We have money in banks all around the world. Only sixty percent of our funds are in US dollars donated by Americans. The rest are international. The fund handles billions of dollars' worth a year."

"Call for an outside audit, then keep your ear to the ground, looking for someone who is running for cover. That will be your person."

"What kind of organizations are getting the charity's, OdaPresent's money?"

"Ones that like killing American military using weapons they shouldn't have. That takes money, lots of money."

"And Gadsden?"

"Called a friend in the FBI. Nothing is a lie. Jenny and I run the Club. We get a great number of private contracts that fall outside governmental scrutiny. Maybe you can help with that here, introduce us to people who have problems. For you, I don't want any dirt to fall your way. I need help to find who it is. Your help."

"Why are you telling me this?"

"Because I'm a good judge of character. No, I'm better than that. I know if people are dirty or not. I know you are, but you're not a terrorist unless they have something over on you. Are you being leveraged?"

Finally, the color started returning to his face. "No. Dirty? Used to be. I'm trying to clean the skeletons out of my past. My children make me want to be a better man. They deserve me to be."

"And your wife."

"Would it sound corny if I said I did it all to impress her and give her the life of a queen?"

"You like it too much for it to be all about her."

"You are correct, Ian. You *are* an excellent judge of character. Are you going to kill me?"

"Probably not, unless you admit to sandbagging on Wednesday's round so you could take my money on Friday."

"Maybe a little," Max replied.

"Max, my associates and I only remove problems who are bad people. Criminals of the worst sort."

"People pay for that?"

"They pay a great deal for that. A drug dealer who moves in next door. A hedge fund manager running a Ponzi scheme. Terrorists. Serial rapists. We give discounts on those guys."

"How do you make sure?"

"That is the hardest thing we do, Max. Just like me,

right here with you. I have to be sure. If it was cut and dried, anyone could do it."

"Why only criminals?"

"You know the answer to that."

"The authorities don't look as hard for those who do in the worst society has to offer? Is Jenny... Is she one of you?"

"Yes. In all ways. You saw the video." I left enough ambiguity. Never give away the whole truth.

"Thank you, Ian, for being open with me. I believe you. Aren't you afraid I'll tell someone about you?"

"Not in the least because you won't. Your world has changed from the one you woke up to this morning. You grew up with stories that people like me existed, but you didn't know for sure. Now you do. I'd like to think that you'll respect those boundaries and understand that you are perfectly safe as long as you take care of those in your charge. That means we root out your terrorist sympathizer."

"I can't have that stench attached to my charity. We'll start first thing on Monday. I was going to fly to Europe for a series of meetings, but I will cancel them all. Nothing is more important than clearing my name and the name of my foundation."

"Good call." We shook hands. "For the record, I played the best round of my life and still lost twelve hundred dollars."

"If you played that well despite your impending doom, then you are a person who can deal with pressure. You are the kind of guy I want on my team. Or at least not playing against me because eventually, I fear I would lose." We headed back toward the pool. "Thanks, Ian. I won't take this level of trust lightly."

"Neither will I. By the way, who did you invite?"

"Hedge fund managers, head of a television station, and Mark Gadsden, of course."

"So, run-of-the-mill guys," I countered. "With problems."

"They could make or break your access to this market."

I had to think that over. My charter was to stop the stream of funds flowing out of Max's charity, and now it was his charter, too. I wasn't sure about expanding the business to Max's friends on Rick's dime and time. I'd feel like I owed him. I didn't want to feel that way.

We waited by the front door for the first guests, out of earshot of the catering crew, while the Odenkirks fed their children from the massive spread.

We had our meals lined up for the next week. No Hamptons' restaurants for us.

"I hope they eat the vegan stuff," I mumbled.

Jenny shook her head. "Two nibbles, and we'll get the rest. Vegans don't graze a buffet like you."

"I'm not feeling the love for vegans right now."

"You'll survive. What did Max want? It looked like things got a little heated for a moment." Jenny eyed me closely.

"He asked me if I was going to kill him."

"That's fairly straightforward. Why would he ask that?"

"Because I told him I was here to do just that if it turned out he was providing funding to terrorists."

"You told him our operation?"

"Mostly. I stayed away from the choice bits. He's appropriately respectful now. And he's introducing us to friends with issues. Maybe we'll pick up some new work. I'm okay with coming to the Hamptons every couple months to hammer out some new business. And leave an open invite for the rich and famous to visit us in Chicago if they need something on a tighter timeline."

"I don't know what to say. Using one gig to snag five

others? It's either genius or sending us off the deep end of the pool without a life preserver."

"You think I'm a genius?" I played coy but poorly.

"I think even a blind squirrel might find an acorn. If he's our guy, he already knows too much about us."

"And then he'll die with the knowledge he has because if he's funding those who kill Marines, he won't just die, he'll die ugly," I whispered into Jenny's ear.

The first one to arrive was a young hedge fund manager, Albus Porter, who showed up with the girlfriend du jour. I tried not to laugh at the name. It seemed like he half-expected it.

"I'm thinking your parents were fans."

"No. I'm older than that. It's a horrible coincidence since I was born a few years before my main man Harry appeared on the scene. Albus is an old family name. Coincidence. I make it work. This is Ashley." He pointed at the arm candy. She smacked her gum, and he rolled his eyes.

"I'm Ian Bragg, and my better half is Jenny. We run the Club in Chicago and are looking at expanding."

Albus looked both ways and leaned close. "Max said you might be able to help me with a problem I'm having."

"Maybe. Depends on the problem. We can discuss it later after everyone's had a bite." Ashley was looking around. "We have a variety of vegan dishes."

"I'm vegan. How did you know?"

"Because you have the glow of someone not encumbered by consuming the corpses of less-developed creatures."

"I know, right?"

"They are grilling filets out by the pool," I told Albus.

"What kind of fish?"

I shook my head. "Tenderloin, the best kind."

"Now you're speaking my language. I look forward to

chatting later while Ashley entertains us with her swimming."

"Pool might be a little chilly," Jenny replied.

"Even better." Albus gave us the thumbs-up and escorted his young friend through the food line. She picked like a bird. I made sad eyes at Jenny, which made her laugh.

Next through the door was William Stacy, a much older gentleman wearing a sports coat over a dress shirt with slacks. "Call me Bill. I run a network through my holding company, Chance Enterprises. You probably watch my stations every day."

"We don't watch much TV, but when we do, it's always a Chance station," I replied.

"You don't know which stations those are, do you?" He held up his finger while he waited for my predictable answer.

"Not the foggiest."

"A refreshing attitude. They don't call it the boob tube for nothing. Stay healthy, don't watch it. Do I smell steak?" I pointed. "Catch you out by the pool."

He sauntered away, heading past the food on his way to the pool to engage Max in a brief conversation.

The next three arrived together—hedge fund managers in a chauffeured limousine.

"Can you grab one of the catering folks and make sure the driver gets a chance to prepare himself a plate? Maybe he's a vegan…"

Jenny chuckled while passing the word to the caterers before rejoining me as the greeting party.

The three introduced themselves as Dave Tapper, Federico Leone, and Phil Drayer. They ran the fourth-, sixth-, and seventh-largest funds. Max held down the third spot, and the gap between his fund and the second was nearly a hundred billion dollars. It was a trillion to get into the top spot.

Reality suggested third wasn't a bad place to be.

"A little friendly competition between you guys?"

"We were told you can help us with a problem or two? We hope that's true," the one called Federico said.

I inched closer and stared at him. He wasn't one to back down. These were billionaires and had made their money being alpha males. "We shall see." He finally blinked and looked away. "Please, grab something to eat. Any of you guys vegans?"

They laughed. Dave clapped Federico on the shoulder. "Eat a vegetable and lighten up, Freddie!"

I stepped aside to usher them through. Phil stayed behind and leaned close. "That's the kind of help I need. I'm not a fan of bullies, and sometimes Freddie goes too far, but deep down, he's a good guy. Sometimes he lets his competitive spirit get the best of him."

I nodded. I wasn't sure what kind of help they thought I'd provide. From Max's perspective, it might have seemed like I was running the mob, pushing out competitors and government regulators. I wasn't going to do any of those things. I needed to set the record straight.

The last to arrive was Mark Gadsden with his wife and Bryan Gadsden with his family. More young kids, the same age as Max's children.

"Look at you!" I said to the little kids. "I thought I heard a splash. Maybe you brought your swimsuits?" Bryan's wife held up a beach bag.

"I'm Felicity." She waved an elbow because her arms were full. Bryan nodded as he guided the children past the food. They showed no interest, having eyes only for the party in the backyard.

Mark introduced his wife. "Eustacia. Meet Mr. Bragg.

He cleared the way for our launch. I have a bunch more work where that came from."

"That was a one-off. What I really do is far more refined. I don't ever want to leverage a regulator again. What's wrong with your ships where he wasn't happy letting them sail?"

He looked taken aback. "There's nothing wrong with the ships. It was the loading plan that he had an issue with. Something about being overloaded, but I assure you, they are rated for what we put on them."

"Then why did he have a problem?" I waved my hand. "You have thirty days to satisfy his concerns. I would have a hard time living with my conscience if anything happened to that ship because it was overloaded. Maybe placate us both by reducing the burden on your ships."

"That's not how I make money, Mr. Bragg," he replied.

"High risk, low reward."

"Not low reward. That extra cargo is pure profit. Makes the entire voyage more than pay for itself."

"If the ship sinks, then what?" I pressed.

"Insurance covers both material and ship."

"What about the lives of the crew? What about those you want to continue doing business with you? Lower the risk, improve the return, and see long-term success. You don't need this win today. Get it next month and next year. Be the go-to guy." I felt like I was pleading.

"You have no skin in this game, so why are you telling me how to run my business?"

"Because I did you a favor, and I have no intention of doing you any more if you can't run an upright business. You still owe me, even if that means listening to me so you don't have to keep asking for favors."

"You need to be on his board of directors. None of those codgers will knock any sense into him." Eustacia kissed me on the cheek.

"There's pushing the boundaries, Mr. Gadsden, and then there's dominating your market share because you're the best at what you do. Are you the best New York shipper?"

"It's those low-cost Chinese mega haulers threatening to put me out of business. Our newest ships are our biggest ever, and they are half the size of our competition."

"How much cargo do they need to dump overboard before they start reducing their loads? I don't watch much news, and I see those stories all the time. Market the hell out of that. Never dumped a load. Gadsden because you need your goods to get to market."

Mark Gadsden smiled. "And here I thought you were a tough guy. You're all about the business."

"Who is also a tough guy." After filling plates and thanking the catering staff for helping, we joined the others at the pool. No one had the vegan dishes, not even the one avowed vegan. I looked at Max. "You're taking the dishes home that you recommended."

"You mean the vegan stuff," he said. "I wasn't sure who was coming."

Jenny nudged me. I asked the catering staff to take a break out front, thirty minutes, paid. When they were gone, I took center stage. "Thank you, everyone, for coming. Thirty minutes to talk business, then no more of that for the rest of the day."

CHAPTER ELEVEN

"The ultimate measure of a man is not where he stands in moments of comfort and convenience, but where he stands at times of challenge and controversy." –Martin Luther King, Jr

Jenny strolled through the house to ensure the staff had gone out front. She counted heads while the group enjoyed a meal with the chauffeur. Ian's butt-grabbing friend had sidled up to the driver and was chatting animatedly.

The assembled group watched me closely. "I don't know how to say this without being specific, but here we go. Jenny and I work with good people to help remove the criminals from their lives. Drug dealers, thieves, murderers, and rapists. Those who flaunt the law. Sometimes there are alternative ways of finding justice."

"Clear as mud," Federico said.

"It's clear as day," Max replied. "You were complaining about Black Stock stealing your best employees. If you paid your people more and were a better leader, they wouldn't leave. Ian isn't going to help you with that. You need to help yourself."

"Thanks, Max. I'm not going to help you with your healthy competition. Business advantage is in your wheelhouse. A pedophile harassing your kids is in mine."

"What kind of fees do you charge?" Federico asked.

"Two million and up. Our current contracts are in the realm of eight to ten million."

"I remember when you could have someone knocked off for fifteen hundred." Mark Gadsden shook his head while his wife elbowed him.

"You've never had anyone knocked off." She stared at him. "Have you?"

He shook his head so slightly it looked like a tremor.

"For people in our position, Mr. Bragg, money is not the problem. It's the possibility of being exposed."

"That's why the prices are high. Nothing will come back to haunt you. All financial transactions go through a series of accounts in the Caymans. Untraceable. We have agreements. All contracts are verbal. There are no electronic footprints to follow. And then we have no further contact. Jenny and I are the faces of an organization that can handle your needs, should your needs be criminals making your lives hell."

"That's a pretty narrow focus."

"We own the entirety of this market for our clients. We only deal with those who can afford us. We have as much work as we want. I don't need contracts from any of you to have a great year, but since we're here, why not? It's good to be busy delivering the utmost in customer satisfaction."

"You sound like a condom salesman," Federico said.

"Providing security to only the finest pricks," I replied. The smile disappeared from his face.

"He's just mad because he's number six and soon to be number seven in hedge fund value. Loser," Max taunted.

"What's holding you back?" I asked.

"Top talent is moving on!"

"Promote your best person to take over for you, change the leadership dynamic, and start another fund that focuses on high-tech out of China." I shrugged after my statement.

"Hey!" He stood before taking notice of Albus Porter's girlfriend, who stood in the hot tub, skin glistening as she stretched languorously. "That's not a bad idea. Authorize raises. I maintain my stake on the board, fifty-point-one percent, and then dominate the crypto market. Not high-tech, you Neanderthal."

I laughed. "There you go. One problem solved, and a new challenge rises."

The group looked at the ground as if participating in a soul-cleansing session with a favorite yogi.

"My daughter's boyfriend..." Mark started. Eustacia paled. Bryan and Felicity clenched their jaws. "He's a dealer and has her hooked. She's a shadow of her former self."

"Is she still in your will?" I wondered.

He nodded.

"We'll need some more details."

Jenny gestured for him to follow her. Mark trailed along, completely changed from the shipping magnate of earlier. He'd become a sad old man. His wife stood and hurried after her husband.

"That sucks," I said. "No one should have to deal with that."

"Can you help him?" Max asked.

"We shall see. We've rescued children from the scum of the Earth quite a few times and delivered them back to their parents. Our track record is impeccable. And no. We don't have references."

"It's hard to believe what you're saying," Dave said.

"You *should* be skeptical. We'll see what we can do about Mark's problem. That will be our testimonial and business card in case you have some work that falls within our narrow skillset."

Max stood. "Your skills don't seem narrow at all, Mr. Ian Bragg. I can work with a man like you, and I will."

Once we clear up that other issue, I thought.

Despite our best efforts, no one wanted to take anything with them. "I hate wasting food."

"Freezer bags, and we extend our rental for another week?" Jenny suggested.

"That's why you're the brains of this outfit. We need more mustard and some barbecue sauce if I'm to eat *those* leftovers."

"You'd put barbecue sauce on vegetables?"

"How long have we been married?" Jenny stared at me. "I'll run to the store and get the bags."

I hugged her fiercely and kissed her passionately. "I'll be right back."

I snagged the keys off the table next to the door and headed to our rental car, a Jeep Grand Cherokee. We liked what we liked. I put Rush on for the short drive to the store. I pulled up to the narrow street and looked left and right. Down the street to the right, I saw a person sitting in their car.

Everyone in this area had driveways with parking areas. There should have been no cars. I turned in the opposite direction from the grocery store and drove toward the car. Inside was the woman we'd seen following us on Fifth Avenue.

"Enough!" I snarled and yanked the wheel to put the Jeep right in front of her. I was out in a flash. The engine revved, and the car screamed backward. I jumped back in as the car angled off the road to start a power slide that spun it toward the far end.

I raced after her, hammering the accelerator to the floor. The Jeep responded as desired, but her vehicle was faster. The Subaru WRX was driven by a person who knew what she was doing.

It made me think she was trained, an agent watching me at Rick's behest. A lady pushing a stroller appeared at the end of a driveway. I jammed on the brakes and slowed quickly, then rolled down the window. "Sorry, ma'am. Just chasing a thief. I didn't get close enough to get the license plate."

"You're not the police. Don't be speeding through here." She gulped air quickly to get through her fright at the screaming car chase happening before her eyes.

"You are correct. My apologies. It won't happen again." I rolled up the window before she could continue trying to extract her pound of flesh. I drove at the speed limit to the main road and then back.

It reminded me too much of when they were watching Jenny's house. We'd ended up running for our lives, and people ended up dying. I didn't like to be on the wrong end of surveillance.

I returned to the house. The door was unlocked. I found Jenny. She knew something was wrong right away.

"Our tail from the city was outside the gate."

"The guy or the girl?"

"The woman. The dangerous one."

"Why would she let you see her?"

"I don't think she expected us to leave. I'm sure she cataloged who visited today." I thought for a moment and pulled out my phone to pound the buttons. Rick answered on the first ring. "Call your damn surveillance off."

"Ian? I don't have any surveillance. What are you

talking about? You are the surveillance, and you have the insider's view."

"None of your assets know about us? Where do you think we are?"

"New York City. Why?"

"We're in the Hamptons because this is where the big-time business gets conducted. Not on Wall Street. Not on Fifth Avenue. None of your buddies at the company are watching me?"

"No. No one knows about you. No one. The DCI gave me my orders directly. He told me to cooperate because it was national command authority level. No one in that group would undermine their own project. You have my word, Ian. It wasn't me, which begs the question, who is following you that you think it was the pros?"

"That is the question." I hung up.

"I take it that Rick's not the culprit." Jenny returned to the kitchen, bringing in the last items from outside before closing and locking the door.

"Come to the store with me. We still need those freezer bags." I watched out the window beside the front door. "I wish I had a piece."

"Mark is willing to pay three mil to never see the drug dealer and his brother again. I bet they're packing. I have an address." She waved a piece of paper.

I looked at it to memorize the address, doused the paper in the grease in the bottom of the near-empty meat tray until the writing disappeared, then lit it on fire and dropped it into the sink.

"Let's hit the store, take care of this mess, and pay our client's daughter a visit."

"Not going to bid it out?"

"Like I said, I need some hardware, and that scumbag is likely to have it. I get paid to snag something I was going to take anyway. And now we have an address. Maybe we can get a drone at the store, too."

Armed with our unmanned aerial vehicle and an address in Queens, we found our way to I-495 and drove west.

Jenny played Rush for me. *Between the Wheels* started with its haunting lead-in. It was time to stop playing corporate exec and start earning our keep. My thoughts wandered to the bad reverend.

"Can you check the net for anything on Gil Pickle?"

Jenny tapped on her burner phone. "Nothing in the news besides his usual carefully cultivated positive image."

"Come on, unknown bidder. Make us proud."

"Anyone who'd ask for six mil has to have chops," Jenny suggested. She tapped her phone back to the GPS directions for a house nearby but not the one we had the address for. She watched out the window.

"They wouldn't be an operator on our payroll if they didn't."

We rolled through the neighborhood. Houses on top of houses, small yards, some in good repair, others not so much. The dealer's house fell into the latter category.

"Do you think she's in there?" Jenny asked.

"I hope not, but I hope so. I feel for Mark."

Jenny continued to stare out the window. "What's the plan?"

"Standard surveillance. Check the neighborhood for watchers and cameras, then avoid them while maintaining eyes on the target. I'm sure there are gunfire sensors throughout, so if the opportunity to make the hit happens tonight, then I have to do it without a sound."

"You're looking at tonight?"

"Only if there's a clear opening. Probably not. We need

a few days to spot trends, maybe more. We could get our reconnaissance guy on it."

"You gave him an impossible job," Jenny replied.

As they passed the house, a couple walked hand in hand toward it.

"Not her," Jenny said. I stopped at the stop sign and stayed there. No cars came up behind me. I kept looking ahead while Jenny watched the house five buildings down. The couple walked up to the front door and knocked. Our target's brother answered the door. They made a drug deal right on the stoop. The couple strolled away as casually as they had arrived. I turned the Jeep around the corner and pulled over two blocks down.

"Are you up for buying some drugs?" I asked.

"No, but if it's what we have to do…"

"I want to get a look inside that house, and there's only one way to do that."

"I'm with you, Ian. We'll act just like that other couple. Nonchalant, out for an evening stroll to buy our smack."

"Is that what they call it nowadays?"

"Meth? Vitamin M? Ice, white cross, cotton candy?"

I furrowed my brow as I studied my wife.

"Don't forget, until I became an international woman of mystery, I taught eighth grade. The last stop before high school, or as some of the students called it, *get high* school."

"I was a nobody," I replied. I stayed away from discussing my past even with my wife, except for my time in the Marines, and that only because of the endless source of humor those memories provided.

Jenny knew not to press me on it. I was more embarrassed than anything. The truth was simple. I was a nobody when I had been somebody in the Corps. I had done things that mattered, but I had rubbed the right people the wrong way.

I parked between a couple of other SUVs, although

there were plenty of open spots elsewhere on the street. We climbed out and began our casual stroll back the way we'd come.

A Prius like a million others backed into a spot on Hanover Street in front of the US Naval Academy chapel on the other side of the fence delineating government from private property. A second Prius pulled up, a vehicle of the same color.

An angry man jumped out and tried the door handle, but the vehicle was locked. His spouse pointed at something. He threw his hands up in frustration. "They took our spot! Damn hippies."

His wife kept pointing. "Look at the license plate."

He looked at the Prius in his spot and realized what his wife had seen: it was their license plate. He checked his front plate. They looked nearly identical, except the impostor's plate didn't have the reflective look of a real plate.

The man's wife shrugged and headed for the house. "I'll call the tow company," she said over her shoulder.

"I'll wait right here for them to show up. They deserve a piece of my mind!" he shouted at the sky, shaking his fist at the twin Prius. It was a year older than his. Who wouldn't recognize that difference?

He moved his car to the side of the roadway, still in the driving lane, but only two people lived past him. Both their cars were parked. He could move out of the way if they needed to go somewhere. In the interim, he waited. With his arms crossed and leaning against his car, he stared at the impostor as if the purveyors of this joke would materialize to accept their tongue-lashing for messing with the wrong man.

The pop, like a gunshot, made him jump. The rear hatch flew open, and a series of rockets streamed out of the vehicle and into the domed chapel beyond. The first two exploded against the wall, blowing a hole big enough to drive a car through. The next rockets flew through the opening to explode inside.

Like a firecracker in a fist, the windows blew out, then the dome started to waver. The sides fell, the building's demise happening in slow motion.

The man took a few steps forward.

The impostor Prius' final act had yet to play out.

The explosives that lined the rear compartment and the floor detonated as one with the power of a five-hundred-pound bomb.

The man was vaporized in the blast. The closest houses overlooking Naval Academy grounds succumbed to the concussive force. What didn't fall burned. Six houses gone, eight more on fire. The remaining chapel walls collapsed under the force of the final blast.

Ten seconds from start to finish.

Sirens sounded on the academy grounds as well as from the city proper. A call to the Joint Chiefs was already underway.

Five minutes later, Rick Banik knew about the blast and jumped into his car for the drive to Annapolis. He needed to see this one firsthand. Failure loomed over him —terrorists in America.

Well-funded terrorists.

And it was his job to prevent exactly what they were doing.

CHAPTER TWELVE

"If you want to be a legend, you have to fight with legends."
–Aleksei Oleinik

We both scanned the area. Jenny took from one o'clock to six o'clock. I took six to one because I was walking on the street side and had less in my field of view.

No cameras. No looky-loos hanging out the windows. They probably don't want to be seen when it comes to living next door to a dealer. We turned and walked up the short sidewalk to the front door of a nondescript single-story house that was about five years beyond when it had last needed painting and probably ten years past when it had needed repairs.

I knocked casually on the door and looked away as if only mildly interested. Someone answered the door. I gave him my full attention.

The pictures Mark had shown us confirmed this was the brother. Movement behind begged to draw my eye, but through sheer force of will, I held the man's eyes and hoped Jenny had a view inside. "I heard this was the place to get the good stuff. The couple that just left sent us here."

"That's a load of crap. You look like a cop."

He started to close the door, and I blocked it with my foot. I tried to look desperate. "I have cash and need a rock." I hoped that was right.

"Go away, or I'll kill you where you stand." He eased a hand inside his light jacket. The bulge suggested he had my future weapon. I hoped he had extra ammunition. I felt like I was going to need it for this one.

I launched a finger strike into his throat and grabbed his jacket with my follow-through before he could go down. I pushed forward and moved inside the house. Jenny followed us and closed the door quietly behind her. I twisted the brother around to brace my forearm across his throat, cutting off whatever air he had left. I bore down on him with my body weight to keep him from flailing.

He struggled to get to his gun, but his arm was pinned, and he was starting to black out.

Jenny headed into the hallway. "Wait," I said in a heavy whisper. *Hurry up*, I urged the brother to pass out. Once I let go, he would recover quickly, but at that point, I'd have his gun.

He went limp. Jenny held back, cocking an ear toward the closed doors beyond. I removed the man's nine-millimeter Glock 26 subcompact and one spare magazine. A quick check showed everything to be new. I stuffed the pistol into my pocket and pounded a right into the brother's face to discourage him from waking up too quickly. I wrapped his hands with the power cord from a lamp and yanked it tight.

I hurried to Jenny's side. She pointed at the door on the right. "Definitely someone in there," she whispered toward my ear.

"I'll kick the door in and move left to stay out of the

line of fire. Depending on what we find, prepare to breach the door behind me."

I eased past the room and to the end of the hallway. One door was open to show a room that looked no better than a dive for squatters. I listened at the other door and couldn't hear anything.

"Bathroom," I whispered and pointed to the closed door opposite the one with the sounds. I waved Jenny toward the room at the end of the hallway.

Once she was in place, I reared back and kicked beside the doorknob. The door nearly ripped off the hinges. I pulled my foot back and jumped to my left.

"Hands up!" I shouted, not taking my eyes from a naked young woman on the bed who looked unconscious.

Jenny kicked the door to the next room in, detaching it from the house that shouldn't have been standing. She pounded inside, but my focus was on the man in the room. No shirt, blue jeans, hands reaching for a gun on a table that also included a dish, a candle, and a syringe.

I moved close to discourage him from thinking he could get the gun before I killed him. "You won't make it, but I invite you to try."

"Cops!" He spat toward me, but I dodged it. He put his hands up.

I surged forward to backhand him across the temple with the barrel of the gun—a glancing blow, but enough to knock him onto the bed. He tried to come up, but I was over him and had already started my second swing. It connected with its full force. His head snapped to the side, and he fell across the woman.

I tucked the pistol into my pocket and lifted his limp form by his head. With a quick twist, the man in Mark's picture was finished.

But the woman in the bed wasn't the one from the picture. She wasn't Mark's daughter.

"Jenny?"

"Back here," she replied in a normal tone of voice. I jogged the few steps down the hallway to find her with a second unconscious woman. Strung out. She looked like a ghost of a person with nearly translucent skin.

It made me sick to my stomach.

"I think this is Brianna," Jenny said softly. Brianna Gadsden. She sat next to the woman and patted her face, trying to get her to wake up. I stormed down the hallway and used my shirt to turn the knob on the bathroom door. It was empty.

I returned to the brother and found him still unconscious. I looked around. We needed an exit plan so the police wouldn't feel the need to look for us.

The brothers had to kill each other in a fight. In the kitchen attached to the living room, I used a dishtowel to remove a dirty knife from the sink. I undid the power cord around his wrists, plugged it back in, and wiped it down.

I carried him to the bedroom so it didn't look like he'd been dragged. I wiped the subcompact pistol down, including the magazines, and positioned it in his hand, holding it by the grip with the finger alongside the barrel.

The dealer had been reaching for his gun with his right hand. I faced the brother, plunged the knife into his abdomen, and pulled it across, yanking the knife out before blood could get on the dishrag or me.

The brother groaned as he fell. I flipped the pistol onto the floor and into the growing pool of blood. I put the knife into the dealer's dead hand and squeezed it tight to either smudge the prints or leave new ones. It dropped from his nerveless fingers. One killed by a stab wound and the other by a broken neck. Not optimal. They needed to be swimming in blood. I arranged them to be twisted up together.

The woman was out cold. A vein throbbed in her neck to let me know she was still alive.

I took the other pistol, a Glock 26 nine-millimeter subcompact. The magazine had six rounds. A quick search using the dishrag to open drawers yielded nothing. I stuffed my new pistol into my pocket, appreciating the good taste in weapons by the drug dealers, unlike the hit in Chicago where the dealers had carried junk.

Jenny shuffled down the hallway. The woman was still unconscious.

With one last wipe of key surfaces, I tossed the dishrag next to the sink.

"She's not waking up, Ian. It's going to look hokey carrying the woman from the house."

"I'll carry her on my hip. It'll look like she's stoned, which is what everyone should expect from this neighborhood. You get the Jeep and meet me around the block to the right. You go the way we came. Follow me closely in case anyone is watching. It might still look like two people arrived and two people left."

"Move fast without running." Jenny stayed close behind me. I wrapped my arm tightly around the woman's almost nonexistent waist and pulled her to my side, hoisting her onto my hip. I walked slowly while her head leaned against my shoulder.

When we reached the street, I broke right, and Jenny went left. I tried to ignore it when I heard the catcall followed by "Hey, baby!"

I looked over my shoulder. Two men were bearing down on Jenny. I could feel my anger rise. They might be too much for her. I turned Brianna around and hugged her to me, running my hand up and down her back so I could watch without anyone being the wiser as to what I was really doing.

The men bracketed her, giving her nowhere to go, no

way out. She lifted to the balls of her feet. The first man nonchalantly reached for her arm. Jenny blocked it and went low, delivering a rabbit punch into his groin. She tried to get him between her and the other man, but she hadn't hit him hard enough, and he managed to grip her forearm.

I looked for a place to put an unconscious woman. It was all sidewalk with little grass.

Jenny knuckle-punched the one who held her, leaning in close to deliver a nearly simultaneous sidekick to the other's chest.

"Bitch!" the first man howled, but he let go.

Jenny hopped to the side away from the second man, crouched, and came up with as much force as she could deliver with her knee to her first assailant's groin. He lifted up and fell backward, breaking down a picket fence that someone had thought had looked nice thirty years ago.

The first man was out of action. He wouldn't be getting up anytime soon. The second hesitated before reaching into his pocket and pulling a butterfly knife, then spun it to open it. Jenny snap-kicked it out of his hand.

"Must suck going through life as a dumbass," she told him. I shifted Brianna to my hip and started ambling away. I glanced over my shoulder two seconds later to find the second man on the ground with his hands holding his bleeding face.

I picked up my pace. Jenny was on her own again.

Years of training. I couldn't have been more proud.

Now all we had to do was get out without anyone else taking note. I doubted those two men would complain about getting beaten up by a girl.

By the time I rounded the corner, I was sweating. It was harder than I'd thought it would be to carry a hundred-pound girl with one arm. She was dead weight, but I kept up my pace. I continued down the main drag until I reached the next corner and took a right, ambled to the first open parking spot, and waited.

Jenny was there with the Jeep one minute later. I deposited Brianna Gadsden in the back seat, put on her seat belt, and climbed up front. Jenny drove the speed limit.

Neither of us had Mark Gadsden's number, but I knew who did. I used my burner smartphone to call Max.

"Ian here."

"A phone call? It's like we just met in a bar," Max replied.

"We have Mark's daughter. I'd like to take her to him. She's going to need medical help. Let him know for us, will you? Text me an address where we should take her."

"Will do." Max's voice was all business. He hung up without me having to say anything else. Two minutes later, we were heading east toward the Hamptons when the phone vibrated with an address.

King's Point. I accessed the GPS and immediately directed Jenny to turn off. We hit the ramp, and at the bottom, turned left to drive north toward the Merchant Marine Academy. It made sense to me that a shipping magnate would have a home on the water not far from others who wanted a sailing career.

We drove in silence until I realized Rush wasn't playing. "What happened to my tunes?"

"Stolen," Jenny replied.

My small phone that had been deactivated and only contained mp3s of all Rush's music was still plugged into the radio's aux port. I turned the sound up to the soothing lullabies in *Fly by Night*.

"Nice try. By the way, I'm proud of the way you handled those guys."

"I thought you'd come flying to my rescue. Imagine my

surprise when my knight in shining armor was sauntering away with another woman."

"Train to win," I replied. "Strike hard and strike first. I hate bullies maybe even more than bureaucrats."

My other phone rang.

"Speaking of bureaucrats, I bet this is Rick." I answered the call but didn't say anything.

"They hit us again, Ian," Rick said without preamble.

"Who and where?"

"They blew up the Naval Academy's chapel, the hallmark of the academy. A massive bomb that wasn't just a bomb. It fired rockets first to soften up the building. The bomb then leveled it, along with a bunch of houses. First reports show eighteen dead."

"We're working it, Rick. I don't like these scumbags any more than you do, but even if we stop the funding today, everything that's in the pipeline will still come to fruition. We could see attacks for another year or more."

"The higher-ups believe the terrorists would go to ground afterward despite me telling them what you just said. The pointy end of the terror spear may not even know their funding is cut off."

"It sounds to me like a bunch of different terrorists with comparable missions. Wreak havoc on the Marines."

Rick breathed heavily into the phone. "*Semper fi*, Ian. I'm at work. If you need anything to help expedite your job, let me know. Maybe we need the person providing the funding to talk with us. Would you consider a capture order as a modification to your contract?"

"That was already my plan. I'll call when I have something." I hung up and stared at the blank screen. "They hit Annapolis."

"I heard," Jenny said. Her ears were so good, I wondered if she could hear what I was thinking.

"I need Max to find the one diverting the funds. Forensic accounting is not in my job description."

"I've seen you crunch numbers. You love it."

"Not like what we're talking about. Tens of millions buried within billions. They'll look legitimate because the person knows what they're doing. It'll take someone with inside knowledge and who knows their way around corporate numbers. It'll take someone like Max and his hedge buddies." I pointed at the next turn. Jenny rolled up to a stop sign. I pointed left. She turned into traffic and headed north. "We start first thing tomorrow after morning rush hour. OdaPresent, here we come."

We followed the directions to a house on the water with a massive barred gate. Jenny faced the intercom, but before she could speak, the gate started to open. The short driveway was occupied by Mark's oversized Mercedes and a private hospital's emergency vehicle.

We pulled up beside it. I jumped out and waved the medical technicians to the back door. They leaned inside and took care of handling the patient. The two carefully moved her to a wheeled stretcher, where they inserted an IV.

Eustacia cried while Mark held her and watched the medics work.

They sprayed Narcan into her nose before replacing her oxygen mask. They quickly moved her into the ambulance. "I think we've gotten to her in time, but follow us to the hospital."

Mark finally looked at me. "My daughter," he said softly.

I nodded. It was hard to speak.

"I haven't even paid you yet." Eustacia pulled at his arm.

"You can drop the whole amount into the account because the other part is taken care of. She has no one to go back to. Go on, now. We'll follow you out. I'm glad she's alive. Her situation was less than ideal."

Mark held out his hand, but we were already climbing into our vehicle. He hurried to the driver's seat and barked the wheels as he raced after the ambulance. Jenny drove close behind the Mercedes to get out before the gate closed.

We stayed behind them a short way before they turned off. The ambulance was running with lights but not the siren, and it wasn't speeding. That gave me hope that Brianna would come through.

"What makes the Naval Academy special to you?" Jenny wondered.

"Marine officers come from there. A bunch of them anyway. Ring-knockers. To me, it's America. Despite only four years in the Corps, I believe. I'm a patriot. These guys are attacking an institution I respect—the Marines. They are hamstrung, but I'm not. I'm in the right place to do something that they cannot."

"And you need Max's help to find the person. How would you know if the bad guy is Max?"

"Dissembling. Excuses. And all of a sudden, he fingers some lackey without the chops to make it happen. Someone expendable. I'll be watching. I don't think I'm wrong about Max. If I am, I don't want to set myself up to fail. And now I've got a piece." I tapped my pocket. "And six whole rounds. Who on this planet only carries six rounds?"

"The Lone Ranger?"

"He had two pistols and a full cartridge belt. Nope. Just this loser. His brother was stacked, but unfortunately, I took that weapon out of play by using it as a bludgeon."

Jenny knew not to ask about the caliber. She had seen the pistols, but only that they were black and small, not that they were Glocks or which models.

"Two more scumbags off the street," I noted.

"What if Mark balks at paying eight million for something that you accomplished in one day?"

"Then we let him know of our discontent. And we pull the plug on the thirty-day approval for his ships. Then again, maybe I wouldn't. I like *having* leverage. I detest *using* it."

I turned up the music and tapped the controls to bring up *Dreamline*. "It's our song, beautiful."

She grunted her approval while checking the GPS to make sure we were on track to our rental home. I wanted to check in on Gil Pickle. I needed to call Gladys to see how the Club was getting on without us, but everything could wait until tomorrow. The wind-down after a hit was intense, even after all these years.

New contracts. Keeping the pipeline filled so our people stayed gainfully employed. We needed our full stable for flexibility.

It had been less than a week since we were last in the Club. Sometimes we went weeks between meetings to get new contracts, and then we'd get five in a day. They could wait.

Absence made the heart grow fonder as long as they didn't try to take their business elsewhere. We had a job to do for the vice president that was nothing short of saving the Marines from a silent and hidden enemy who wouldn't give them a chance to fight back.

The high-tech weapons the terrorists were employing seemed like something out of a James Bond movie. That gave me a different tack for dark web research.

Where could one acquire such exotics?

CHAPTER THIRTEEN

"If I charge, follow me. If I retreat, kill me. If I die, avenge me."
–USMC Motivational Quote

We cruised the neighborhood in the Hamptons. The WRX was nowhere to be seen. No cars looked out of place. The house hadn't been tampered with, not that we could tell. The alarm system showed no interruptions since we'd departed for Queens.

I turned on the light in the pool and opened the door to the patio. The hot tub hummed as the water cycled.

"Naked hot tub?" I asked.

"If I must." Jenny winked and left a trail of clothes on her way past me. I followed her in, hugging her to me while we sat and looked into the darkness of the night. Sometimes, we didn't need to talk.

I had killed two men that day, men who destroyed others' lives. It wasn't like they lived in luxury as a benefit of their crimes. How a rich heiress got mixed up with men of their ilk defied logic. We also left one woman behind who would probably be the one to report the deaths. We couldn't save everyone.

"Why did she do it?" I asked.

"The allure of something she wasn't. Maybe rebellion against her father."

The answer would elude us but not Mark Gadsden. He'd find out when Brianna was in the ugly stage of withdrawal. But that contract was finished, and Mark Gadsden owed me. Maybe I'd ask him to lighten the load in his ships, placate everyone, and make sure his people came home, not just this time but every time.

"Max..." I started but had nothing else. He remained an enigma. A self-made billionaire. Self-made by convincing others to invest their money in his fund. Then he convinced them to give him their profits. After meeting him, I wasn't swayed. I had seen the best and worst of him. He struck me as a normal rich guy.

And I owed OdaPresent two million. "Are we going to give the charity two mil?" I asked.

"Not when we don't know who's funneling the money where," Jenny replied.

"That is the challenge, isn't it?" Jenny ran her hand down my chest. It made my body tingle. "I need to search the net for things but not today. We should celebrate life, the ones we live and the ones we've saved. Rich guys and their daughters. They need to have better relationships."

Jenny chuckled. "I second that." Her green eyes sparkled in the lights shining from the pool. Sometimes it was best to put everything else aside to enjoy life. In our line of work, we never knew when our last day would be.

I spent the morning exhaustively searching for high-tech weapons sales, but even the dark web wasn't forthcoming.

Those must have taken place in person. It came back to following the money. We needed to find the transfers. Millions of dollars shouldn't go missing, not for very long.

Even after waiting until nearly lunchtime, the drive into New York City from Southampton was a long and painful affair.

We finally made it to Fifth Avenue and pulled into the garage supporting the building within which the charity was located. Despite the number of larger vehicles, the parking spaces seemed to be made for nothing bigger than a subcompact. Jenny had to get out before I backed into a spot with an inch between the mirror and the wall so I could leave the vehicle without crawling through the window. I didn't back in all the way in case we needed to climb in through the back window when we finished for the day.

Thinking of such contingencies added yet another reason why I hated big cities.

We kept our ticket so we could pay our debt to humanity the instant we reentered the garage. A driver eased past us, looking hopeful and thinking we might be on the way out. I wasn't sorry to burst his bubble. There was a certain rite of passage in finding a parking spot.

The next time we came, we'd park outside the city and take a taxi, but then I'd need a briefcase to carry the pistol. I had to leave it in the car because the weather was warm and a jacket would stand out. I hoped I wouldn't need it in the OdaPresent offices or between the garage and the offices. Using it out there would tie us to the drug dealer.

No. The pistol would serve a unique purpose: close out the contract by eliminating the sponsor of terrorism.

We hit a coffee shop before taking the elevator to the offices.

"I feel like a day dweeb," I whispered.

"These people could take offense at that. Look how

miserable they are. Every single one of them could be an axe murderer," Jenny offered.

They did look miserable. I smiled at the barista and ordered a simple medium roast in a large cup. She used the urn to fill the cup and pushed it across the counter. I tossed her a ten and told her to keep the change.

We strolled into the building and to the elevators. A group of tourists jostled their way in front of us. We stepped aside and waited for them to clear out before attempting to get an elevator.

The press of humanity. The sense of urgency. The dire nature of everyday life. And millions of people loved it. With intensity came vibrancy. With the din of constant traffic came familiarity and the comfort of never being alone.

I was good with being alone, as long as I was alone with Jenny.

When we finally arrived at the office, we were greeted like long-lost family.

"We are so happy to see you again." The young man removed his headset and stood. The phone rang, and he ignored it. "I will take you right back to Mr. Odenkirk's office."

We followed him back. This was the second time, and that was enough to get my bearings. We wouldn't need an escort after this.

The receptionist outside Max's office had two mimosas ready and handed them to us as she ushered us inside and closed the door behind us. Another woman was in the room, sitting at a long table that had been added since last we were there. She had three monitors and continued to type, seemingly oblivious to our presence.

"A different treatment this time around," I said.

"They know that you are my special guests."

"I suggest anyone coming in here to donate money is a special guest."

"True. I'll discuss perception at the next staff get-together. I have a pizza day on the first Friday of the month, and they all go home early after we've talked about the successes of the previous month."

"I like that. You know what made you stand out to the feds and not in a good way?"

Max looked at the other person and gestured at the window, from which we looked upon the massive city.

"I'm curious to know what gave the feds a bad impression of me and my charity?"

"Beside the funding thing, the office entrance imagery is all about you. Nothing personal. You made all the great things happen with the charity. Seventy-one percent of the funds go to the causes, only twenty-nine percent to overhead. That's good, considering the office location. Maybe have the pictures be about the help first."

Max nodded.

"Who's she?" I asked.

"An outside accountant. She's looking for which money didn't go where it was supposed to, starting two years ago, balanced against who authorized the transfers."

"What is your threshold for approval?"

"Ten million or more," Max replied.

"How many are in the approval chain?"

"Only five, but they will sign off on almost anything that clears their review teams, which act like mini boards of directors. I fear there are about fifty of those individuals."

"I'll need all fifty-five names and other employee data."

"Why?" He realized I wouldn't reply. He had to know what I was going to do with the information. "Additional resources. I get it. Maybe we can narrow things down first."

"How many transactions do you have to look through if you start from everything under ten million down to one million?"

"Somewhere between one thousand and three thousand."

"That's moving a lot of money." I tried to do the math in my head, but it failed me.

"This *is* a successful charity." He hung his head instead of looking proud. "A successful charity that's helping someone kill Americans. I'm from the former Soviet Union but was only a baby when my mother left. I am an American, even with its problems. I wouldn't be where I am without the opportunity this country afforded my family."

"Is that what we're looking for?" the woman piped up.

"It is, Ms. Nagunova. Someone has been using this charity to funnel funds to bad people. We need to cut off those funds and find the person responsible. And of course, now that you know, you are sworn to secrecy. I believe your company is obliged to adhere to the secrecy required of fiduciary relationships."

"I will not share your secrets, Mr. Odenkirk." She didn't seem amused by the turn of the conversation.

"Then why did you ask if that's what we're looking for?" Max pressed, moving next to her table. She stood to prevent him from looming over her.

"Because I already see the transfers. What will happen to the individuals authorizing them?"

"We want to talk with them," Max replied smoothly. "See where we went wrong, detail the programs that were not funded because the money went where it shouldn't have. Show me, please."

He took a knee next to the table, and she sat down. She clicked through the spreadsheets. "The effort was not to hide the transfer, but that the recipient is a false charity. I am surprised by the ease with which I've found this."

Max looked at me.

"I suspect it's a ploy to cast suspicion on another. We can look into that one, but I suggest we keep digging."

Ms. Nagunova shrugged and went back to work. The small printer attached to her system hummed to life and spat out a page bearing the details of the transfers and who approved them. Nine transfers of two million dollars each to a charity called Doctors Beyond Borders, which was in no way associated with Doctors Without Borders.

Max accessed his own computer and pulled up the transactions, then traced the approvals back through the key five to the head of the committee supporting the international health arm of the charity.

He blew up his screen so Jenny and I could both see it.

Arthur Wiggins the Fourth. "I'm thinking old money?"

"A most distinguished New York family," Max muttered.

"Let's go talk with him," I suggested.

"They don't work in this building. Like a board of directors, they come together once a week to discuss the applications and champion any proposals. They usually do it remotely, which means I have no idea where to find Mr. Wiggins." He faced me. "I expect your associates would have no such challenges."

"My *associates* probably would give him no benefit of the doubt. We need to talk with him first."

Max headed to the door. "We'll do this the old-fashioned way." He opened it and called to his executive assistant, "Frances, can you ask Mr. Wiggins to come to the office tomorrow morning, please, around eleven? Tell him that Mr. Johnson has decided to retire, and I'm interviewing people that I will consider moving into his position."

"I didn't know Mr. Johnson was retiring," Frances replied.

"It's a rumor I just started. Get Mr. Wiggins to my office tomorrow, please. It'll become clear at that time. Thanks, Fran."

He closed the door.

"She knows you're lying," Jenny said.

"How can you tell?"

"Women can always tell."

"I was honest that he'd figure it out tomorrow."

"There's no doubt about that," I added. "Frances will make you look good, but if there's nothing on Wiggins, then he'll not be pleased with the subterfuge."

"He'll deal with it because I'll tell him I lied to Frances to get him here. He gets paid a great deal of money to give us a few hours a week of his time. And that is why he'll come, and why he'll be a captive audience when he gets here because he will hold out hope that I am considering moving him up."

"Are you?"

"Not in the least. The guy brings nothing to the table."

"Then why does he work for your charity? This is fascinating as I never see this side of the executive team." I sat on the couch and listened carefully. Jenny moved next to me.

"Family name and connections, so he does bring something, but it has nothing to do with his personal abilities, which I find limited by his lack of drive. His ambition far exceeds his abilities."

It wasn't adding up. "Why would he fund terrorists?"

"Now, that doesn't make any sense. He had to believe that something was in it for him personally. I can't see him turning into a crusader. I look forward to hearing what he has to say for himself."

I bobbed my head while I tried to think through

scenarios of what would entice him to take the kind of risk he had. Nothing came to mind. I, too, looked forward to tomorrow's conversation. We'd have to get into town early.

"Anything else brewing for today?" I asked.

Max returned to his computer and pulled up his schedule. "I have six meetings between now and five this evening. Unless you want to watch over Ms. Nagunova's shoulder, I suggest there is nothing more to accomplish today."

We waved as we headed for the door. I stopped. "Does the charity have any private investigators that you use?"

Max frowned. "No. Why?"

"I think we have one watching us who I suspect is working at the behest of our target, the one we're looking for."

"Won't that make things harder with the one you're looking for already on to you?"

"That's one way to look at it," I said. "Or, we could accept it as an opportunity."

Jenny and I took the elevator down and walked quickly to the parking garage. "She's here," I whispered. "Across the street, larger than life. I'm going to circle around. You get the Jeep. There's a loading zone half a block down. Pull in there and wait once you're out. I'll be along shortly."

Inside the parking garage, we paid the ticket. Once out of sight, we ran to the Jeep and were thankful that no one different had parked next to us, blocking the door. Jenny climbed into the driver's seat and handed the pistol to me. I put it in my front pocket and ran for the back exit, out of the garage, and around the block. I hunched my shoulders and blended into a mob of people crossing the street. She was still there in a shadow between two buildings, wearing a cap and big sunglasses that covered half her face.

I hugged the building's wall as I approached. For the last twenty feet, I waited for the sidewalk to clear, then I ran. She jumped back a step before I had her by the wrists, pushing her backward off her feet to remove any leverage she could get to break free.

"Why are you following us?" I snarled before lifting her and spinning her around to face the wall. I held her arms and pressed in close behind her. She smelled faintly of violets. Her blouse had a Prada tag. Her shoes had the distinctive red sole of Louboutins. "Who the hell are you?"

I let go. She was wearing a couple of thousand dollars worth of clothes. She wasn't a PI or a common thug.

I stepped far enough away to keep her from kicking me, but she wasn't going to outrun me if she tried to bolt.

"Not answering?" I took out my burner phone and took her picture. "We'll figure out who you are, and then your life will get much more difficult."

"Is that a threat, Mr. Bragg?"

"A threat is where I tell you that I'll beat the hell out of you, but I had my chance right here and didn't take it. No. I'm not threatening you; otherwise, you'd be a bruised and bleeding mess, curled up on the ground crying. What I want is for you to not follow me."

"What are you afraid of?" she shot back, chin raised in defiance.

"Afraid? Who opens their life to a stranger? No. It's not fear but a healthy embrace of my personal freedom. And you've infringed on that."

I moved close, and she backed against the wall. I ripped the purse off her shoulder. She reached for it but was too slow. I hit her in the breastbone with the heel of my hand to drive her back against the wall.

"What are you afraid I'll find in here?" Turnabout was fair play.

I raised the purse so I could look over it at her while digging for identification. "A pistol? Shame on you." I could feel the derringer without having to look to know that it was a twenty-two caliber, probably a single shot. Just enough so that if she had to use it, she had better make the shot count. A thin wallet held an identification card.

"Miss Anastasia Milford from Manhattan. Ritzy." A stack of business cards was in the opposite slot. I helped myself to one, stuffed everything into the purse, and handed it back.

"Aren't you concerned I'll shoot you?"

"No. Your job was to tail me, and kudos; you did a good job. But you're not out here to kill people. Lawyers don't do that, do they, especially not high-dollar defense counsels. Just because you know how to get off doesn't mean you will. By the way, bonus points on your driving. Where'd you learn that?"

She stared at me, lips turning white from forcing her mouth closed.

"It's killing you not to tell me about an ex-boyfriend race car driver who showed you the tips and tricks of high-speed driving. You know you want to say it."

"I'm pretty sure I don't." She stood with her feet apart, her pose defiant.

It came to me like manna from heaven. "You work for Babs." I threw my hands up and walked away.

"So what? Sometimes it's better to conduct a trial in the court of public opinion. It's caught many a guilty man."

I stopped and turned to face her.

"And it's snared many more innocent people. Many, many more. Innocent 'til proven guilty. That's not a premise the media abides by. Get the story today, issue a retraction at the bottom of page seventeen tomorrow. You make me sick."

"I took this gig because you're black ops. No one fights like you two if they aren't. I've seen too many special operators not to know the difference. What are you doing with the charity?"

Special operators. If she only knew the truth. I wondered how close she'd gotten and what conclusions she'd drawn from the meeting of the bigwigs we'd had at our house.

"Donating money because we've been successful and we're giving back."

"The Club has been sued three times in the past ten years. Each time, the person bringing the suit didn't survive to see it come to trial, and the cases were dismissed."

"Before my time. There have been no legal proceedings since Jenny and I have been in charge."

"Where did you get the money to buy something as exclusive as the Club?"

"From the bank. Where do you get your money?"

"That's not an answer." She had her hands on her hips and glared at me.

"It's the only answer you're getting. Here's a real threat. I doubt your employer is good with this kind of freelance work since I'm not a case your firm will ever handle. I am a waster of the partners' time. I expect your position there is tenuous at best, like all younger associates. Thanks for the business card. Don't call me, and I won't be calling you. Oh, and stop tailing me. Your job here is done." I thought better of it. "Are you a vegan?"

"I can be. Why do you ask?"

"Come to the house in the Hamptons tonight. We have a lot of leftovers, and not a whole lot of it has meat in it."

"When you say it that way, yeah, I'm a vegan."

I walked onto the sidewalk and called over my shoulder, "I bet you do CrossFit, too." I continued down the street to find the loading zone filled with trucks. I waited behind them for Jenny to complete another loop around the block.

Milford walked casually down the street, swinging her purse and watching me stand there looking helpless.

It was five minutes before Jenny appeared. I waved before I jumped in.

"A new girlfriend?"

"She's coming for dinner tonight because she's a vegan."

"Ian?" She turned the radio down because she knew there was a story attached. "You're not dropping that nuclear depth bomb on me without an explanation."

CHAPTER FOURTEEN

"My actions are my only true belongings." – Thich Nhat Hanh

While we waited, Jenny and I had learned everything there was to know about Anastasia Milford, esquire. Top of her class at Chicago Law School, where she had two different articles published in the school's journal. One was titled, *Self-Help in Tort Law Versus Self-Help in Criminal Law*. Her take on vigilantism.

Her article suggested a solid defense for a victim who sought justice when the system failed to prosecute a crime. In the real world, very few crimes made it to court, but the rule of law still applied. How could it be enforced when communities were woefully understaffed?

Enter the Peace Archive. Different, but the idea was the same.

To protect those who were not getting justice elsewhere.

An added bonus was her silence. She shared little on social media, not even reporting her junior associate status until after she'd worked there for a week. She had few if any real friends. Her phone records showed that she talked to few people, but no one on a regular basis except her mother, who lived in rural Illinois.

Someone with no close friends, the ability to keep a secret, and a willingness to consider the advantage of vigilante law.

I had no doubt what I needed to do. Jenny remained skeptical.

Help was on its way, someone who knew both New York and Chicago and supported an alternate system of justice.

The knock on the door came exactly at seven in the evening. I'd been hungry for a while. Jenny made faces every time my stomach growled like an angry pitbull.

We found the young lawyer waiting on the stoop, dressed as she had been earlier in the day. We had changed to casual.

"Ms. Milford. Welcome to Casa Bragg, where you'll get to help yourself out of the refrigerator. We'll eat out by the pool if that's okay. My better half, Jenny."

"Happy to meet you," Jenny said neutrally, offering her hand. The women shook in a cold, unemotional manner.

"Call me Stacy, please," she replied, a well-practiced phrase.

My stomach growled afresh. "We usually eat a little earlier," I explained. "So, let's grab our plates."

We retreated to the kitchen, which was clean. We had three plates on the counter. "Help yourself."

She looked around, confused.

"It's in the refrigerator. I wasn't kidding. I'm not hauling it all out just to put it all back when you inevitably nibble."

Anastasia Milford sported a slender physique but was cut in a way that suggested aerobics or yoga versus the weightlifting and full-contact sparring Jenny and I employed to keep us fit. Jenny and Anastasia could not have been more different. I didn't care about her blonde hair or alabaster skin; I only cared what was inside her head.

Jenny had her back up immediately as if the woman were a contender for my affections.

I slipped an arm around Jenny's waist and pulled her tight against me as I turned away from the lawyer. I ran a finger down the side of Jenny's face, holding her gaze. I kissed her until we heard a dish clink on the counter.

My favorite. A sausage pasta with cheese that was to die for. She took half of what was left and stuffed the plate into the microwave.

I stared at the plate turning within, the light highlighting the cheese bubbles. Jenny started to laugh.

"What's wrong?" Stacy asked.

"Ian said you were a vegan."

"After the disgusting way he described what was available, of course I told him I was a vegan. Vegetables with meat stuffed into them…"

"That's not what I said." I looked from face to face. From mortal enemies to friends in a matter of seconds, they'd teamed up against me.

Sometimes retreat was the only way to save one's dignity. "I'll set the table."

I took the silverware and paper napkins to the patio. It only took a moment to put them out, which wasn't enough time to recover from the assault on the one dish I liked out of everything we'd bought. I put on my music and let it play in the background. *Test for Echo*, a good intro to the evening.

In the kitchen, I found the rest of the dish empty and a second plate in the microwave. More dishes from the refrigerator were on the counter.

Looked like beef jerky later. I had some in the Jeep. I

picked up the last plate and moved in beside Stacy. Jenny nudged me and gestured for me to give her the plate. "That's mine. Yours is in there." She pointed at the microwave.

I smiled. "I put on some music for us."

"He means Rush," Jenny explained.

"Is that Geddy Lee? His voice sounds like fingernails on a chalkboard."

My eye started to twitch.

"Jenny is way too good for you with your blue-collar ways."

"There's no doubt about that. You don't like Rush?" I was appalled every time I heard non-believers speak the words out loud.

"Ian Bragg's weakness is bagging on his favorite band. His wife is a close second, along with food, and there's probably no other way to get under his skin," Stacy said as if logging details into a file.

"Privileged information protected by client-lawyer confidentiality."

"I don't work for you. No privilege. I'm telling everyone." She added enough of my least favorite dish to her plate to almost make her violation of Bragg household protocols okay.

Almost.

When the microwave dinged, I split the remainder with Jenny and kissed her fiercely.

"What's with you?" she wondered.

"I'm softening you up."

She pushed back and sized me up. "For what?"

"What if we hire her to be the Club's legal counsel?"

"What? You don't even know her chops. She might be a horrible lawyer."

"She trailed us around the city and all the way out here.

She could be a player in the big game. And she's packing heat."

"Interesting. You've never recruited an operator before. You think she could do it?"

I shrugged. "We'll have to find out, one small step at a time."

"You're not good at small steps."

It was hard to argue with that. We joined Stacy on the deck.

"Babs hired you to follow us. What was she looking for?" I asked.

"No small talk first?" She took a bite of the sausage pasta dish and chewed slowly.

"I'm not good at small talk, so I don't even try. You've spent two minutes total talking with me, which means you should have already figured that out."

"And you've talked with me for two minutes and should know that I avoid straight answers because I'm a lawyer."

"Fine, you're a lawyer. Babs. Why?"

"Because she wanted to know if you were worth doing an exposé on. In my opinion, you are, but not for the reasons she thinks. She thinks you are rich people trying to be Batman or Iron Man. I think you're black ops with a cover of being rich people and that you're not actually rich."

I didn't change expressions. "I'd like to put you on retainer for the Club. You've shown talents that we find useful."

"You don't even know if I'm a good lawyer or not."

"Retainer. What's your price?"

She stood and gestured toward her outfit before turning like a runway model. "I have expensive tastes."

"I don't care about your tastes. Price."

"Retainer of ten thousand dollars a month, and all work on top of that is at two hundred and fifty dollars an hour."

"Twenty thousand a month, and you join the Club full-time. We'll pay for your move to Chicago."

"Hang on. Who said anything about moving to Chicago?" She put her fork down, leaned back, and crossed her arms.

"Body language. You heard the offer, and it rocked your world. You were completely unprepared for this conversation, and you're embarrassed. You think you're better than that. I think Jenny is the master when it comes to negotiating a contract, but I can hold my own. This offer expires by the time we finish eating."

She wrinkled her brow and got to her feet. She strolled around the pool, mumbling to herself. We kept eating. I meant the end of my dinner. That was within my control.

"And housing?"

I looked at Jenny. She made the final offer. "You can stay in our guest house, no cost. We have a full gym too, so you can add some meat to those bones."

"So, you are rich?"

"We are," Jenny confirmed, "but I married into it."

I nodded.

"Retirement plan?"

"You're on your own for that, just like a vehicle."

"Incentive bonuses?"

"You can't find out about any of that until we have an agreement and you are under a fiduciary duty to us and the Club."

Stacy sat down. "Letting me in on the secrets? Already?"

"I'm a good judge of character. And if there are any issues, then you'll get to see what it means being on the wrong side."

"That's not very enticing." She crossed her arms again, realized she was doing it, and threw her arms to her sides. She decided to clasp her hands in her lap.

"You can walk away now and miss the lifetime of an opportunity."

"Opportunity of a lifetime," she corrected.

"Just like I said."

Jenny finished her meal. I had two bites left. "Clock is running out."

She pursed her lips, then blew out a breath. "Admirable negotiating skills." She thrust her hand across the table, and we shook. "It's a deal. I'll draw up the contract."

"We have our own contract for employees of the Club, but thank you anyway."

She returned to her meal. "What did I learn today?" she asked, but it sounded like she was talking to herself. "Never take anything for granted."

"I learned not to trust a vegan with no taste in music."

"But you hired me anyway."

I finished what was on my plate—the cold vegan salad. Rush played in the background. Stacy waited.

"I know I should have asked this question before, but what do you guys really do? The meeting with hedge fund managers, a shipping magnate, and a media tycoon was telling."

"What did it tell you?"

"You're moving into the big players' market, and you need them on board for a club you want to open here."

"That's an interesting take. Yes. Let's go with that." I pushed my plate away. Jenny reached to pick it up, but I wrestled with her briefly and ended with her plate on mine and me taking them both to the kitchen.

"Is he always like that?" Stacy asked.

"Yes. Out of the entire world of people, Ian is the first one you want on your side," Jenny replied.

"This isn't just about lawyering for the Club, is it?" Jenny shook her head. When I returned, I found her smiling.

I turned my attention to Ms. Milford, esquire. "It's good that you know the Club may not be our primary source of revenue."

"Do I know that?"

"You do now. We solve problems for people. Sometimes they are major problems, but it's usually just a single person who is creating the strife in our lives."

"Are you the mob?"

"We are not the mob. We are not organized crime in any way, but we don't always comply with the law. You have to be good with that."

She waved it away as if it were nothing. "Laws are meant to be broken, and all of them can be challenged in court. And I mean *all* of them."

"My sentiments exactly." Jenny excused herself and returned inside the house.

"You adore her, don't you?"

"I am unapologetic about it, too. I am head over heels madly in love with my wife. Even the Elvis who married us thought so."

Stacy chuckled. "I was going to take the job because I would prefer working for a power couple versus the partners I currently have. Young and pretty associates are a dime a dozen for obvious reasons. I took side gigs with Barbara Jaekel because I was never going to move up for the simple reason that I wouldn't sleep with any of the partners."

"It's like that?" I wanted to think better of the world.

She shrugged.

"You won't have any of those concerns with us. I'll transfer the first sums to your account in the morning. Well, not me. I have people. You'll get to know Gladys well. Drop your notice and leave your firm behind. You're on the Club's payroll now."

"And what exactly do you do?"

"We have a mix of government and private contracts. None of our contracts are ever written down, so there are no contested clauses or reinterpretations."

"What exactly do you do?" Stacy pressed.

I leaned close and stared hard into her eyes. "We remove people from existence."

"Like, fake IDs?"

The naïveté of our new lawyer was refreshing.

"No."

"Then what?" I stared until understanding dawned on her. "Oh." Her face dropped.

"But only bad people," I clarified. "Making the world safer one scumbag at a time."

"You said government contracts?"

I nodded.

She held her head in her hands while wincing as if fighting off a headache.

"I think that's enough revelations for the day. Oh, and your time working for Babs has come to an end. She doesn't need to know anything about us. Nothing at all besides what she already has. We're nobodies. Being in the news is not our thing, so Babs needs to stay away. Boring people trying to climb higher than their abilities will carry us. Period."

"You work for the government? What does that look like?"

"It looks like good money with a little bit of top cover. The wrong people aren't looking to get into our business. They accept that some ways of handling an issue are quicker and cheaper. We provide a secondary check to ensure that justice is served. Think of us as a safety valve in the inner workings of the world."

"Refusing to let evil get a foothold?"

I pointed at her. "Bullseye. Welcome aboard."

CHAPTER FIFTEEN

"People sleep peaceably in their beds at night only because rough men stand ready to do violence on their behalf." –George Orwell

The Buxom Blues bar in Jacksonville, North Carolina, was filled every night, weekday, and weekend. It didn't matter.

Home to the Marine Corps' Camp LeJeune and its storied Second Marine Division, over one hundred thirty-five thousand Marines, retirees, and their families called J-Ville home.

A dark man with a short haircut strolled from the overflowing parking lot to the front door, where he bumped his way inside. Ninety percent male, one hundred percent beer-infused, the Marines had landed. Country music blared from a small stage where a female lead singer held the rapt attention of the audience as she lamented the loss of love.

The crowd cheered wildly.

The swarthy man pointed at the tap and ordered a draft. The beer arrived, and he tossed a five at the bartender and walked away. Not memorable enough for anyone to take notice, but enough to forestall questions.

Head bopping to the beat, he worked his way around the dance floor, which was hosting a spontaneous line dance. Marines in their cowboy boots and hats tucked their thumbs and moved to the beat. At least twenty men but only one woman, too drunk to stay in rhythm. A valiant soul held her up as they danced together.

To the wall the man went, grabbing empty space to watch. He tipped the mug to his lips but didn't drink. The song ended, and a new one started. The man strolled away, depositing his mug on a table when the occupants were looking the other way. He continued outside, where he found a small group of Marines huddled in a group, complaining about their gunnery sergeant.

He waited in his car until they broke up and the lot was once again occupied only by cars. He removed two backpacks and lugged them around the side of the building, where the smell of urine was nearly overwhelming. He dropped one pack by the back wall almost directly behind the stage. He placed the second behind the wall behind the bar, then returned the way he had come, past the outdoor latrine.

More Marines meandered into the parking lot. When they spotted him, he checked his zipper and nodded toward the side of the building. They gave him the thumbs-up and piled into a truck. None of them should have been driving, but one fired it up and spun the wheels in the gravel on his way out of the parking lot.

He climbed into his car and tapped the remote to set the timer, then drove out of the lot slowly and headed toward the highway out of town. He accelerated once he was out of the city limits until he was happily driving at sixty miles per hour. A fireball rose into the sky two miles behind him.

"You sound like crap," I told Rick when he briefed me on the latest.

He was losing patience. I gave him the name of our first mark, but I warned him that I didn't think Arthur Wiggins was our terrorist sponsor, although I was suspicious of Doctors Beyond Borders.

"I'll look into both with all the resources at my command," Rick said ominously.

"We're still searching. I hope to have something more for you very soon."

"Define soon," Rick requested.

"No can do." I lowered my voice to just above a whisper. "A forensic accountant is dissecting the finances right now and has been since yesterday. I won't give you an artificial date because you'll rely on it for something important. I can't have you doing that."

"I'm tired. I just want to know there's an end in sight. And you'll take care of our person when you know mostly for sure?"

"I will secure him for your people. In the interim, I will be speaking with our first person of interest."

Rick grunted unintelligibly before hanging up. I returned to the office from the empty break area with two coffees that I had snagged from the Keurig. One for me, one for Jenny.

We'd sip while we waited for Wiggins to show.

I looked out the window of Max's office. I could feel the power of the corner office, looking down on the tangle of humanity busy with their individual tasks but moving en masse like a machine that needed the people to grease its gears.

In a way, they did. The economic engine that was Fifth Avenue counted on the people to produce and the people to buy, even if that production was capital for an entrepreneur or a store for fashionable clothing. And all the offices where people worked the lines, internet and phone, to align production with shipping until the customers had their treasures, no matter where the buyer or seller could be found.

The economic engine. So much money moved through the city that millions went missing and no one had noticed. I glanced at Max. He looked like he'd aged since I met him.

When a good thing goes bad, the philanthropist pays the price.

A knock on the door signaled the arrival of the eleven o'clock visitor. Five minutes early.

"Ms. Nagunova, if you would take a break now, we'd appreciate it," Max said, pointing at the side door. She made her exit, so Arthur Wiggins would never know who was doing the accounting work.

Max opened the door for his guest and invited him in.

Arthur's smile evaporated when he saw me.

"What is this?"

"Take a seat, Arthur." The man sat in the chair in front of the big desk. Max leaned against the front and looked down at his suddenly worried colleague.

"I'd like to introduce you to my associate, Mr. Ian Bragg. He's helping me with a little problem I have, and that's about twelve million dollars to an organization called Doctors Beyond Borders. I'm going to need an explanation, and then I'd appreciate the return of that money."

"It's gone," he whined in a high, nasal pitch. "Doctors Beyond Borders is me. I sent the money to myself and threw it all into a corn-based ethanol project that promised a five hundred percent return."

Max closed his eyes. "Corn-based ethanol takes more energy to produce than it yields. Even with depressed corn prices, it's a losing proposition, but you found that out the hard way rather than ask someone with a clue."

"I'll pay it back…somehow."

"Yes, you need to pay it back. I'm not going to turn you over to the police for embezzlement because I don't need anyone else crawling up my butt with a microscope. You disappoint me, Arthur. If I were you, I'd find a different city to work in. Wait. Find a different state. Go to Jersey. They'll kill you there if you steal twelve million dollars. Now, be on your way. Your employment here has come to an end, and I want that thirteen million dollars."

"Twelve," Arthur said in a weak voice.

"No, Arthur, it's thirteen because there are penalties for such behavior. I want it in my hands one year from today. If you haven't paid by then, you'll never pay it, and I will simply have you killed. Do you understand that? I can't tolerate people stealing from me."

"You wouldn't!"

"Don't try to show a backbone now. It's too late for that. One year. Thirteen mil. Or make sure you have your will updated. Do you understand me?"

Arthur nodded without looking up.

"Get out." Max moved away. I waited. I had no intention of being the muscle for this exchange. It had nothing to do with me except it was a red herring distracting us from finding the real perpetrator.

Arthur moped his way to the door. He stopped with his hand on the knob. "I'm sorry, Max."

"Out," Max reiterated.

He left and carefully shut the door behind him.

"I may need your services in a year *when* he doesn't pay. We'll see if I'm still angry."

"In the meantime, we have a bad guy to catch," I said. We needed to focus. "Did anyone convince you to make a big transfer, all in one?"

"We better look. I shouldn't rule anything out," Max said.

I can't rule anything out, or I'll have the pleasure of getting second-guessed even more by the bureaucrat. Rick makes me feel like I'm not carrying my weight on this contract. This is why I should never talk to a client between signing the contract and completing it, I thought.

"I've asked people to look into Arthur Wiggins at a microscopic level. If he's lying to us about Doctors Beyond Borders, we'll find out soon enough. And then we'll go get him. Running from me won't be anywhere near as bad as trying to run from the terrorists. They'll want their money. Either you're all in on the cause, or you're the enemy."

Max leaned back. "Is that how they think?"

"I've had limited experience with terrorists, so all I can say is I believe so. They are dangerous because these are the types who are willing to die for their cause, even though they haven't so far."

I paced in the office. The accountant hadn't returned yet. "Where's Ms. Nagunova?"

Max hurried to the outer office. His executive assistant gave him her full attention when he appeared. "Ms. Nagunova?"

"She left with a man who arrived with Mr. Wiggins."

The color drained from Max's face. He turned to me, but Jenny and I were already moving. He ran out of the office and through the outer office to the elevators, but there was no one there. "You take the elevator." I pointed and ran for the stairs.

Jenny jammed the button and waited impatiently. I could feel her eyes on my back.

The pistol was in the Jeep. The warm weather precluded wearing a jacket. I'd have to start wearing baggy khakis with cargo pockets.

I took the stairs three at a time, jumping to the landings

and continuing down. Twenty flights. I descended as quickly as I could without risking blowing out a knee. I kept my legs together when I hit airborne-style, but I didn't roll, just touched down and moved on.

I came out the ground floor and headed through the lobby to the street. At the edge of what I could see, I thought I saw her tight bun. There were no other brunettes sporting a bun.

"Gotcha!" I sprinted half a block into the back of a mob at a light that had just turned red. Traffic filled the street. I watched for an opening while working my way to the front, keeping my hands on my wallet and phones as I elbowed and nudged my way forward.

From behind me, I heard a shrill voice scream. "It's Jenny Bragg!" The man and Ms. Nagunova were long gone. When the light changed, I could sprint after them, but I expected phones were capturing everything. The chase was over. We needed to locate Arthur Wiggins and find out the identity of his man-pal.

I suspected he was leveraging Wiggins and there was no ethanol plant except on paper. A shell within a shell within a shell.

I thumbed my untraceable phone, itching to call Stacy Milford and turn her loose on finding Arthur Wiggins the Fourth, or I could call Rick. Or both, but I liked having my own resources.

With one last glance down the street to where the target of my ire had disappeared, I joined my wife in the middle of a mob of women, some much older than us. Jenny made cow eyes at me. I felt her anguish just as she knew mine. At least we had focus now.

Wiggins and his circle. Phone records. Meetings. Anything and everything to find him before anyone else.

"Can I get a picture?" a teenager called and muscled her way close. Someone captured the image for her.

This seemed to be choreographed. I strolled beyond the circle of people until I found her.

"Babs. The gutters getting a cleaning today, and you were flushed out?"

"Nice to see you, too, Ian. Jenny is a celebrity for the ages."

I didn't want to continue the conversation. Barbara Jaekel was annoying and needed to go away. I got Jenny's attention before moving to the side of the street and hailing a taxi by waving a hundred-dollar bill. The vehicle crossed two lanes of traffic to cut off another vehicle hurrying to make the pickup.

Jenny excused herself and waved before rushing across the sidewalk and diving into the cab.

"Drive!" The driver took off. The meter was already running.

"Anywhere in particular or just a spin around the block?"

I handed over the bill. "You can turn off the meter now."

"We got rules here in the City. I don't want to lose my cabbie license."

I flopped against the headrest and stared at the cab's filthy roof. "Take us to Queens." We'd get our vehicle and start making phone calls.

"Max. I need the address to Arthur's home."

"One minute." Maksim Odenkirk was all business.

Manhattan. An apartment. Not optimal. I pulled over to put on my nondescript hoodie. It was the middle of the day. I wondered how many people would be home.

Too many thoughts. We took a different bridge to get back to New York City.

"Feels like we were just here," I joked as I always did when we returned somewhere. Humor in times of stress was my key to making it through.

Once on track, Jenny tapped the number of our new employee into the untraceable phone. Once Stacy answered, Jenny put the call on speaker.

"We could use a hand finding an individual we need to talk with. You have those mad research skills and a VPN to hide behind, right?"

"Of course," she replied.

"Arthur Wiggins the Fourth. He's a person of interest in an ongoing contract. What's that sound? Are you writing this down?"

There was a hesitation. "I'm new to this. You'll have to give me a little bit to get used to the cloak and dagger."

"It's pure survival. Write nothing down, ever. Once you're settled in Chicago, we'll get you online with our system, where work product can be stored as safely as humanly possible. Arthur Wiggins the Fourth. We need to find him right-freaking-now."

"I'm at work and on a project, but I'll slip away in an hour and see what I can gin up."

"That will work this time, but in the future, the world moves too fast to wait an hour when we're in pursuit of a suspect." I gestured for Jenny to hang up, but she didn't.

"Once again, I'm new to this. And I know I'm on your dime—thank you for the payment, by the way—but I still have my other job. I'm leaving with my dignity intact and not under a dark cloud. You will have one hundred percent of my attention in thirteen more days. I have to go. I'll be in touch as soon as I find anything."

I calmed. "Work from the outside in. Look for his credit card to see if he bought airline tickets or used his toll pass somewhere. You have those here, right?"

"Yes, but getting access will take a warrant…" Her voice drifted off.

"You heard yourself, didn't you? Welcome to a new world. Find him. We'll contact you if we've found him first."

Jenny hung up. I grumbled a thanks for not hanging up in the middle.

"She'll be a good addition to the team if you ease her into it. It's what it will take to move the organization in a more professional direction."

"We are at the top of our game in two things—fulfilling the contracts and not getting caught. She's a safety valve and an extra pair of hands because I could feel the pressure bearing down on me. On both of us. Keeping the company running isn't anywhere near as easy as doing what got us to the top. Isn't it called the Peter Principle, where everyone gets promoted one level beyond their capabilities? That's me. I'm better at what we're doing right now. Chasing a target and rocking his world. We need information that only he has, and I'm determined to get it."

"I'm worried about Nagunova."

"Me, too. There is no advantage in keeping her alive. If these are the terrorists, then they will have no qualms about killing her even though I think we have everything we need. Once we get into the Fourth's accounts, I think we'll see that he never invested in ethanol."

"It was him, or it wasn't him?"

"He was being manipulated, probably coerced. He might be running from them as much as from us." We took an exit ramp and turned toward the residential district where Wiggins lived.

"How did they know about the accountant?"

"She walked through the front door just like the rest of us. Someone else in that office knew she was there. The receptionists out front, maybe. Or they talked about it. I don't see Max's EA talking. It's probably in her contract not to talk with anyone about what she sees or hears."

"Beyond the contract, I don't see Max keeping someone close to him who can't keep a secret," Jenny replied.

We drove past a modern building with a guard at the front door. Parking on the street was limited to those with passes if there had been a spot, which there wasn't. We continued down the street and to the next block, where a parking garage beckoned.

We rolled in and went around and around until we reached the top level outside. Good enough. I would have preferred the anonymity of the inside, but it wasn't my plan to hit Wiggy, my new name for him. I only wanted to know who took Ms. Nagunova.

He had information we needed. It was much easier to hit the targets than to serenade them as part of a bigger plan. Like Max. This contract had involved too many people. No. I couldn't hit Wiggy even if he deserved it because too many fingers would point at me. I changed out of my hoodie and back into my dress shirt.

We strolled toward the apartment building at a quick pace without looking like we were walking fast. Since we weren't going to hit him, I used the straight-up approach. We'd announce ourselves.

It reinforced that we needed fake IDs.

The guard at the front looked more official from a distance than he did up close. He was both aging and overweight, neither of which was a bar to performance, but he also looked bored and distracted. "We're here to see one of your residents," I tried.

"Do you know which floor?"

"We do."

"Go on in," he said and looked at the street.

"Thank you." I held the door for Miss Jenny.

"Whodathunk that looking respectable gave us an all-access pass?"

"Multipass," I said. Jenny didn't get it. I felt like a failure as a husband.

We took the elevator to the tenth floor, careful not to leave our fingerprints on anything just in case. We hadn't had to announce ourselves, but the cameras trained on the front doors had to have captured us despite looking down.

It would have been much easier to just kill him. Relatively no risk compared to marching up to his apartment door.

A man stepped off the elevator, looking away as he walked past. I stepped in, then held out my hand to stop Jenny from boarding. I hurried back into the lobby. "Hold up," I called.

The man bolted. I dashed after him and dove when he tried to pull the door open. I hit his waist with my shoulder and drove him into the heavy glass of the second door, which was locked and braced.

He elbowed me in the head to get me to relax my grip, but I wrapped my arms around him and lifted.

Jenny came in from the side and swung, but he twisted wildly in my grip, trying to get free. The security guard came to life and forced his way inside by pushing the door open and grabbing Jenny's arm.

Still holding him in the air, I tried to force him into the wall, but he fell over my shoulder and drove the point of his elbow into the middle of my back. My arms went numb for an instant, and he pulled free, backed out the door, and ran for his life. The security guard blocked the door. I straightened and tried to get by, but the impact on my back still stung, and I knew I'd never catch him with his growing lead.

"Let us go, you idiot!" I shouted in the guard's face.

"I should shoot you for attacking someone right here in the lobby!"

"Call the police. I suspect they'll find Arthur Wiggins the Fourth has been done a disservice and that you made sure the perpetrator escaped. That'll look good on your résumé."

Jenny pulled her arm free when he released her. She used her burner to call 911. "Since you aren't."

She told them what we thought they needed to know and hung up.

We stared at the guard, who stared back at us for nearly thirty minutes before the police arrived—a single car with a single officer.

He tucked his nightstick into his belt as he checked out the area before coming to the door. The guard opened it for him.

"I caught these two attacking someone in the lobby."

"Where's that someone?" I asked

The officer held up his hand for me to be quiet. If he only knew what I did for a living. Shush yourself. We needed to go to the tenth floor.

When the guard finished, the officer turned to me.

"Let's go to the tenth floor and see what the perp left behind," I said.

The officer seemed fine with less talk and more looking. There was nothing to argue about. With one last glare at the guard, we returned to the elevator. There was room for the three of us and a dozen more.

We didn't talk. When the elevator arrived, I had to look at the numbers to figure out where Wiggy's place was, but the officer took off. The door was open, and the wooden door frame was shattered where it had been kicked open. Inside, Arthur Wiggins the Fourth lay in a pool of his own blood.

The officer accessed his microphone and called in a

homicide. "I'm going to need some information from you," he said in a tired voice.

"We had him. We had the perp!"

"How did you know it was him?"

"Mr. Wiggins had just been let go for activities inconsistent with his duties, funneling money where it shouldn't have gone. We suspected the ones he was working with might be a little bit miffed at their sudden loss of revenue. We came here from the offices of OdaPresent Charities to check on him. And then the perp got away."

The officer frowned. "Not everyone is as diligent in their duties. He tried, but he guessed wrong. At least he tried. Do you know how many would have held the door open? The answer is, too many."

I didn't have anything to say to the officer's revelation. My back hurt, and Jenny rubbed her arm where the guard had held her.

"Can we go?"

"I'm going to need full statements," the officer replied.

"Sure. Can we email them?"

"This is the twenty-first century." He gave us a business card. "Each of you send your own, from your own email, please."

"Of course." I hadn't intended to do that but revised my plan with the officer's request.

We strolled down the hallway as a crime scene team arrived. A woman in a disheveled suit walked behind them.

"Detective," the officer said by way of greeting. She glanced at us, but her focus was on the door and apartment. She was given a pair of protective shoe covers that she put on and entered. We hit the elevator. I dialed Stacy's number on the way down.

"We found him, but keep digging. Maybe we can

determine a link to our bad guys, the ones who had him killed."

"He's dead?"

"We were too late. Had our hands on the perp, but intervention by a well-meaning security guard ensured the perp got away."

"I've only been at it for five minutes, but Mr. Wiggins led a low-profile life. I'll dig much deeper before I'm finished with him."

"Let us know if you find anything good."

The elevator reached the bottom floor, and we left. I had no idea where we were going next, but there were angry terrorists in town that I had been paid to eliminate. At least one—the guy in charge. I thought that was the guy who'd arrived with Arthur but not the one who'd killed him.

The worst part was that they looked just like everyone else. Nothing stood out about them, except the one I wrestled with was in shape. His body was hard, and he was every bit as strong as me.

Stymied twice in two hours by people with their own agendas. It made me feel like there was a massive conspiracy against us in finding the terrorists.

It was no longer just about financing. The terrorists had moved into the active phase of their campaign.

But we didn't know the strategic goal of the campaign, and worse, we didn't know who *they* were.

They held all the cards.

CHAPTER SIXTEEN

"Out of suffering have emerged the strongest souls; the most massive characters are seared with scars." –Khalil Gibran

I drove angrily, darting into small openings and dodging as if driving in the Indy 500. Jenny grabbed my hand.

"Slow down!" She wasn't a backseat driver, so when she complained about my driving, it was for the right reasons. I stayed in the lane I was in and crawled along with the traffic. "I know. I'm angry, too. I missed connecting with him; otherwise, he wouldn't have been able to run."

"I should have body-slammed him. Shoulda, woulda, coulda. We lost our best lead."

"We'll find another lead. Or Rick will. He's got to be able to give us something. He has the entire CIA and FBI at his disposal, and he can't give us a name?"

"Call him, if you wouldn't mind," I said.

Jenny used my phone and clicked it over to speaker.

After Rick answered, I got right to the point. "They killed Wiggins because we were on to him. It was him, but not him. They had something on him where he did the dirty work. Almost had him, but a good Samaritan stymied us."

"That's not good." Rick was less than empathetic.

"Give us a name or a contact. You have to have something. I feel like we're doing all the heavy lifting here."

"You're on the inside. Of course you're doing the heavy lifting. You are the best resource I have, but you just lost a key witness. I'm not feeling warm and fuzzy about this."

"Neither is Wiggins. He's on his way to a slab in a hospital basement. You paid us a lot of money. We're going to get this right, but this is Twilight Zone stuff, not a criminal infiltration of the daughter's bedroom. These guys are well-funded, fit, and motivated. I don't think they needed Wiggins anymore, and once he was on the outside, they pulled the plug."

"What do you mean, on the outside?"

"Max confronted him, called him out, and fired him when he gave a lame excuse on what happened to the money."

"I would not have recommended that since now you can't keep an eye on him."

"Max was pretty mad because he caught the guy stealing millions from the charity."

"How much did he get?" Rick asked.

"At least twelve million, maybe thirteen."

"They have to have received double or triple that. Some of the weapons they are using are easily a million each on the black market."

"Where did the other money come from?"

"Looks like it was the same source." Rick sounded confident.

"And our forensic accountant going through the books at the charity was kidnapped. They took her and killed Wiggins," I explained

"Not our best day," Rick replied. "Did you hear about

the bar that got blown up last night in J-Ville? Forty-three Marines killed, another fifty injured."

"I hate losing, Rick. I hate it. Give me something I can run down on this end, someone I can high-stress. Give me a name, someone working with Wiggins who was frequent in his life but on the down-low. Send me his phone records, credit card bills, something."

"I can't. I've got my team on it, but now that he's dead, we'll fire up the forensics machine and see what we can find in bank & phone records. Give me a few hours."

"We're going to grab a late lunch. We'll stay in Manhattan all night if that's what it takes. Don't let anyone go home until you give me a name."

"Now you sound like a Marine and just like me. Welcome to the bureaucrats' club, Ian. Paperwork to follow." Rick hung up, having delivered the last word. Humor. Crisis. It's how we rolled.

"Look for a place to eat if you would. I'm not that hungry, but I could use a couple ibuprofen and an ice pack."

"Then you better eat first."

"If I must," I agreed. My thoughts descended into the darkness where someone held Ms. Nagunova, an independent accountant whose job was to dig through disbursed funds and find where millions had gone astray. She knew we were looking for a terrorist, but her only crime was helping us find them. "I wonder if they're coming after us, too?"

"Or Max," Jenny said. She took my hand and gripped it tightly. "Not all jobs are straightforward. We're doing the best we can with what we have, which is, thanks to Babs Jaekel, having to do it in the open. That's not our style. We need to operate outside of the public eye."

"That we do." I couldn't think of a way to leverage our new high-profile status to our benefit. I needed to return to the underworld, a place where I thrived against the addicts, the mentally unstable, those who were down on their luck, and anyone else who found themselves on the streets.

I fit in there, could blend in, but this time, the target was different. He was invisible until something needed to be done. Then he reappeared, executed his plan, and was gone again. I needed to change my thinking about how to approach these people.

Targets who were fanatically loyal to their cause.

What *was* their cause? Kill Marines? Was it that simple? I knew Rick was struggling with the question, too.

Find the motivation, find the supporters, and find the group.

We ate in silence. To the other diners, we looked like everyone else who was unhappy with their existence. I needed to think, and Jenny was thinking right along with me.

"Love," I blurted. "These attacks are revenge first, and then they're to change political strategy. Where have the Marines been over the last five years?"

Jenny stated the obvious. "Middle East."

"Attacks over there brought more troops, not less. They didn't achieve the goal of removing the Marines."

"Then why did they run campaigns over there?" Jenny wondered.

"Good question. Amateurs talk tactics. Professionals talk logistics. They couldn't project their power. Make a bomb, ride it out on a bicycle. Then plant it, and hope for the best. Thanks to a secret benefactor, this small group, and I'm sure it's small, now have the means to move their violence away from what they're trying to protect. Force

America to collapse its defensive rings. Chase our tails, as it may be. Their fight is here to keep it away from what they're trying to protect: the people and lifestyle they love."

"And they're willing to die for it." Jenny didn't smile at me, but she held my eyes with her gaze. Our revelation didn't get us any closer to someone we could reach out and touch. The clock was ticking on Ms. Nagunova. The group had no value in keeping her alive except to more easily transport her out of the city.

We finished our early dinner quickly so we could go outside and make a call.

When a happy voice at the other end of the line picked up, I started right in. "Stacy, we need to dissect Doctors Beyond Borders to find any addresses associated with the charity. This means any other names tied into it and where they live. Are there any addresses in NYC or Manhattan? We need to know right now."

"That could take a bit. I'll get started and call you back."

"Sooner rather than later, Stacy. A woman's life depends on it."

"I'm beginning to see how you work. As soon as I can, Ian."

She disconnected. I thought about calling Rick again, but that wouldn't hurry anything he was doing. I called Max.

"Wiggins is dead. They killed him in his upscale apartment. We missed the killer by about two minutes."

"I'm sorry to hear that. Was it because I fired him?" The tension in his voice increased.

"It's because he wasn't useful to them anymore."

"Will they be coming after me or my family?"

"I don't know, but if I were you, I'd be sending my wife and kids to her mom's house."

"Not her mom's, but I'll tell them to head upstate. We have a private place that's not on the books."

"Go help her get on the road and then meet me at the Loneham Hotel. We'll snag a suite and make it our command center. I have a feeling that what and who we're looking for are on Long Island."

"I'll be back in two hours." He clicked off.

We returned to our Jeep in its parking spot on the street. Luck had delivered us into the spot as someone pulled out. A ticket was under the wiper. I looked for a sign that suggested we shouldn't have parked there. Two-hour parking. We'd been there less than an hour. I wanted to crumple the ticket, but no. We'd get a money order and pay it, mail it in. Stay under the radar for what that was worth.

I guessed parking fees made up a significant part of the local constabulary's budget. I gave it to Jenny. She stuffed it into her small purse and smiled at me.

"You didn't tell me not to park here," I countered.

"I've never gotten as much as a parking ticket, so my record is still intact. I can't believe I'm married to a hardened criminal like you. That doesn't look like your first ticket. That's the look of a man who just got caught. I should probably take a cab."

"Signage. Labels to make it clear. I'm not a fan of the City and am pretty sure I'm not opening up the Club East anywhere near here. It would cause me a great deal of consternation to give money to these people."

"Put it in the Hamptons. That's where the money is, and open it three days a week. One staff that puts in all their time on those three days and we pay them for forty hours. We don't have to manage shifts. Three on, four off. That's a worker's schedule."

"You've been thinking about that a lot, haven't you?"

"Only because I can't get my head wrapped around the cat and mouse game when we're not the cat. You are great at seeing routines and finding weaknesses. What is holding you back here?"

"Information. Private targets have digital footprints. I couldn't find anything on these people."

"Wiggy was a private person."

"Fire up your data plan, and let me see what we can find."

Jenny created a hotspot, and I dug my computer out from under the driver's seat. I powered through the VPN and the myriad of logins and misdirections necessary to avoid anyone tracking me, then started my search for Arthur Wiggins. The Third was an upstanding citizen now living in the Hamptons. The family home was a four-story brownstone in Manhattan. I couldn't find a record of anyone living there. "Why did Wiggy have his own apartment if the brownstone is available?"

"Because there *is* someone living there, but our boy wants his freedom."

"No sisters, no other siblings. It's only two blocks away." I showed Jenny the address, and she poked it into the phone's GPS. I closed out of everything and shut my computer down. Once it was back under the seat, I merged into traffic and fought my way across the street to get into the turn lane.

There was much honking and finger-waving.

But not by me.

"I hate this place."

Jenny laughed. "We'll have an unlimited amount of work from here. Grow the business. Right here. Because there are criminal scumbags and money."

"I know you're right. We need to meet with the regional director. See what Lenny Goldman thinks, but he shouldn't be miffed about more work. How many operators do we have here?"

Jenny shrugged. We didn't have that kind of information readily available. Lenny would have an idea.

I pulled past the brownstone and was able to park right

in front of it, where three spots stood empty on an otherwise packed street. I stuffed the pistol into my pocket before I got out. An older lady sat on her stoop next door. Jenny and I approached her before checking on the house. I thought I knew the answer to my question but wanted to confirm.

"Why are there three empty spots? I'm not going to get towed, am I?"

"A moving truck was just there. A bunch of them Mediterranean boys."

She had my interest. "How many is a bunch?"

"Six."

"You wouldn't have been able to get a license plate or something from that vehicle, would you?"

She held up her phone with a picture front and center. I dialed Rick's number. "We have them on the run. I need to know where this truck is right now." I gave him the details from the picture. "If I were to email the picture, where would we send it?"

"Rbanik at cia dot gov."

"Can you email that to this email address?" Jenny helped the woman attach it and send it.

"The CIA! How exciting. What did those boys do?"

"Can you tell me what they carried out?" I asked.

"Boxes, big and small. A lot of boxes."

"Would you happen to have a key?"

She shook her head.

I thanked her, and we excused ourselves. Jenny stayed for a moment longer to give the old woman a hug.

The front door was unlocked. I turned the knob with my sleeve covering my hand and went inside. Jenny followed me in. I pulled the pistol and aimed into the rooms as I checked them slowly, walking toe to heel to avoid making a sound. The furniture in the ground floor living room had been piled to one side, and tables stood empty in the middle.

They had left their furniture behind.

The scuff of a shoe made my body freeze. My pulse raced for a moment before settling down. I waved Jenny back while I slowly climbed the stairs, placing my feet on the brace to maintain my silent approach. It sounded like at least one person, maybe two were moving furniture with the grunts and scrapes. I hurried forward.

The second floor. Two men. Swarthy. Packing more boxes. I watched them over the barrel of my Glock.

CHAPTER SEVENTEEN

"Difficulties are meant to rouse, not discourage. The human spirit is to grow strong by conflict." –William Ellery Channing

The occupants of the brownstone hadn't been able to get their materials out in one load. I moved into the room and would have given them an ultimatum since we needed the information they had, but they were both armed. I fired a single round at the closest one's face, but he straightened and took it in the throat.

I lined up on the second man, but he was already moving laterally to my line of fire. I snap-fired two rounds, hitting him in the hip with one and missing with the other. He crashed to the floor and struggled to bring up his weapon. I kicked him in the face to dissuade further efforts to fight back. The pistol fell out of his waistband. I toed it away from him before bending to pick it up.

Another nine-millimeter. I tucked it into the back of my waistband and stuffed the Glock 26 into my pocket. I grabbed the man by the hair and dragged him halfway across the floor. He screamed the whole way. I rolled him off his damaged hip. His legs twitched and shook, which I thought was his attempt to kick me. He howled in pain.

His pelvis was probably shattered. He wouldn't be kicking anyone for a while.

"Where did they go?"

He spat at me. I dodged the projectile.

"All okay?" Jenny called.

"We're good. One down and one damaged. Come on up."

The injured man started shouting in Arabic. From my time in the desert, I thought it was the Iraqi dialect but couldn't be sure. Our interactions with the locals had been limited, but we had worked with a smattering of international troops. There were subtle differences when one listened, and native speakers of the language could tell right away.

That wasn't me.

Jenny came up the stairs two at a time and hurried into the room. I spoke softly. "Anything to secure this guy with? I want to check the rest of the house." I gave her the nine-millimeter.

"Cute toy," she said, pleased with how it fit in her hand.

I picked up the hand cannon, my term for a Colt M1911A1, then helped myself to the corpse's pistol and checked his pockets. "What's with the kids of today? No extra magazines and no extra bullets." I check the magazines. Both carried five rounds. I consolidated them into one. I disassembled the second pistol, wiped the parts off, and put it aside.

I walked quietly through the rest of the second floor to find that this was where they'd been sleeping and doing other work, while the bottom floor had been the main production. I checked the closets carefully, dipping low when I yanked the doors open. It had my heart racing. I had never enjoyed house-clearing during my time in the

Marines. It was a gamble every single time. Kill or be killed. Innocents could have been hiding behind the next door, or an innocent with a future martyr hiding behind them.

Up the stairs to the third floor. In the master bedroom, I found an unconscious woman, Ms. Nagunova. Her pulse felt strong to me. I thought I smelled chloroform, small amounts of which were harmless. It took breathing a fair amount over a longer period of time to render someone unconscious, unlike what television shows suggested.

I continued my quiet search of the floor and then went to the top floor. They didn't appear to enjoy climbing stairs since the top floor was undisturbed. I returned to the third floor and hoisted the accountant over my shoulder.

Jenny helped me put her on one of the cots that had been set up, turning the second-floor family room into a barracks.

"Is there anything downstairs to bind our guy? Duct tape, shoestrings, or maybe zip-ties?"

Jenny smiled and gave me a kiss. "There are a couple rolls of packing tape they left behind."

"And boxes that need to be filled." I pointed at the operation that filled the room where I'd found the two still working. Tables with electrical wires, cutters, chemicals, and electronics. Timers and detonators.

I called Rick. "You got anybody that can translate this?" I repeated my question to my injured captive while nudging his groin with the toe of my shoe. He started shouting again.

"He is questioning your lineage," Rick replied. "Where did who go?"

"A truck with boxes and six guys. 'Mediterranean boys,' as the lady next door called them. And this guy. There were two. First one died an untimely death. The second one won't be walking for a while. Maybe the FBI wants these two. It would be easiest if I just eliminated him. I can work my way up the chain until there are none left. That's what you hired me for. I've got a baby-sized nine mil that I took off a drug dealer. That, and now two forty-fives that the bad guys have been generous enough to donate to the cause."

"I kill you!" the man growled through gritted teeth. I kicked him in the face, and he went limp.

"Wait until they come back and take them down. You are working for me, so we'll fight off any DA who tries to get involved."

"You gotta stop with that sexy talk, Rick. People might think we got something going. I'll take care of it. No innocents will be harmed."

"I'll contact the field office and see how quickly they can get there."

"They were making bombs, and judging by the size of the operation, we're probably talking a couple hundred pounds of C4 or Semtex along with timers and detonators. They were still in production mode, so I'm not sure if they're ready to pull the trigger on the final solution or whatever they intend to do with this stuff. Ain't no Marine units besides recruiters in New York City. Let me look around. They had to be doing their planning in here."

"Roger," was the only answer Rick gave me.

I didn't know what his "quickly" meant, minutes or hours. Probably the latter. When would the terrorists be back? In the meantime, I had a semi-conscious scumbag breathing the same air as me, and I didn't like it.

With a well-placed nudge, pain brought my captive back to life.

"What's the target?" I asked.

"I kill you." He was less vociferous in his claim this time. I pulled his arm toward me and started twisting two of his fingers. I was happy Jenny wasn't watching.

"I will break your fingers one by one. Where did they go?" He started to howl. "Where are the maps?"

He twitched, but I thought that was him fighting with himself as his head tipped toward the side of this room. I couldn't torture him. That was different than killing him, which was easy in comparison. I did not revel in other people's pain.

I rolled him onto his face and used the tape to bind his wrists together. He screamed into the carpet. I bunched a fold of clothing over the bullet wound, which hadn't bled too heavily, and taped it down to hold it in place. I wiped the blood on his pant leg. "Don't bleed on me, scumbag. You need to save yourself for the pros, who will have a field day with you. You know what's going to happen to you? You'll disappear off the face of the planet. Your family won't know what happened to you. Love? Whoever you love, you failed them by bringing your war here. You went up against me, and you lost."

I taped over his mouth but loosely. He needed to breathe for the next hour or two. I was surprised he wasn't in shock. Good for him. His anger kept the adrenaline flowing. And if he died?

Not my problem. He was a terrorist. I knew that with every fiber of my being.

My phone rang. Rick.

"Where?" I asked.

"Another address in Manhattan. A garage not far from you. Freedom and Sons."

"How far is not far?"

"Ian!" Jenny shouted. "Truck is back."

"Gotta go. I hear it's raining men." I hung up. With one last pistol check, I headed down the stairs. Jenny watched from the top of the stairs. "Watch over Nagunova. I'll take care of this."

Jenny nodded and stayed where she was. She checked

her pistol, too. The safety was on. She had three rounds left. No one had expected to get into a protracted gun battle.

No one except me. I never felt like I had enough ammunition.

I rushed down the stairs. Only two men. They had double-parked beside our Jeep. I expected that. There were no other spots, and they didn't look twice.

I couldn't fire my pistol in the open; the gunfire monitors would register it and bring the police.

Probably too quickly. I still needed time.

As they came to the door, I stepped into the side room and out of sight. They entered and kicked the door closed behind them.

Their backs were turned since they were going upstairs. From around the door, I fired at the nearer target's left shoulder. At point-blank range, the forty-five caliber bullet felt like getting hit by a sledgehammer. It spun him around, and he fell. The remains of the round slammed into the side of the second man. He grabbed the wound and arched back until he fell over. I jerked my aim back and forth between the two men, looking for who had retained enough wits to pull a weapon. The first man slumped, unconscious.

The second man spotted me through wild eyes and tried to get his hand behind his back. I cuffed him in the head with the pistol barrel, then rolled him over and took the military-special, an M9 Beretta nine-millimeter, from his waistband. A quick check found a knife clipped to the side of his boot. I took that too, along with the moving truck's keys.

The first man had gone pale and was sweating profusely. The shattered bullet must have hit something important. He didn't look like he was going to make it. He carried a thirty-eight-caliber revolver.

I shook my head. How dare my enemies refuse to arm me properly! I took the thirty-eight, rotated the cylinder out and dumped the ammo and threw them behind the stacked furniture. I wiped down the pistol and tossed it in the garbage can.

On top of a small stack of papers.

I pulled them out to look.

A map with notes in Arabic. I took a picture with my burner phone and sent it to Rick with a burner email address, one of the dozens I maintained.

"Grab Nagunova. We're leaving!" I called up the stairs. Jenny had remained ready to fire if the men broke free and headed upward. She was the accountant's last line of defense.

While Jenny retrieved Ms. Nagunova, I pulled the magazine out of the nine-millimeter, ejected the round in the chamber, inserted it into the nearly full magazine, and put it in my pocket. I wiped down the pistol and sent it to join its brother in the trash.

With the packing tape, I bound the second man while leaving the first to his demise. His breathing was rapid, and his heartbeat was barely noticeable. I wiped down the tape and tossed it aside. Last thing I did was take the hat that had flown off his head when the round hit him.

Jenny had the accountant over one shoulder in a fireman's carry. She navigated down the stairs without touching the railing. I had trained her well. She had never been a small woman, but with years of weight training and sparring, she'd become as fit and capable as any professional athlete. Just like me.

Our job demanded it.

When she reached the bottom of the steps, I kissed her.

"You take the Jeep and follow me to the garage where these knotheads went. We'll go in with the truck, and if we see the boxes," I pointed at the unpacked ones, "Blanchard Moving, then we'll go in hot."

Jenny fumbled with her pocket to pull out her burner phone. I typed in the address and looked at the directions before holding the door for Jenny. With one last look, I dragged my sleeve across the knob and shut it quietly.

The old lady sat on the stoop facing us, looking mesmerized. I waved. "Men with suits should be here shortly. Tell them there are four inside, and two are desnogulized."

"Desnogulized? What does that mean?"

"They'll know. Very hush-hush." I put my finger to my lips and hurried to open the back door of the Jeep. We belted Ms. Nagunova in. I handed Jenny the keys and kissed her once more before taking the driver's seat in the twenty-foot rental truck. It was like driving a van. I put it in gear and rolled slowly down the street. With the mirrors, it was hard to see if anyone was trying to squeeze in beside me.

I'd crunch them if I had to. I needed to get to that garage.

My phone started to ring. I was in traffic, but I slowed down and took the call.

It was Rick. "Looks like the World Trade Center."

"What? What the hell are they going to do with a couple hundred pounds of plastic explosive?"

"I don't know, Ian. That is a far cry from attacking Marines."

"Red herring?" I turned the corner and dropped the phone. It bounced on the floor. I yelled, "Dropped the phone, Rick. Hang up. I'll call back when I can. I'm heading to Freedom and Sons Garage. I think they've restaged there."

I kept driving, signaling to change lanes and then speeding up to start merging. I heard a horn. Too bad; I was coming over. I heard a screech from brakes that locked up. I thought newer cars all had anti-lock brakes.

Maybe it was an older car. I never saw it.

The garage was on the left. I slowed as I approached to find the best way in. It looked closed, but there were two cars in front. I pulled around them and headed toward the single bay. Somebody rolled the door up before I got there.

CHAPTER EIGHTEEN

"When adversity strikes, that's when you have to be the most calm. Take a step back, stay strong, stay grounded, and press on."
–LL Cool J

I pulled the hat down over my face. There was only one of me, but neither of the two men inside seemed to notice. I was expecting four.

There was at least one room off the bay, and the door stood open. I stopped the truck and turned it off. One man rolled the door down. I tried to envision where Jenny would park. I hoped it would be a long way from here. I bent down to recover my untraceable phone, but it had slipped under the seat. I'd get it later.

Speed and violence had to be my weapons. I opened the door when the second man rolled up the back door on the truck. The closest man stared at me in surprise. I swung the pistol up and tagged him on the chin. He staggered back.

I ran for the one opening the back. He was reaching for

his weapon. No time for a silent takedown. I fired once at his face and a second at center mass.

Both hit. He was dead before he hit the dirty floor. I rushed back to the man with the broken jaw. He'd started to moan. I checked him for a weapon—another thirty-eight. It made me want to put them through a four-hour class on optimizing logistical support so they could be punished as much as I was in learning about the benefits of being able to exchange ammunition with your fellow Marines.

I hit him on the side of the head with the pistol barrel. The sickening thud and crunch told me I hit him too hard, and he would probably never wake up. I moved to the side of the door to the reception area and leaned around, looking down the barrel of my weapon. Nothing there.

In the back was parts storage with leftover bits and pieces from the garage's previous operators. In the space to the side of the bay, the boxes from the house were stacked. Two of them were leaking. I wanted to look for more information, but the leaking boxes of chemicals used to make explosives put me on edge. I checked the two men to see what they carried.

One had an entry pass to the 9/11 Memorial. I took it. The other had a forty-five. "Praise be," I told him before adding, "I'm not sorry I killed you." I checked the magazine from the dead guy's M1911, and it fit into the pistol I was carrying. That wasn't a given, so I was happy to have something swing my way when it came to arms and ammunition.

I returned to the truck and dug my phone out from under the seat. It was still live. "Rick?"

"No one survived, did they?"

"So judge-y. Every one of these toads was armed. I had no choice. I'm getting out of here. That leaking stuff is giving me the willies." I used a garage rag to wipe down the truck and used the same rag to open the roller door. I tossed the rag behind me as I let the garage door fall to the ground, then headed to the street, looking for Jenny. She was nowhere to be seen.

"I'm going to have to call you back, Rick. In the interim, you might want to get a bomb squad here before this place blows." I hung up and stuffed my phone into my pocket. With my shirt untucked and a forty-five in my rear waistband, two phones, and a spare magazine, my pants bulged like a chipmunk's cheeks.

I was still dressed in office clothes. I wanted tactical gear or my homeless outfit. I wandered on the street in front of the gas station, feeling exposed. Finally, the Jeep appeared around the corner. I waved at Jenny to pull to the edge of the garage lot.

If the place blew, we'd be hurt, but we couldn't let anyone get near a ticking bomb, so Jenny jockeyed the vehicle to block the driveway. If the authorities showed up, they could have it. I hoped the ones who showed were EOD types. If not, they could still have it.

We waited fifteen minutes. No one came.

"World Trade Center. I want to take a look, so the feds can have this place when they get here as long as it hasn't been looted, which would probably set off whatever they have."

"Makes me wonder if the bomb is here still. The other guys might be at dinner or something."

My eye started to twitch again. "You're right. We better stay. Move to the far end. It's closer to the building, which would suck if it blew. Hang on. Is that somebody getting ready to pull out?"

Across the street and one building down. An acceptable view of the garage front. Jenny blasted in front of the cars coming down the road and pulled in nose-first, leaving the tail end sticking into traffic.

I winced at what I assumed would be the inevitable crash into our rear quarter panel. Once the traffic cleared, Jenny backed out, evened up to the car in front, and properly parallel parked. I hitched my leg onto the seat so I could watch the garage.

A long groan came from the back seat. Jenny and I bumped heads as we leaned around the headrests to look. Ms. Nagunova struggled to sit up. I jumped out and opened the back door to help her.

She smacked her dry lips. "Such a headache." She held her head. "Water, please?"

There wasn't any in the cup holders. Only an empty coffee cup held a spot there. "We don't have any. You're going to have to hold on," I told her in my most sympathetic voice.

She groaned louder, and I had to shut the door. Jenny pointed out the windshield. "Is that a deli down there?" Almost a block away. "I'll go. I'll be right back." Once the traffic cleared, she hopped out, ran across the road, and kept running to stay clear of the garage. She slowed to a walk after putting a building between her and the explosives.

Five minutes, then ten. Nagunova continued to groan. Nothing I said would placate her. She probably needed more than a jug of water. She needed medical help. I assumed she had no identification on her since her purse was in Max's office. We could drop her off at a hospital.

We needed to do that. I pulled out my burner smartphone and looked for the nearest medical facility. Three blocks away, but we'd lose our spot and eyes on the target.

"If we drop you off at the front door, can you get yourself checked in to the emergency room?"

While talking, a car pulled to the front of the garage.

Two men jumped out. They looked like the others in their clothes and other features.

Nagunova was instantly forgotten. In about ten seconds, they were going to figure out their operation was blown.

All six men accounted for. I took a deep breath and stepped out of the Jeep. The traffic was heavy, with no letup in sight. I did my best Frogger imitation to get from line to line until I was able to run the last bit to get across the street.

The two lifted the garage door and made it to about head-high before letting it crash back down. They ran for their car, and I ran at them. The two didn't try to pull weapons. They had a two-ton Mercedes at their command.

They had it running and in gear in an instant. I skirted wide as they backed toward me, then transitioned into a power slide to swing the front of the vehicle at me. They didn't have enough momentum to get all the way around. I crouched, aimed, and fired. The passenger bucked as the round took him in the side of the head. The bullet punched straight through and busted out the far window.

The car swung wildly toward me. I dove to the side, and the car jerked the other way and accelerated into traffic. I rolled to my feet and smoothly tucked my pistol into the back of my pants. Jenny appeared to be angry that she had missed it. She carried a couple of bags.

"Got away," she said. But she had been right that they were coming back. She repeated the license plate, which was the same as I remembered. I texted it to Rick's phone with the note **Bad guy inside**.

"We're down to one. We started with eight. I think this guy will do his best to get back home."

"We tangled with Wiggy's killer. Were any of these guys him?"

I shook my head. "Crap. That means they still have at least two."

We returned to the Jeep and gave the accountant three bottles of water. She chugged the first and the second and took her time with the third.

"Where to?" Jenny asked.

"The hospital up ahead and then the Loneham," I replied. Before we drove off, I called Max.

"We have Ms. Nagunova. She's a little drugged up but alive."

"That's good news. Where'd you find her?"

"We'll answer those questions in person. We want to drop her off at a hospital, but she'll need her wallet. Can you go to your office and get her purse?"

"Will do. I'm at the Loneham right now. I rented the two-bedroom suite. I hope you don't mind company."

"I think you're in the clear, Max. We have this group on the run. After you get us Nagunova's purse, you can join your wife. Your role in this has come to an end. I'm sure you're in the clear. You have a major business and a charity to run."

"What about you, Ian?"

"My job is not done. Jenny and I have a few loose threads, but I hope we'll be able to declare victory in a day or two," I lied. I had no idea how long it would take to hunt down at least two men in an urban sprawl with tens of millions of people.

"I'll meet you in the Loneham lobby," Max replied and hung up.

I turned toward the back seat. "We'll get your ID first and then send you in a cab to the hospital, if you don't mind," I told Ms. Nagunova. "Do you have a first name?"

"Okay," was all she managed to say.

She sounded miserable. Maybe I could talk Max into going with her.

My phone rang. I figured it was Rick.

"What's going on, Ian?" Jimmy Tripplethorn asked.

"It's madness up here, sir. We've beaten the body of the snake until it's black and blue, but the head is still out there. We've cut off funding, but at this point, I think that's almost irrelevant. I wish I had better news, Jimmy."

Jenny raised her eyebrows and leaned close to listen.

"I look forward to hearing the full story. Is a threat imminent?"

"It is. We believe the World Trade Center is the target."

"Again? Why?"

"I wish I knew. I think the entire effort against the Marines was to distract us from the real target. The heart of American commerce, maybe. Who knows? Maybe they'll just plant explosives and send a letter touting that they can do it any time and any place. Public fear is a great political motivator. *Pull your troops out, or else...*"

"Could be. That's why you're on this job. Rick seems happy working with you," the vice president said.

"Jimmy, your time has to be too important to make small talk. What did you call me for?"

"The FBI is raising a stink about a madman leaving a trail of bodies across New York City."

"That can't be me. I'm not mad, not angry at all. At least not every one of the bodies is dead." I waited to see if I got a chuckle, but Jimmy sounded tired. Everyone was tired. The terrorists were wearing down the people they needed to wear down. "These guys are here in force, Jimmy, and they mean business. As for functional resources, we have to assume they have the means to carry out this attack. They are at their endgame."

"I'll make sure we get extra bodies around the trade center and the memorial too, just in case."

"We can't let them get close enough to scratch the paint, Mr. Vice President."

"No, we can't. Keep doing what you're doing, Ian. I need you." Jimmy clicked off.

I looked at the blank screen on the phone before jamming it into my pocket. It mirrored my mind—endless possibilities but blank on the surface. I didn't know where to turn.

"What's next?" I asked.

CHAPTER NINETEEN

"You'll never find a better sparring partner than adversity."
–Golda Meir

Jenny put her hand on my leg while I eased into traffic. "Give Stacy a call and tell her to get some rest and start fresh in the morning. These locations have been tied together somehow. I think their support structure is limited, but they are using everything related to it. Like Wiggins. A useful idiot for whatever they had on him."

Jenny held out her phone but didn't make the call. "What if she wants to keep working? You have already paid her for this month. What would she look for?"

"Tendrils and ties to the garage. Other Wiggins properties. We might find the garage was one of theirs in some odd way."

"Then why didn't they use the garage to begin with?" Jenny wondered

"Too obvious. A bunch of guys working in a closed shop that doesn't open up. There was no place to sleep. No kitchen. This was their safety valve to move stuff. No one would question someone moving in. They might have a staging area near the tower or not. They could already be there or not. Or it could be another diversion."

"That's a lot of ifs," Jenny replied. She tapped the buttons. Stacy answered on the first ring. "What are you working on?"

"The many tendrils of the Wiggins real estate machine. Most of their properties are mortgaged for the full value and occupied by renters. Odd that the homestead wasn't and that the only property in the Fourth's name was his upscale apartment."

"Even the family didn't trust him?" Jenny wondered.

"Not exactly. The word 'trust' is correct in that all the property is in the name of the Wiggins Family Trust, but they've gone to great lengths to keep much of the information private. I'm digging through it."

"Make sure you get some rest," Jenny said. "You can get back to it in the morning because there are still members of the group running free, and we still need help."

"That sounds like the best thing to do. I'm sorry I couldn't get you the information sooner."

"Sometimes things move pretty fast," Jenny replied. "All we can do is our best to keep up after we've done everything we can to stay ahead."

"Cryptic and deep. That's probably everything you do, isn't it?"

"Mostly."

I smiled. Every job was different. Every job was life or death. We never had the option of not staying on our toes.

This was the most challenging contract I had ever had, and I still couldn't see the end. What would it take to finish this?

How would we know when we'd cut the head off the snake?

We dropped off Ms. Nagunova with Max, who said he would get her to the hospital. She never did give us her first name.

We used the Loneham's valet and headed to the suite. Once there, we ordered room service. I hadn't realized how tired I was until I sat down. I was almost asleep by the time our food arrived.

The morning brought a new opportunity to lack information. I could find nothing on any of our suspects. No information regarding the men who had died had made it into the press. That was good. I had top cover, something I wasn't used to.

But this one was different, hunting terrorists. It was almost legitimate.

I decided to wear the clothes I had worn the previous day since I had nothing else. Jenny did too. There might have been a time when that bothered us. It wouldn't have, but I was going to pack heavily until the last of the serpents was gone. I wore the hoodie with my slacks, even though it was going to be warm. It would hide my piece. Jenny carried hers in her purse. At least she had a full magazine with more spare rounds.

In this job, improvising was critical since we rarely carried the equipment we would use. We determined what was best based on the situation. Traveling without being armed was the only way we could travel. We were business owners.

The knock on the door came as a surprise. Jenny drew her pistol and moved to the side. I didn't look through the peephole since that was a good way to get shot in the eye.

I called, "Who is it?"

"It's Max."

I opened the door. "You look like hell."

"Slept in the hospital waiting room. Got any coffee?" He pushed past and waved at Jenny. He glanced at the pistol but was too tired to care or say anything.

I checked the corridor before closing and deadbolting the door.

"How is she?"

"Riding a chloroform overdose. She needed a lot of fluids plus pain meds. She had bruises, suggesting she fought back. They hassled me because it looked like domestic violence. I couldn't just leave her there."

I smiled and clapped him on the shoulder. He stared at the room's coffee maker. "Sit down. I'll get you a cup." I took the pot to the sink to fill it. "Where is she now?"

He flopped on the couch. "I left her there."

I didn't push him despite the opportunity for humor. He wasn't like us. Intense situations didn't bring out the best of the worst jokes.

Jenny put the pistol in her purse and took a seat on the cushioned chair opposite him. She held up two fingers. We had been heading out to get a designer brew, but the plan had changed.

"She said they wanted to know what she'd told me. She didn't answer them. They beat her, but she stayed quiet."

"Her fiduciary duty saved her life," I replied.

"What do you have on the schedule for today?" he asked, closing his eyes as he slouched low enough to rest his head on the back of his cushion.

"No schedule, just a goal. Find the runners."

"And then what?"

"And then we'll take care of it." I didn't want to say out loud that we planned to kill people. I could imagine the recording in court as Stacy tried to convince a jury it was self-defense.

"What happened yesterday?"

"Bad guys tried to kill us."

"What happened to them?" Max pressed. The first cup of the hotel's special blend finished brewing, and I put it on the appropriately named coffee table. I nudged his foot with mine.

"They are no longer trying to kill us."

"What?" He leaned forward and scratched his head before taking a sip. "You paid them off or something like that?"

"Or something." I started the second cup and leaned against the counter. "We have to focus our energy on the two who got away, keeping in mind there could be more. We've done some damage to the cell, but how much? We don't know."

"A cell that was running with money from my charity."

"That you didn't know was going to them. We have to trust people, Max. Without that, we'd be insane. And most people *are* trustworthy. Have you heard from Mark?"

He nodded. "It's going to be a long and painful road. She's in bad shape but getting the care she needs. Mark will be forever in your debt."

I had checked that morning. He still hadn't paid. I couldn't bring myself to nudge him on the payment. Maybe we'd do that one gratis. No one had to know. I hated bureaucrats, but drug dealers were worse. They deserved what they got. Their business destroyed lives.

The Peace Archive could be accused of being in a comparable business, but the lives we destroyed made the world a better place.

As soon as I questioned that, I'd be out of the game. Moral superiority only worked if one had the ethics on which to stand. It wasn't a sliding scale.

My burner phone rang. Stacy.

"Tell me you have something good," I said as soon as I answered.

"I found one more property buried deep. Lower Manhattan, Soho area."

"Text me the address. We'll take a look. Thanks, Stacy."

"I'll keep digging, but I think that might be it for their portfolio. Twenty properties, excluding the Fourth's apartment, and only two are showing as unoccupied."

"Your logic is sound. Next steps are that we check the properties one by one. Prepare a list based on rented most recently to oldest tenants and send it as a different text."

We finished the call. I pulled up the text.

"Where are we going?" Max asked.

"Jenny and I are going to check out whatever is at this address. You're going home."

"I need to see this to the end," Max took a big swig from his coffee.

"Jenny and I need to see this to an acceptable conclusion. You need to run your business and your charity."

"Not today, I don't. Do you have an extra weapon?"

"No." I couldn't get any more definitive than that. It was a solid "no" to all of it. We couldn't have a strap-hanger getting in our way. Jenny and I worked seamlessly together because of years of training. "You're not coming with us."

"Ian," Max started. He stood to make eye contact, but we'd already been through that. His battles were fought in a different space. Mine were more hands-on. Max recognized the difference.

"Maybe you can go keep Nagunova company."

"Do you think they'll come after her?"

"Not anymore. Her information is meaningless now because they know someone is coming after them. From my experience in the Sandbox, they don't like playing defense, but they are experts at playing the long game. It may sound like a dichotomy, but it's not. They are fine as long as they know they'll get to wield the scimitar of retribution. They are patient but offense-minded."

"Do you think they'll come after me?"

"I'm less sure about that today than I was yesterday," I replied. "Go to your family and wait it out."

He smiled. "I have a contract with a private security company. I activated it yesterday. There are two burly men in dark sunglasses in the lobby, waiting for me to return."

"You're definitely not coming with us. It's their job to stand out. It's ours to blend in."

"Does that include spots on the local news?"

"Yeah, that." I was less than amused. "Sometimes the spotlight is unavoidable. They shouldn't have tried to steal from us."

"It was a setup by our favorite gotcha reporter, but she made Jenny Bragg look like a hero."

"Jenny Bragg *is* a hero." I didn't explain further. What she had done in the Quresh compound had taken nerves of steel, a keen eye, and lightning-quick actions. We were making a name for ourselves by carrying damaged daughters back to their fathers.

Rich fathers who wanted a second chance.

I'd take their money while also encouraging them to get it right in the first place. And tell all their friends to get it right.

But I enjoyed hurting those who hurt the innocent. Sometimes, deep in my mind, I saw myself as an avenging angel. It wouldn't be anything I said out loud.

It helped me reconcile the bad part of a hard job so I could keep doing what needed to be done.

Moral superiority.

It came with a pinch of guilt. My conscience watching over me, prodding me.

"We better go," I said. Jenny had taken two sips and made a face after both.

Max drained his cup.

"Stay here if you like. Get some shut-eye. You are paying for this place. You still have a key, right?"

"I do. I didn't just come in because I suspected you might be on edge. Or naked. I don't want to see you naked, Ian." He held my look.

"You say that now," I replied cryptically. Max stood and made to walk out with us.

"You're not going with us."

"I most assuredly am."

I looked at Jenny. She shrugged and shook her head.

"The lovely lady wouldn't deny me…"

"You can't go with us," Jenny enunciated. "I don't want you to get hurt because I like Clarice and your kids. They deserve to grow up knowing their father."

He made a face. "I can handle myself."

It took all my self-discipline not to snort and roll my eyes. "Not against these guys. We'll take care of it."

He glanced at Jenny.

"She's as good as any operator out there. We've trained for years, and we're under contract on this one. I want to get more contracts. I promised the head shed that no innocents would be injured. That means you. Nagunova was a surprise, kidnapped out of the waiting area outside your office. Brazen. And what they're doing? You don't want any part of that."

"Who contracted you?"

"If Ms. Nagunova won't talk to terrorists who beat her and probably threatened to kill her, I'm not going to talk about our clients. We can't. That would put us out of business quicker than anything. Understand that we are under contract, and we'll take care of it."

"Strange world we live in. Only the government would

know about terrorists. The government has hitmen in their employ? That's got to be illegal."

"It's only illegal if you're not working for the ones who enforce the law."

With one last look to make sure we'd left nothing behind, I quietly unlocked the door and yanked it open to look out. The cleaning person in the hallway nearly jumped out of her skin.

"Sorry," I mumbled. "I thought someone was going to play a practical joke on me."

Jenny walked into the hallway, and then Max. I closed the door after myself and tipped my head to the older lady on my way around her cart. I snagged a handful of the nitrile gloves and stuffed them into my pocket. "You don't need to do anything with our room. It's fine."

"Not even clean towels?"

"We're way good." I slipped her a twenty-dollar bill. "It was immaculate when we moved in, and it's still clean. We'll be here for a few more days, so plenty of time to get fresh towels if we need them."

The woman made the twenty disappear like magic before smiling at us.

We headed for the elevator and to the ground floor. In the lobby, we found the two men Max had described. He looked smug.

"Still can't come," I whispered.

"I'm a private citizen. I can go where I please."

"Max, we're trying to protect you."

"And I'm trying to protect my reputation."

"Hedge fund managers have good reputations?"

"Ouch! Don't confuse me with Federico. The charity, my friend. I'm not saying I'm buying my way into heaven, but I'm paving the stairway and lining it with cheering fans."

"Stay out of our way." He bristled. I changed my tone. "Please, do not get in our way."

"I'll do what I can. We'll ride with you." He waved at his bodyguards. I wasn't sure how they were going to fit in the back of the Jeep.

The click-clack of high heels strolling across the marble floor drew my attention, as it was undoubtedly designed to do.

My face fell. "Babs! Had I not ever seen you again, that would have been too soon."

She ignored me. "Jenny, it's great to see you looking so fit. A testament to womanhood and a role model for young girls everywhere."

Babs wasn't wrong, but it made me angry to hear it from her. It wasn't about celebrating Jenny; it was all about Babs.

"The only person you care about is yourself. Why don't you leave us alone?" I waved to the valet with my ticket.

"Fifteen minutes, sir," he called back. "You can call ahead from your room, and we'll have your vehicle waiting." He sent one of his people running to the garage a block over where Loneham leased space.

I felt like a moron. "Can I get anyone a steaming cup of designer java?"

Jenny nodded. "Mocha. Large."

"Sounds good to me," Babs said.

"Not you." I frowned. Jenny gave me her look. "Fine. I'll get it for the bloodsucking leech. Max?"

"I'll come with you." He made a wide berth around the reporter. She blew a kiss at him. He gestured for his bodyguards to stay behind. They backed away from the women. "What do you think they're going to talk about?"

"Us. No doubt. I have a deep dislike for that woman."

"I like that she's latched onto you and is staying away from me. On a side note, since you like security, how do you feel about someone in the hotel tipping her off that you're here?"

"Didn't have to be an employee," I replied. I had no intention of complaining to a manager. "I don't need any other reasons to be angry, so I choose to be happy instead." I smiled.

"You don't look happy."

"Because I'm not." I ordered three mochas, and Max ordered a double-shot latte with almond milk.

We waited for our drinks and watched Babs speak using extravagant gestures. Jenny tensed.

"Can you get it all, Max? I think the cavalry is called for."

I hurried back. Jenny looked at me. "Miss Jaekel has an interesting theory."

"I know what you are, Mr. Bragg, Mrs. Bragg. You're assassins." Babs crossed her arms and tipped her head back with her victory.

I tried to show a shocked face. I expect it was less than convincing. "I like it!" I declared. "I'm going to add that to my curriculum vitae. Babs Make-Up-The-News Jaekel has designated me as an assassin. Where's the camera, because this has to be a joke. There is something seriously wrong with you, Barbara. When your investigative skills are bad, you resort to the next best thing. Fiction."

"You haven't denied it!" She continued to look down her nose at me.

"I haven't denied being Santa Claus either, an alien from Mars, or a billion other things you could come up with. It's not my job to deny things. If I understand my rights, I'm a private citizen, and you don't get to make slanderous claims. Those could negatively impact my business opportunities in the great state of New York. Just because you manufactured an event that targeted us doesn't mean you get to use us. I'm tired of your games."

I took my phone out and dialed Stacy's number.

"Stacy, do you have a classmate out here who takes civil cases? Babs Jaekel is here in the hotel, making fantastic claims that I feel need to be addressed by a higher power. Can you have a suit filed against the station and her personally by this afternoon?"

"I'm sure we can. It'll cost you probably fifty thousand to get the ball rolling that quickly, but it'll get their attention. Will that work?"

"Fifty grand to start?" I repeated for Babs' edification. "File the suit. You can recover the Loneham lobby security video to confirm that she was here. Her claim was simple. She called Jenny and me assassins in front of at least two other people. I will not stand for it."

"Consider it done, Ian. I have no other information. Still working up the prioritized listing, but that'll be ready soon."

I turned back to Babs. "I like having a local lawyer on retainer. You should probably consider it. We're going to expose your purse-snatching scam and illegal gathering of information by the cop. He'll get fired. You'll get fired. The studio will pay my legal fees. And we'll disappear from the news, where we never should have been in the first place. We only want to go about our business. Nothing nefarious. Expanding the Club to a potentially lucrative market is boring business stuff. And we stay fit because if we let the mind-numbing side of what we do get to us, we'd be slovenly and brain-dead."

Babs held up her hands. "Jenny is still a hero among the girls. I'm sure middle or high schools would love to have her come and talk with them."

Jenny tried not to perk up. She would do that, but we had a contract. That took precedence over everything else.

"Be on your way, Babs. And that wasn't a bluff. We are going to file suit because you can't be creating the news.

The world is sensational enough. It doesn't need fiction masquerading as fact."

She didn't say another word. Babs Jaekel stepped back, nodded at Jenny, and clacked her way to the front door and out.

I didn't see a cameraman lurking but assumed the cameras were still rolling.

CHAPTER TWENTY

"When we long for life without difficulties, remind us that oaks grow strong in contrary winds and diamonds are made under pressure." –Peter Marshall

When the valet summoned us, we hurried to the door and got into the Jeep. Max squeezed into the middle between his two bodyguards. They were impressive in size. He didn't have time to regret his decision since I pulled out immediately, letting Jenny's GPS guide us to the supposedly empty building.

I knew we wouldn't find it empty, but would the squatters be the ones we were looking for? Jenny dialed up the first side of the landmark 2112 album and fast-forwarded to *Temples of Syrinx*. Always play Rush before going into battle. It soothes the soul.

We weren't surprised or disappointed to find two vehicles parked by the side of the building.

"You'll find the one has its passenger window shot out," I said while checking the building on our way past. I continued another block before pulling into a parking garage. I circled to the top of the structure to check for exits before returning to the third floor, where there were available spots. I let the passengers in the back get out before pulling in because of the tight space.

"Time to go get them!" Max declared.

I didn't reply to him but to the bodyguards. "To protect him, you're going to keep him across the street and halfway down the block. Don't let him anywhere near that building."

They both looked at Jenny.

"That's right." I pointed at Jenny and then at myself. "*We* are going in. You are not."

"How many times do you need to say it? I'll watch from across the street. Give it a rest, will you?"

"I want there to be no doubt." I nodded, and we took the back stairs. I checked for cameras and found the mounts, but no hardware remained. A ball mount hung outside the garage that would have recorded our entry and our departure. The ticket machine camera had a Joe's Pizza sticker covering it.

It hadn't gotten a look into the Jeep.

The rear stairs deposited us on the ground floor of the garage. There was no way out except through the front. "Keep your heads down. Don't make it easy on them."

We mobbed out. I pulled my hood over my head. The others couldn't cover up enough to make it worthwhile. Still, anything less than a positive identification would work to our benefit if this went south on us.

Then again, if it went bad, we wouldn't be walking away.

The bodyguards crossed the street at the light and waited on the other side. Jenny and I strolled hand in hand until we could see the edge of the building. It was a fairly large two-story brick structure, double the size of a normal home, so pushing five thousand square feet. The building to the left was tight against it.

The alley on the right side was wide enough for a single vehicle. The one we'd shot into was blocked in by a similar vehicle, a black four-door.

We continued past the building, purposely not looking at it. Once by, we leaned against the wall of the neighboring structure. I took Jenny in my arms and nibbled on her ear while studying the front of the target building. I couldn't see through the windows since they were covered on the inside with newspaper. The windows on the second floor were uncovered and open to the cool morning air.

A rusty fire escape let into the alley behind the two vehicles.

I didn't like it. We had no intel. I whispered into Jenny's ear, "And now we wait."

She nodded just enough to let me know she heard. We leaned against the building and made small talk about my golf game until Jenny laughed. The owner of the building we leaned against popped out of his front door and waved a large wooden spoon at us. "Go away!"

I wondered if he was old enough to have served in the First World War.

"Can you tell us what's going on in the building next door?" I asked.

"First time in New York?" he shot back. "Best not to ask those kinds of questions. Friendly advice. Now take your smutty bodies and go someplace else."

Jenny chuckled, turning away so as not to offend our new friend. I pulled a bill from my pocket. It was one of my last hundreds. I folded it so the 100 was showing and reached it forward.

"What's this for?"

"I just want to know what's going on next door." I gestured with my head.

"Not worth it."

I pulled a second hundred and handed them over. He took both and waved us inside. We followed him but stayed near the door since we could no longer see the target building.

"I'm not a criminal." That wasn't exactly true. "I'm working with the authorities." Mostly true. "The men inside are persons of interest in a rather extensive case. We don't have time to set up surveillance and do things the normal way." That was completely true.

"Yes. Men inside. Trucks making deliveries. Trucks taking stuff away. Very busy the last week."

"Trucks taking stuff away? Where did they go?"

"Are you kidding me? How in the hell would I know? In my generation, people as dumb as you didn't last long."

"I appreciate your patience." I needed what he had. "How many people are in there?"

He shrugged. "Six, ten, maybe two." The money had disappeared into a pocket, and he held his hand palm up in front of him.

It was only money, and his shop was hurting by the looks of it. Antiques. No customers. Dust everywhere. I pulled a bunch of twenties out of my pocket and handed them over. "That's it. This isn't a well-funded operation." That was a lie.

"At least six. More come than go. Yesterday was a busy day."

"How do you know this?" I couldn't ignore his hand. "I don't have any more. Just tell me."

"Fine. Upstart and impatient, just like all the young people nowadays. I smoke out the side door. Unfiltered Camels. Like I said, my generation is tough. I don't look too bad for forty-five, do I?"

"You don't look bad for a hundred and forty-five," I answered before I could stop myself.

He croaked what passed for a laugh before leading us to his side door. Jenny turned sideways to get through the aisles, doing her best to avoid touching anything. I kept my hands in front of me and my eyes moving.

Out the side door, we stood in the alley beyond the car with the shattered window. I casually moved close while the old man lit a cigarette. Jenny stayed upwind from him. There was blood in the seat and splattered in the back. More than blood. It had been a clean headshot.

The body had been removed.

I glanced at the upstairs windows, then turned around and walked back to Miss Jenny. These downstairs windows had been papered over on the inside too. In keeping with the broken windows approach in reducing crime, the windows were intact. It had survived being empty. The upstairs windows were dark. The side door had a hasp and a lock.

"You wouldn't happen to have a crowbar, would you?"

"Crowbars are for amateurs. I have a bolt cutter." He casually finished his cigarette, having no sense of urgency. I didn't want to rush him because he was the best friend we had when it came to casing the building, even though it had cost me a few hundred dollars.

A pittance in the big scheme of life.

He disappeared inside while we waited, playing the groping couple again while we waited. When he returned with a bolt cutter half his height, I had to give him a hearty thumbs-up.

"As soon as you make the cut, you get back inside and lock the door." He smiled. This day was the most excitement he had had in a long time. Jenny and I pulled on the latex gloves I had lifted from the cleaning cart while I talked to the maid.

Jenny slipped the nine-millimeter out of her purse and gripped it, ready to enter when the door was open.

He made short work of the lock and strolled back toward his building. As soon as he was inside, we worked the door, but it didn't come open.

"Must be blocked on the inside." I wasn't amused.

The old guy opened the door and looked at us. He held a hammer and a punch. "Just pop out those hinges. Door will come right off."

"You deserve a bonus, my friend." He handed me the tools.

He was right. A few light taps punched out the hinge pins since the door had been recently used. I stuffed the claw part of the hammer into the rings and torqued it, and the door slid away from the frame. Two deadlocks twisted within the frame while I levered the door open. I dropped the hammer and punch on the ground and pulled the forty-five.

I went inside first, moving the pistol barrel with my eyes as I snapped from left to right to take on anyone who was waiting.

Someone had to have heard the door, but there was enough noise from the front part of the building to cover it. I stalked forward, then eased down the hallway. We passed two closed doors, hesitating to listen at each but hearing nothing.

I didn't like leaving them closed, but we couldn't give ourselves away since we had penetrated the building without being noticed. I motioned for Jenny to stay on the far side of the rooms while I continued down the hallway.

Only one bulb was lit near the open side door. The rest of the hallway was dank and dark and smelled of rotting wood. Light outlined the door I was heading for. The loud voices and the sounds of small equipment came from the other side.

As I reached it, the door was flung open. The individual standing there was just as surprised as I was. I was happy I didn't jerk the trigger and blow his head off.

"Who are you?" he asked in Arabic, a common phrase when I was there. It came through clearly.

"*Habibi, as-salamu alaykum,*" I replied while aiming my pistol at his face. He took a deep breath and started to turn. I fired once into the side of his head and stepped forward to take in the room. I found an active workshop and counted six people. Four had ducked at the sound of the erupting forty-five.

Two were pulling weapons and taking aim. I double-tapped the closest target and jumped back before the second man was able to get off a shot.

Seven. Two down. Five to go. I stayed out of the line of fire. The first three shots of return fire dinged off the inside brick of the outer wall.

A door flew open behind me. I dropped to the floor and started to turn. The unmistakable sound of the small Glock popped twice, followed by the thump of a body hitting the floor.

The hiss of a grenade preceded it bouncing off the brick and into my body. Had I not been on the floor, it would have skipped past. I flung it away from me and covered my face with my hands the instant before it exploded.

I scrambled to my feet and leaned around the corner, looking for anyone moving. They were spread out, and I didn't count on the grenade having removed any of them from the equation.

A round chipped the wall a finger's breadth from my head, sending chunks of plaster into my face. I drew back and blinked quickly, hoping I could still see.

I wiped my face with my sleeve, and it came away wet. I

was bleeding but didn't feel hurt. My eye cleared with the tears washing away the dust.

A sound beyond the door suggested they were closing in. I heard a grunt and replied by slamming the door. A grenade hit it and bounced back into the workshop.

Lucky twice. I couldn't count on that again.

I opened the door and dove toward a drill press to the left. Once inside the shop, I stayed on the floor and looked for legs or feet. I saw a pair of shins below a low conveyor leading into a boxy machine. I had no idea what it was for, and that didn't matter. Much of the equipment wasn't in use. They didn't need it for their purposes.

I assumed it was bomb-making. It was always bombs, the ragtag army's weapon of choice. When a mouse defies Goliath, he needs a weapon of equal power. If not to destroy, to create fear.

Explosions. Debris. Smoke.

I took aim and fired. The man screamed and fell. I fired twice more, and the screaming stopped. I didn't have enough ammunition for a firefight. There was a scuff and the telltale pop of a subcompact.

I leaned upward to look and almost had my head blown off. I caught the fleeting image of a man holding his bleeding arm.

He was the one who had killed Wiggins the Fourth.

I aimed into the small gap between equipment legs and pedestals. He staggered past, and I fired. The forty-five ripped through the back of his leg. He started to fall. I couldn't see more since a flurry of rounds impacted around me. Sounded like at least four shooters, and two carried AK sub-machine guns limited to semi-automatic fire. The short barrels made them woefully inaccurate, but the high volume of fire, even limited to how fast the shooter could pull the trigger, made up for it. The banana magazines were big thirty rounders. The others carried semi-autos. Looked like Glocks from the glimpse I'd had.

Shouting near the front door.

I didn't dare try to get a better look. I stayed low and searched for a way out. This had gone on for far too long. The police had to be on their way, given the two grenades and the fifty to one hundred rounds fired. No one could mistake the noise for anything other than a firefight.

A piece of scrap wood on the floor gave me a thought. I tossed it over my head and scooted across the floor, closer to the hallway. Rounds tore through the air over my head. One even managed to hit the piece of wood, sending it flying off the wall behind me.

I was tensing my muscles to run for the opening when a barrage rained fire on the equipment between the shooters and me. I covered my head and tried to become one with the concrete floor.

It took a couple of seconds of silence to realize the firing had ended. It sounded like a Marine platoon's final protective fire when everyone fired at their maximum cyclic rate along set fields of fire to completely embroil a target area, slicing and dicing anyone unlucky enough to be within.

I peeked around a machine pedestal, then jumped to the next machine and brought my pistol around the side of it, looking for a target. The front door was open, and two men ran through. I dodged from cover to cover, checking the area as I went in case they'd left someone behind to deal with me. The black car raced into traffic, carrying the two I had seen plus two more. It immediately got caught up and stopped. I moved to the doorway, aimed, and fired. It wasn't that long a shot, maybe thirty yards. It caught the driver in the shoulder.

I fired a second round, staying out of sight. The door strut was in the way and the round splattered off it, shattering the back window and peppering the passenger on that side of the car. The doors popped open on the far side, and the other two men jumped out and ran for it. They headed in the direction where Max and his two bodyguards stood.

CHAPTER TWENTY-ONE

"I love those who can smile in trouble, who can gather strength from distress, and grow brave by reflection. 'Tis the business of little minds to shrink, but they whose heart is firm, and whose conscience approves their conduct, will pursue their principles unto death." –Leonardo da Vinci

Max couldn't distinguish between the different weapons being fired but knew that a major battle raged within. The explosions told him it was more than just handguns.

"Should we go help?" Max asked. He didn't know their names. "Bob?"

"Lawrence," the man corrected. "The last place you want to be is in there."

A massive amount of gunfire made it sound like multiple machine guns had simultaneously unleashed their fury.

It ended suddenly, and the front door popped open. A stream of men ran out and jumped into the car. Even before the last door slammed shut, the car raced into traffic but immediately came to a halt.

A single flash marked a gunshot from the doorway, and the getaway car crunched into the one in front of it. Then another shot came from the shooter in the shadow of the doorway.

Max was mesmerized. His mind raced. It meant Ian was still alive and fighting!

The passenger doors kicked open, and two men fell out and ran low across the stalled traffic and onto the sidewalk.

They started running toward Max. "Guys?" he asked and started backing up. The two bodyguards blocked the sidewalk. "Stop them!"

The big men leapt into action, but only at the last second.

Lawrence swept a forearm into the path of the incoming, keeping his elbow tight to maximize the impact. The runner's feet went out from under him and he went down, landing flat on his back. The bodyguard drove a piledriver of a fist into the man's face.

The second bodyguard grabbed an arm as the man tried to get by. He started to spin and completed three hundred and sixty degrees to send him flying past Max's face and into the wall. He followed and pounced on the crumpled soul, turning him on his face to kneel on his back and hold his wrists. The passenger behind the driver pushed his door open and staggered out.

Ian was nowhere to be seen. Max ran through the stopped cars, with drivers and passengers all using their cell phones to record every action taking place around them. He made a beeline for the staggering man, preparing to take him off his unsteady feet with a body block—right up until his target pulled a sub-machine gun out from behind him. Max's eyes shot wide, and he dove into traffic.

A single shot came from the doorway, and the last man went down.

Max got up, dusted himself off, and gave the body a wide berth on his way into the building.

"Nice shot, Ian."

"It wasn't me. There was another guy in here." I clapped him on the shoulder. "And now it's time to leave. Come with us." I waved dismissively at the door. "Leave your bodyguards to deal with the bad guys."

I ran to the doorway where Jenny watched the rear in case more terrorists appeared behind me. One door was open—the one with the dead body in front of it.

"Damn, Ian. A one-man wrecking crew."

"That one wasn't me either."

Jenny shrugged.

I looked into a room where a lamp shone on a wall. "What the…"

On the wall was a schematic of the new world trade center. Technical details of the air-handling system were taped to the side wall. The writing was in Arabic, but the image taped beside the graphic told me all I needed to know.

I used my burner to take pictures and texted them to Rick's phone.

Then I used my other phone to call Rick's number. He answered on the fourth ring.

"Looks like nerve gas in the air-handling system of the tower," I said. "Not a bomb. The minions are neutralized. Twelve over the last two days."

"I'm looking at the pictures now. Holy crap, Ian. I need to go. I'll get the right people on this." He hung up.

"Looks like we're finished." Sirens got louder. More than one vehicle. "Run!"

Jenny bolted for the side door, ran out, and turned left to run away from where the action had taken place. We took off our gloves as we walked and pocketed them. We cleared the alley, slowed down, and walked along the sidewalk the next block over until we ran into an Italian place gearing up for lunch.

"Shall we?" I asked.

Max looked flustered.

I leaned close to him and whispered, "People running from a scene stand out. We'll stay here, eat, and then walk away slowly after the initial tension dies down. Call your bodyguards and tell them not to mention their client, which they shouldn't do anyway."

Max shook his head. "I don't have their number."

"Then I guess you better take the long way around the block and get to them before they start talking."

"I never mentioned your names in front of them."

"I'm sure they know who we are. We need the FBI to intercept any local cops trying to figure out who else was at the shootout." My initial desire to keep it quiet was going to fail, thanks to the bodyguards.

Max walked away, head up, at a brisk pace.

I called Rick back. "We're going to need top cover. I think the police will have our names soon enough. The Bureau needs to take that away from them and not ask questions. We stuck our necks out a long way on this one."

"We already have agents on the scene," Rick replied. "All information will go through DC. We'll intercept what can't be made public. Initial reports say it was a bloodbath."

"Initial reports are almost always wrong," I noted.

"Almost always. We're taking the steps we need to take to make sure nothing comes back to you, Ian."

"I'd appreciate that. We're going to grab some lunch, take a casual drive back to the hotel, and then take another casual drive to our place in the Hamptons, where we're going to hit the hot tub and watch some television."

"I'd love to join you, but I'll be busy for the next few days cleaning up a mess."

"The mess is because the intelligence community let this group get this deep before calling in someone like me to make sure that there wasn't a real mess. Which is still possible unless your people can dismantle that canister. We're grabbing lunch. I don't expect to hear from you again unless agents come knocking at my door, and then you and I are going to have a real problem. You need to be a better bureaucrat than those who would see me as the problem and not those who are the real problem."

My finger hovered over the button to end the call, but I didn't press it.

"I know what you mean. Our hands are tied in a lot of instances. We would have goofed around for a year trying to get the information you were able to acquire in just a few days. Good thing, too. I'm glad there are people like you, and I'm glad that you're on the right side of the people trying to do the right thing."

"That's the best diplomatic weaselly language I've ever heard not come from my own mouth."

I hugged Jenny.

"I do my best. I hope I don't need to call you anymore, but I have you on speed dial just in case."

"In another life, I might actually like you." I ended the call.

"He's just like you," Jenny said.

"Competition for my woman's affections?" I kissed her forehead.

"Your woman?" She jabbed me in the chest with her finger. "What's the plan?"

"Eat, hotel, Hamptons."

"And then?"

"Back to Chicago unless we meet with Max and his heavy-hitter friends. I bet we can get them to join the Club without there being a New York branch. We can rent the place we have for a week or two every quarter and make it an open house. It's not like we need a business license for what we do."

"Look at you with all the sexy business talk." Jenny glanced away.

"Are you okay about today?" Jenny didn't like doing what I did, but she was fanatically loyal to me, as I was to her.

"It's not in my nature," she said softly. "I have to fight off how I feel and perform the mechanics of shooting, the artistic technique of hand-to-hand combat, and not that I'm hurting people. That's not me."

"I know. This one was big. I should have called in backup from the region. Then again, it happened so fast, dominos falling." I had put Jenny at risk from the first day we'd met. She had agreed because love was a powerful motivator. "Maybe you shouldn't come anymore."

"There's no way that's going to happen. Ian, maybe you should let your team handle some of these jobs. Jimmy asks for your help, but he has to trust that you'll get it done. And you have to trust your people. *Do* you trust them?"

I looked into her eyes and was lost. She asked questions that only a best friend had the right to ask.

"You know the answer to that," I dodged.

"Men." Jenny shook her head.

"You married one."

"This isn't about me. I know you're trying to protect me. That's what the weights and sparring are about. But you have grown beyond being the pointy end of the spear, as you like to say. We need to keep the engine running, and the rest of the team does everything else."

I looked at my feet and found a rock close by that I could kick against the wall. "The weights and sparring are something I do anyway. It's something we can do together, and you are egregiously sexy while working out."

"I don't think that's the right word." Jenny smiled and gave me a playful push with her elbow.

"I don't have the luxury of trusting someone else with my relationship with Jimmy," I admitted. "I have to stay in the game as long as Jimmy is personally dropping contracts on me. There is no other way. We have to balance both. We need an office here and probably something in DC, too, to give us a reason to keep visiting."

"My family lives in DC."

"I guess that's reason enough."

"Just because you don't like them."

"Not true, but if I get their sister killed, my life won't be worth living. And it won't be because of them."

"That's sweet, but I'm still coming wherever you go."

I conceded the field of battle, having won the mental chess match. I needed Jenny watching my back. I didn't trust anyone else. And if anyone hurt her, there would be no place they could hide.

A reckoning would be unleashed. The dichotomy of having her with me: keep her safe while putting her in the line of fire.

I'd wrestle with that until I was out of the game, which was planned for the second Jimmy was out of office. I didn't owe his successor. I wouldn't be a tool for a scumbag politician. I'd do jobs for Jimmy only.

We would do the jobs.

"Lunch?" I wanted to sit down and decompress. I had too much on my mind and needed to clear things. Lunch, an ice pack, and then the hot tub. I could feel the bruises starting to come out and play from getting bounced around inside that shop.

Jenny nodded and pointed at the Italian place we'd been headed to before I called Rick.

My burner phone rang. Max.

I slid my finger to accept the call but didn't speak.

"Ian. My bodyguards bailed on the unconscious men. They're waiting with me at the garage."

"You guys! I like that better than trying to convince them not to talk. We'll be there shortly." I looked at Jenny and shook my head. "No lunch for us. It's time to go."

Of course, she'd heard the phone conversation.

She started walking without waiting. We bowed our heads when we entered the garage and climbed to the third level, where we found Max and his people waiting. We got into the Jeep and waited for another car to leave before we attempted it. That meant we had to pull down to the first level, pay our bill, and then exit.

Despite my trepidation at being too visible in the area immediately following the hit, we were able to leave the garage and cross a few blocks away before heading north. We stopped on Fifth Avenue near the Loneham.

I waited for the bodyguards to walk away after Max turned them loose, giving them each a cash tip and a caution not to mention him as their client. They vowed not to. I wasn't too sure. I needed Rick's top cover to make me comfortable. I was counting on a bureaucrat to protect me.

We needed to leave the state.

"I'd like to set up another meet and greet with your colleagues, but we need to let things cool off first."

Max held out his hand. I looked at it for a moment before taking it with a firm grip. "I won't forget any of this, Ian. I'll introduce you to the right people if you want to make a go of the Club."

Kill two birds with one stone. "Maybe we'll just come for a week or two every quarter. I'll let you take more of my money on the course, and I'll take more of yours and your friends to help with any problems that fit within our specialty."

"You can count on that. Just give me a heads up when you're in town." I nodded, and Max Odenkirk walked away. He'd once had a target on his back, and now he was a friend. Sounded like someone else. The benefits of allies.

We needed as many allies as we could get. I thought about Mark's daughter. I hoped that someday she'd appreciate what he had done for her.

Jenny used her GPS to help us avoid a jam on one bridge, taking a roundabout route to get to Southampton and the rental house that held my computer and our carry-ons. We didn't need any of it. I debated going straight to the airport when we passed the signs, but I wanted to trust that Rick would protect us.

But trust only went so far. We parked a half-block from a convenience store and ditched our wiped-clean pistols and gloves. I bought a cup of coffee, and Jenny went with orange juice. The all-American couple doing nothing out of the ordinary.

When we pulled into our driveway, a black sedan with federal government plates was waiting.

CHAPTER TWENTY-TWO

"Endurance is not just the ability to bear a hard thing, but to turn it into glory." –William Barclay

I looked at Jenny. "That was a little faster than I would have liked. Curious couple who won't answer any questions without a warrant. Call Stacy and ask if she could join us. About two minutes from now would be best, but as soon as possible after that will have to do."

They opened their doors the second I opened mine. I climbed out, closed it behind me, and leaned against it with my arms crossed, Magnum PI-style.

The man and the woman wore sunglasses. They held out their credentials as they approached.

"I didn't know she was married, honest!" I said and thrust my arms in the air. The two agents flinched at my rapid movement. "Jesus! Don't shoot me. That's right. You lost your sense of humor in Quantico."

"Mr. Bragg. We'd like to ask you a few questions." The female agent moved around to Jenny's side of the Jeep. I could hear her talking on the phone.

"Please get out of the vehicle, ma'am."

Jenny finished her call before getting out. She glared at the agent.

"I don't think so," I answered. "No matter what you're thinking, I don't talk to law enforcement without them showing paperwork and without our lawyer present."

"Lawyer? That makes you sound guilty of something."

"Sounds guilty because I understand the purpose behind the Constitution and the protections it gives the citizens. The Constitution was adopted to protect the likes of my wife and me from big government like you. Using our defense of our rights as a basis for further examination is unconstitutional. You should have a sense of humor because Quantico didn't give you the education you should've gotten unless you're used to railroading people. But to humor us while we wait for our lawyer, why are you in my driveway? Which is an odd turn of phrase because we *park* in a *driveway* but we *drive* on a *parkway*. You'd think it would be the other way around."

"We have information that suggests you might have witnessed an event in Lower Manhattan."

"That's nice." I leaned back and crossed my arms.

"You're not going to cooperate, are you? What happened to your face?"

I resisted the urge to touch the scabs that made it look like I'd been dragged sideways across the pavement.

"I will do whatever my lawyer advises because she has my best interests in mind, unlike you. Patience is a bitter cup from which only the strong may drink."

The female agent was trying to work Jenny, but she refused to say anything, resorting to glaring at the woman. She gave up and came to my side.

"Look, we have a lot of people to interview. Just answer a few simple questions, and we'll be on our way."

"Then come back when you've talked with the others. Not. Without. My. Lawyer."

"This is nothing. We think you have some information that would help us with our investigation. That's it. Nothing nefarious."

"No sense of humor and dense as a box of rocks. Is this how you strong-arm people? It probably works often enough to reinforce that it's okay. But not on me. Lawyer. On her way."

"Who's your lawyer?"

"She can introduce herself when she gets here. In the meantime, we're going inside. You can't come in."

"We'd prefer if you waited out here."

"It's nothing! We're going in our hot tub. When our lawyer arrives, she'll come in, we'll talk, and then we'll meet with you."

"We'd prefer if you stayed out here." The man stepped in front of us and put his hand out. I stared at it, ready to break his wrist, but that would give them what they wanted.

I tossed the keys over the roof to where Jenny stood. "Since it looks like I've been detained, can you put on some music and crank it up?"

"We'd prefer if you didn't."

Jenny ignored him and climbed in. She locked the doors before they could act, put the keys in, and turned the key far enough to activate the radio. She scrolled through the albums and selected Hold Your Fire. I smiled as the first track, *Force Ten*, started to play. Jenny rolled down the windows and climbed out.

The female agent started to reach through the window.

"Fruit of the poisoned tree," I said. "You don't have a warrant; otherwise, you would have already shown it. So, stay out of my car."

"It's a rental," the male agent replied.

"Quantico teach you how the law works? It's a rental. In my name. Which means I have a license for use as if it were my own vehicle. Law applies the same. Keep your mitts out of my Jeep."

The agents looked at each other. The man tipped his chin, and they moved to the opposite side of their vehicle and started an intense whispered conversation. I left the keys in the Jeep while Jenny and I strolled to our front door and walked in.

"Wait!"

I closed the door. "Hot tub?" Jenny looked at me.

"Are you serious?"

"I'd prefer an ice pack and that would be best, but maybe the hot tub will work the muscles. I'm a little sore."

Jenny grimaced. "I'm sorry." She had forgotten. "Sure. Hot tub it is, but not naked hot tub. I expect we'll have company fairly soon."

"Leave it to the feds to take all the fun out of life."

We ignored the pounding on the door and changed into our swimsuits. I lowered myself slowly into the hot tub before using my burner to call Stacy.

"On my way," she answered.

"Just let yourself into the house. The feds are outside and a little miffed because we wouldn't cave to their pressure. If you would be so kind, shut off the Jeep and bring my music player inside with you."

"You are going to be a full-time job, aren't you?"

"That's what I pay you for. I didn't expect anything this soon, but since you're on the payroll, might as well start earning your keep. Gladys from HR will handle your vacation days and such. You will get time off. We don't get in trouble all the time."

"I have a hard time believing that. I'm hanging up now. I should be there in about ten minutes."

"We're in the hot tub. Did you bring your suit?"

"I most certainly did not."

"You're not getting in naked," I replied.

"I'm not getting in at all. This isn't a joke, Ian. What did you do?"

"Nothing. That's our story, and we're sticking to it. See you in a bit."

Jenny eased into the water and took a spot in front of the jets. With a punch of a button, the bubbles began pummeling my back. I laid my head back on an inflatable pillow and closed my eyes.

"Are you going to fall asleep?"

"No. Too much on my mind." I kept my eyes closed as I talked. "You asked about trust. I hate counting on other people because it's too easy to be disappointed. I need Jimmy and Rick to come through for us, restore my faith. What little control I do have over my life involves you and what I myself can touch. Nothing else. Not Max. Not Jimmy, and definitely not the bureaucrat."

"We'll make do, and we'll be fine. You are an excellent judge of character. You haven't been wrong."

"I was right about you, sultry temptress."

Jenny laughed, then found her way across the hot tub and pushed herself against me. "Maybe I was right about you, too."

"Maybe. I might be a bad influence, too. I'm sure your parents would not approve."

"They would not. Until now, and then they would," Jenny suggested. "They trusted me, just not as much as my older siblings."

We didn't hear Stacy arrive. She just strolled onto the deck. I rolled my head to face her. "I guess bubble time is over." Jenny hit the button, and silence returned. "Thanks for joining us on such short notice."

"What do these guys want with you?"

"They probably want to know our role over the past two days in dismantling a terrorist cell operating in Manhattan."

"Do you know anything about it?"

"We might," I answered.

"Will they have evidence of your involvement?"

"Then they don't need me to tell them anything. They don't have a warrant. I'm not keen on answering any questions."

"Since you probably don't have an alibi for the times in question, we want to avoid you talking with them in any way, shape, or form." She smacked her lips. "For my edification, what did you do?"

"Be careful about the questions you ask because the answers may be shocking."

"I still need to know, and this is entirely protected under attorney-client privilege. I lose my career if I tell anyone."

I turned to Jenny, and she shrugged.

"The vice president of the United States hired me to do a job under the direction of the CIA to kill the man funding the terrorist group. At the time of the contract, they didn't know the group was fully established in Manhattan because the attacks were happening around the world, but thanks to information gathered from rolling up the cell members, we determined that the main attack was going to happen right here. The World Trade Center. A nerve gas attack, but thanks to our efforts, agents are working to dismantle the device right now. They have the schematics for it, so it'll make their job easier. And eight or ten terrorists were killed, and the others incapacitated."

"Might have been twelve to fourteen. I lost count," Jenny added.

"Twelve to fourteen, but we left a few alive for the

Agency to question in the special way that they interrogate prisoners." Jenny and I nodded at each other.

Stacy closed her eyes and tipped her head back. "You were right. The answer was shocking." She shook herself free from the unreality of the situation. "If you're working for the US government, why are there agents here to talk with you?"

"Because of what we do, the ones we work for aren't so keen on telling people that we work for them."

"Because you operate outside the law," Stacy filled in.

I pointed at my nose.

"What do you want me to do?"

"Make them go away until our liaison with the Agency and the Bureau calls them off." I slid down until my neck was in the hot water.

"You can get out of the water. We need to get to work on talking through how to approach this."

"Today was a rough day. They didn't play nice, and I'm a little beat up. You making the bad agents go away will relieve a great deal of my stress."

"I'll bring them in here. You don't say anything. I'll do all the talking."

"That's why you're here."

Jenny pushed me toward the steps. "Fine. I'm getting out."

Stacy stepped back to avoid getting wet before going to bring the agents in.

We dried ourselves before taking a seat at the table by the pool. We had just sat down when Stacy brought the agents out. "Special Agents Smith and Johnson."

"Cool. Find yourself an Agent Wesson, and you'll be in business," I quipped.

Stacy held a finger to her lips.

"My clients are ready to address your questions."

I had thought we were going with something else.

Maybe she wanted to hear the questions and would advise us not to answer once the question was asked.

"We have evidence suggesting you were at a crime scene in Manhattan. The Wiggins household, where three men were found murdered, and one was discovered alive but in critical condition."

Critical condition? We'd left the one alive in good shape. The wheels started turning. I schooled my expression to one of passive indifference, hoping I sold it.

"Were you there, Mr. and Mrs. Bragg?"

"Don't answer that question," Stacy told us.

"On the advice of my legal counsel, I decline to answer that question."

Jenny pointed at me. "Same."

"In Lower Manhattan, another crime scene. Four men murdered, two men critically injured, and two men in stable condition. Were you in Lower Manhattan today?"

"My clients decline to answer that question."

"Is that how it's going to go, Ms. Milford?" Agent Johnson, the female, asked.

"Yes. It's going to go exactly that way."

Agent Smith's phone buzzed. He looked at it. "I'm going to have to take this."

He stepped toward the kitchen. "Not in the house," I called. He waved and answered his phone while walking around the pool to the farthest point from the house.

He talked in a hushed tone while we watched. Agent Johnson tried to distract us with more questions.

"You didn't exist before three years ago. Who are you, Mr. Bragg?"

"My client declines to answer that question," Stacy said in a cold and hard voice.

Agent Smith returned. "I have to go. Deputy Director Rohrbach is arriving at a helo pad just up the street. I'll be right back. Make sure they don't go anywhere."

"Interesting," Stacy said. "Maybe you shouldn't ask any more questions. We'll just sit here quietly and wait."

"While listening to music," I offered. Stacy pulled my music player out of her pocket and slid it across the table to me.

"Let the torture begin." She gestured at the agent to put her fingers in her ears. The woman had no sense of humor as she stared blankly.

I put on *Losing It* to set the mood. I stayed by the music console while Jenny and the agent sat at the table. By the end of the song, I could hear a vehicle pull into the driveway. I turned it off. I wasn't going to play the upstart routine on the deputy director of the Bureau. I wondered if Jimmy had sent him.

He walked in wearing a suit that might have looked fresh two days earlier. "If you'll wait for me in the car, I won't be long."

Agents Smith and Johnson didn't question the order. They deferred and hurried out. Stacy moved to the kitchen but stayed where she could watch us.

"I'm Ian Bragg, and this is my wife Jenny." I moved closer to him. He didn't offer to shake my hand, so I didn't push it.

He sat down before I could ask. I joined him and Jenny at the table.

"I've come here at the attorney general's request as part of a joint operation called Viscous Leather. Don't ask. We're given the names. We've been investigating terrorist activities on US soil but were running into roadblocks. It appears that you were able to remove those roadblocks and dismantle the organization over the course of two days. You don't need to deny anything. I've been read into the Agency's program. I want to thank you on behalf of a grateful nation. We have found the nerve gas, thanks to you. It has been quietly rendered inert and removed from the World Trade Center."

"That is good news, Mr. Deputy Director." I hadn't thought we would hear what the Bureau had done with the information. We would have known had they done nothing and the device flooded the tower with deadly gas.

"I know what you do. I find it distasteful. I have been a servant of the law for thirty-seven years. Delivering capital punishment without benefit of a trial makes my head spin, but I know our government will take that action on occasion for the ubiquitous reason of *national defense*, a term bandied about as if it were the get-out-of-jail-free card. That's when we must adhere to the law, not throw it away when it is needed most. Convenience does not trump the foundation that this nation is built on. Crisis does not a monarchy make."

I wasn't sure what point he was making besides trying to distance himself from the Peace Archive's relationship with the government, but calling off the agents, followed by a private meeting, inextricably linked him to me.

He continued. "I have no doubt that someone will call on you again. Ask you to do things that are convenient, outside the law, because you were lucky this time. Next time, who knows how many innocents will be killed? I wish there wouldn't be a next time. Not for me. You are the catalyst that will bring my retirement, Mr. Bragg. This isn't the nation that I have served my entire career. It's time for me to move on. I can't abide mercenaries working outside the law."

"People like me stopped a terrorist attack despite the billions of dollars funding your agency. As much as it may grate on your soul, none of this comes cheap, and I'm not talking a house in the Hamptons. I'm talking an organization capable of doing the hard jobs at the risk of their own lives. And Jenny and me? We could have just as easily died today fighting your war, but we were going to fight nonetheless. Even though I get paid a great deal for what I do, I believe in this country, and I will do what I'm paid to do. You get paid for what you do, don't you? Same difference. Making the world a safer place. The people get to live free while we take the risks. As George Orwell said, *'People sleep peaceably in their beds at night only because rough men stand ready to do violence on their behalf.'*"

"I'm not like you."

"No. Your organization asked a guy like me to do what you can't. Don't look down your nose at me, Deputy Director. You vetted the target. I only guaranteed conviction and punishment."

He screwed his face into a confused mask of pain. "Maybe it is time to retire because that makes too much sense. Whatever they paid you on the last job, they got their money's worth, which will make it too easy to do it again."

"Then maybe it's your responsibility to make sure that if someone is approved for targeting outside the law, that there is no doubt they are the right person. Unlike this time. They told me to go after the wrong person. Good thing we did more research from the inside. Have you ever supported someone going undercover and they committed crimes as part of the operation to get deeper into the target? Did you prosecute your undercover officer?"

I knew the answer, and he knew I knew. He shook his head.

"No difference except that what I do doesn't hurt innocent people. You need to make sure that is *always* the case."

He stared at the table with his shoulders hunched. He looked old and tired. He finally straightened, then stood.

"I'll take my leave now, Mr. Bragg, Mrs. Bragg. We will

make sure that your names stay out of all reports related to Operation Viscous Leather and its related cases."

He walked away without a further word. We stayed at the table, not bothering to escort him out. He didn't want anything to do with us, but he needed us. The seed had been planted to grow a tree of liberty, a tree that sprouted only because hard souls risked all for others.

CHAPTER TWENTY-THREE

"It's not what you look at that matters, it's what you see."
–Henry David Thoreau

After the deputy director of the FBI left, Stacy joined us.

"Don't tell me you were listening in." I brushed the finger of shame at her.

"You make a compelling argument," she replied. "Despite the emergency that turned out not to be, I'm glad that I'm on board. What is next for the Club?"

"The Club is a private place for golf, with good food and superior conversation. It has nothing to do with our side gig. It's the day job that keeps us legitimate."

"I work for an organization that operates outside the law in defense of those who can't protect themselves. I'm good with that."

"That's a good tagline! Don't ever say it out loud again," I cautioned. I clapped her on the shoulder. "You like vegan food, don't you?"

I stood, but my muscles were twice as stiff as when I'd

sat down. I thought the hot tub would have helped. Maybe I wasn't in there long enough, or maybe I had needed ice first.

Jenny watched. "My tough man is all beat up."

"Weren't you there too?"

"Wyatt Earp here put himself right in the middle of it all, where things were a little more active. My job is to watch his back."

I tried to maintain my dignity as I strolled toward the kitchen.

"That's probably the harder job. I applaud you, my sister."

I looked over my shoulder, a much greater effort than normal that only served to reinforce their point. I used the ice dispenser in the refrigerator to fill a glass with cubes, then wet a dish towel and put the cubes inside. I contorted an arm to get it into one spot. The cool started to take the edge off.

"Lay down," Jenny ordered. "All you had to do was ask for help."

"Have you forgotten that I'm a man?" I handed her the dishrag, gave her a kiss on the cheek, and returned outside to drop face-first onto one of the lounge-style chairs by the pool.

Jenny prepared a second ice pack and joined me. Stacy helped herself to the wet bar. "You said you had a room for me?"

"It's somewhere in there," I pointed toward the house.

"I think there are three or four extras. Help yourself."

Stacy finished mixing a rum and coke using the last ice cube the dispenser ejected.

"Can I get you something?" Stacy asked.

I mumbled a negative. Jenny nodded. "Perrier in the fridge if you don't mind."

Stacy returned with it and her glass to relax into the lounge chair next to where Jenny held the ice packs on my back.

"How often does the law get involved?" Stacy wondered.

"First time for us having to do the rug dance in front of the authorities. We had an operator arrested but were able to free him thanks to a technicality. Otherwise, none. Our people are good at what they do."

"How do they get good?"

"A couple years ago, I asked that same question. After that, we've had a couple retreats, believe it or not. Training and camaraderie, but we all use pseudonyms at the events. Unlike the Babs Jaekel debacle, our faces usually aren't in the media. Which means that we won't be able to attend any other retreats, but like I said, we have good people."

"An assassin retreat? I can't imagine what that looks like."

"We never use that term. We're operators. It's ambiguous enough. No one can have a clue unless they're on the inside, which means they are complicit. If one person turns, they take themselves with us, but there's no evidence. No one can get to the deep dark recesses where our information resides. Nothing is ever written down in any other forum, and the little scraps of evidence here and there are nothing more than circumstantial."

"Are you confident it works?"

"We don't usually work for the government, and our jobs aren't free-for-alls like you were just a party to. A single problem that needs to be removed. Which reminds me, have we heard anything about Gil Pickle?"

Jenny handed me her phone, and I did a quick search using the phrase 'Gil Wright latest sermon.'

The news popped up, showing his untimely demise.

The reporter had heard it was a heart attack. None of the reports suggested anything different. He had been overweight by a great deal, and it made sense. "Memorial service was today. The ex-president was in attendance, along with a legion of weeping followers. I wonder if this was the coincidence to end all coincidences?"

I handed the phone back to Jenny.

"He was an upstanding citizen," Stacy remarked.

"Not so much." I rolled my shoulders and stretched my back. "Thanks, beautiful. I think the hot tub is in my immediate future. Maybe…"

"We have company," Jenny interrupted. "No naked hot tub."

"I'll lock myself in my room!" Stacy declared. "You won't see me until morning."

I waggled my eyebrows.

"Still no." Jenny winked at me.

In this rare instance, "no" meant "yes."

"Max, how are you feeling today?"

"Slept like crap."

I ignored his personal distress for the moment.

"We extended the house in the Hamptons for another week. If you and the good folks who might be interested in joining the Club want to come by for a grill out, we can do something. We have a plan to expand the Club's membership without opening up a new brick-and-mortar facility. We'll remain based out of Chicago but will hold events at a vacation home here. We're looking at a couple properties today."

"Holding business meetings in a private home? You might need a license for that." Max was in poor humor. Maybe this sleepless night wasn't the first.

"Thanks for the tip. We'll never hold a business meeting. The people who attend will be there for the camaraderie of like-minded souls."

"Fun words. I might have to start using them. You don't mind if I do a little business too? I don't have a place in the Hamptons and don't want one. I prefer the French Riviera."

"That's a little far for the New York people. Critical mass. Getting the most opportunities in the least amount of time. We'll have to balance between Chicago and here."

"I'll put the word out to the right people whenever we have an address and dates. I'll join, of course, whatever the cost. Maybe I'll bring my family to the Windy City to experience a little of what you have."

"Wind. We have more of that than anything else. Sometimes it's warm, unless it's a cold breeze blowing to suck the life out of you. San Francisco is worse, but not by much. Still, we call it home, and the Club has a most excellent golf course. I'd love to treat you and take more of your money."

"That's how it works. You didn't call to make small talk, did you?" Max wondered.

"No. I called to check on you. A day like we had tests the strongest souls. You've not been around that kind of thing before, so I expected you might not feel right today. I only wanted to take your mind off the past by selfishly pitching the Club. The way is forward, not back."

"You are a strange man, Ian Bragg. Very strange indeed. I'll be fine. Maybe I'll take a day or two off to gather myself."

"Cancel your appointments. Reflect, unwind, and enjoy the world that we were able to recover. No one needs to know how the sausage was made, only that the end product is good."

"I'll keep that in mind. Thanks for showing me a world

outside of my world that I never knew existed. You're like James Bond."

"Flattery will get you everywhere. I'll text the details of another bash. If you bring any vegans this time, they'll have to eat the lettuce and tomato off the hamburger-making bar."

"I expect Albus will have a new girlfriend by now, but if not, then he'll bring Ashley."

"I see." I was hungry, already thinking of the good dishes we'd have in addition to one small option for the rest. Besides dessert, of course.

"We all got to see, and I'm not embarrassed to say that."

"Only because your wife isn't standing right there. You're sounding better already, Max. We'll see you when we see you."

"Roger. Over and out." Max's parody of military lingo made me laugh. He was right. He would be fine.

Stacy showed up dressed for a day trapped in the boardroom discussing strategic business worth billions of dollars. I wore my swimsuit for shorts and my workout t-shirt.

"I like my office attire."

"I like mine," she replied and added the side-eye as if I'd insulted her.

"I like Stacy's too," Jenny added, joining us from the kitchen with a freshly microwaved plate of leftovers. I was waiting until we had something that hadn't been in the refrigerator for a week.

"I've had plenty of time to think."

Oh, no. The worst scenarios ran through my mind. She was going to turn us in!

I rolled my finger for her to continue.

"The deputy director of the FBI was acting under orders. Who gives him orders? And I didn't feel like it was the director. The attorney general of the United States contracts work to Ian Bragg?"

"We get a lot of contracts."

"How many are ongoing right now?"

"Six? Seven?" I shrugged. I wasn't sure. We'd been out of the office for too long and needed to follow up on payments for the closed contracts. "And now you know more than any single operator out there. It's called plausible deniability. No one knows anything more than a few basic elements of the work. What's with the third degree?"

Stacy undid her jacket and slouched. "I took this job without knowing a lot of what I should know. With the added information, I'm confident I made the right decision. No one leaves your employ except in a pine box, I suppose."

I snorted. "We have people retire all the time. The game isn't for everyone, and it's not a long-term career. Our best people take one or two contracts a year total so they don't burn out. I hope someday I'll have that luxury."

"You're the boss. How can you not have that luxury?"

I pointed between Jenny and me. "*We're* the boss, but I don't have that luxury because of one man."

"Who?"

I shook my head. "No one gets to know that but Jenny."

My untraceable phone rang. I clicked accept and waited.

"Ian, are you there?"

"Mr. Vice President," I said and looked away. Stacy's eyes shot wide. Jenny poked her in the shoulder and held her finger in front of her mouth.

"Good work, Ian. I'm sure no one ever tells you that. They pay and bury their heads, hoping it doesn't come back to haunt them."

"It's nice to get a pat on the back. That was the hardest contract I've ever completed—sleight of hand with an army of kidnappers, terrorists, and murderers. Despite our success here, we didn't get any of the overseas organizations. I'm sorry about that."

"We have our people looking into that. We have a lot of assets at our command, Ian. Some are more expedient than others. When time is at a premium, we have to access resources that might not otherwise be viable. I'm glad you were with us on this one. I hope I never have to use your services again, but I know that's just wishful thinking. We'll need you again, probably sooner rather than later."

"Thanks for trusting me, Jimmy. This country is too important to put it in the hands of amateurs."

"I think I might use that at the next VP debate. Next year is an election year. I hope I can count on your vote."

"I used to like the non-politician version of you."

"He's still in here, but sometimes, you can't get elected without the votes."

"Only sometimes?" I made a face at Jenny.

"Oops. Never mind I said that. I saw pictures of your work when Justice briefed the president. I'm amazed anyone walked away from that, amazed and happy both you and Jenny survived. I have to go now, Ian. We'll still have you two over for dinner next time you're in town."

"We look forward to it, Jimmy. And yes, you can count on our votes." I ended the call.

Stacy's mouth hung open.

"What? If you tell anyone, I'll have to kill you."

Stacy snapped her mouth shut. "Is that what passes for humor in your world?"

"It does. Now you know our secret, but not the secret behind the secret. Let's keep it that way if you don't mind."

"No one would believe it. *I* don't believe it, and I'm sitting right here."

Food wasn't getting any closer while I sat there.

"We're having a party this weekend, probably Sunday. Come on out. It'll be the first meeting to determine interest in joining the Club, Chicago."

"What do they get for their money?"

"Access to special problem resolution services." I pointed at my chest. "A good meal and great company. It has significant value. Word will get out that it's the organization that's only for members who are at the top of their profession."

"I'm not at the top," Stacy suggested.

"You'll be carrying a tray of snacks."

"More humor?"

Jenny jumped in. "More humor. You're one of the close associates, so of course you're welcome to mingle. Just stay away from that Albus Porter guy. I think he's looking for his next conquest."

"That's his real name?"

Jenny nodded while checking her watch. She looked at me. "You need to change because it's time to go."

I went to change into my less casual casual attire.

"Help yourself to whatever. Lock the door on your way out." I waved over my shoulder one minute later when I was dressed and heading out. Jenny hurried after me.

We were looking at a new home built on the water. Twenty million. I did two double-takes at the price before Jenny brought me back to reality. We could afford it by loaning ourselves the money from our own account in the Caymans. As a business property, we could write it off while getting our money back.

That was the last thought I had about logistics and accounting. Once we saw the place, we made an offer. Life was too short to worry about ten million here or there. We had a business to grow. Next party would be at our house when we returned in the summer. We stopped by a local place after sending ourselves money to restock the cash pile.

We made it back to the rental house to find a black sedan in the driveway.

CHAPTER TWENTY-FOUR

"It's fine to celebrate success but it is more important to heed the lessons of failure." –Bill Gates

"What do you think that's about?" I asked.

"Defeated in round one, they're back for round two?"

I parked close to the house. We got out and headed for the door. The doors popped open, and two men jumped out. Swarthy men carrying US-made but based on a Russian design sub-machine guns, the Vityaz, firing a nine-by-nineteen-millimeter round.

"Get down," I shouted, but Jenny was already diving out of the way.

We had no way to shoot back, so the only course of action was to get away. Jenny hit, rolled, and came up running. The small-caliber round fired from a short-barreled weapon became less lethal the more distance one could put between it and them.

That was us. I hit and scooted forward, trying to put the Jeep between the men firing and me. Rounds embedded in the cedar shake siding on the house. The metallic ping suggested a round hit the Grand Cherokee, then more as they pelted the vehicle, trying to get closer to us. Jenny made it to the corner of the house and rounded it. A wave of fire swept in front of me as the shooters changed their firing position.

I ducked behind the Jeep and crouched to look underneath. One coming toward the front of the vehicle, and one headed toward the back. The Jeep was too low to get under. I had to go around to get to the men.

The magazine release clicked, and a magazine hit the ground. I made my move around the rear of the vehicle. By the time I cleared the rear hatch, the shooter was slapping the new magazine home.

I dove, hands outstretched for the weapon. I slapped the barrel away from aiming straight at me and grabbed the forward handgrip, driving it upward. My momentum carried me into the man, and he staggered back. I got my feet under me to leverage the Vityaz out of his hands.

With a final twist, it came free. I spun it and fired. He started to fall, and I pulled myself around him to use him as a shield. Bullets slammed into his body, but the rounds didn't have enough power to penetrate. The second shooter fired again. I dragged the body backward to get behind their sedan. The man tried to aim and fire. Out of the corner of my eye, I saw the upstairs window open.

Jenny launched a can toward the shooter. It missed his head but hit his shoulder. The weapon nearly fell from his hand. I ditched the body and ran, looking over the barrel and firing well-aimed shots through the windows of the Jeep and into exposed flesh. He tried to raise his barrel, and I finally had a clear shot.

I double-tapped his face, one through the eye and one through his cheek. He was dead before he hit the ground.

The men had almost nothing on them: driver's licenses and enough cash to pay the tolls. I called Rick.

"They sent two people after me and Jenny. That tells me the one calling the shots is here and has access to restricted databases like the ones for rental properties." There were a few people who knew where we were staying. Max and his friends. Stacy.

And thanks to Stacy's private gig before she joined us, Babs Jaekel.

"Barbara Jaekel. We need to look into who she's selling information to."

"Who's she?" Rick wondered.

"TV reporter with an affinity for creating the news."

"That's a tough one. Hard to get warrants nowadays on reporters."

"I have full confidence because if anyone kills me, I shall be very put out. Very."

Rick sounded like he had more life to him than the day before.

"Did you get enough sleep or something?"

"I did. It was a good night."

"What do I do with these two dead bodies?" I asked the second he was feeling good about himself.

"You have dead bodies?" Rick sighed so loud I had to move the phone away from my ear.

I gave him the address. "And send a tow truck, too. They shot up my rental. That'll be a hard one to explain. Good thing I bought the bumper-to-bumper insurance."

"I'm going after whoever sent them, Rick. Be warned. I will not be threatened. I will not be targeted."

"If you find who it is, let us know. We'd love to draw a big red X across that individual's picture."

"I'll be in touch," I promised.

Jenny came outside and examined me from front to back to make sure I hadn't been shot. I was sure I hadn't, but one never knew in the rush of a firefight.

Yet another firefight. How many soldiers served in this army?

"Get his gun. We're taking them, and I bet they have more ammunition." We each picked up a Vityaz and slung it over our shoulder. These weapons, even though they were only semi-automatics, were high-intensity close-in weapons systems slung for guard duty.

Or enemy attacks at their home. The thought made me furious. Targeting individuals where they were vulnerable was my business, but never with terror, and never waiting to shoot it out like a gunfight at the OK Corral.

No more. We were going on the attack.

The car doors were open. Little was inside, but when I popped the trunk, they had extra supplies like body bags, lime, and two shovels. We were supposed to disappear. Too bad they thought we'd go easily.

They also had four boxes of spare ammunition. Nine by nineteen-millimeter rounds weren't common. We sat in the entryway and reloaded the magazines after familiarizing ourselves with our new weapons.

"Not quite a precision weapon," Jenny noted.

"But it's all we have." I rubbed her shoulders. "Nice throw. You saved my life. Again."

"It's what I do. I enjoy the sex way too much to have to go through the rigamarole of finding another. That is exhausting." She smiled. "There are dead bodies in our driveway."

"Not anything you would have ever contemplated saying until you met me."

"And not anything I would consider being okay with, but I am. They tried to kill us. Screw them. They signed their death warrants when they took aim at us."

"Now you're starting to sound like me."

"It was inevitable, but I have to admit, I tolerate Rush. Maybe we can listen to something else on occasion?" She let the thought linger, then recoiled and stabbed a finger at me. "Did your eye just twitch?"

"It might have," I admitted. I wondered if those in cars driving by could see the battlefield that was the driveway.

Jenny went inside to get herself a drink. A black sedan turned into our driveway and parked away from the terrorists' sedan. A panel van pulled in behind us, and a wrecker parked on the street.

"Smith and Wesson," I called after the agents got out.

"I hate you," Agent Johnson said.

"That's the spirit." I pointed at the men. "These bastards came after me and my wife. We've taken their weapons, and we're going to find the one who gave them the orders."

"You see," Smith started, "this is where we would have captured them and questioned them for that information. But we can't do that because Cowboy Ian is on the case. I don't know who you think you are, but we've been told to accommodate you, so we're going to clean up your mess. Again! I saw what you did at the Wiggins house. I saw the workshop, too. You're dangerous, and I'm tired of cleaning up your messes."

"Not sorry. If you had done your job, you wouldn't have to clean up after someone doing it for you. Haul our Jeep out of here and return it to the rental company with your standard 'this is FBI business' explanation. We're taking their sedan."

"It's crime scene evidence. You can't have it."

I frowned. "You seem to have misunderstood your guidance. What I do is not for you to say yes or no to. You just take care of what you're supposed to take care of, like cleaning up my messes. Chop-chop." I headed for the car. "Oh, yeah, they brought this stuff."

Jenny and I pulled the body disposal kit out of the trunk and tossed it on the ground. "Just in case you were wondering what they were going to do to us after they killed us. We're on your side! Maybe you should open your eyes to what's possible. Terrorists. Right here. Shooting up the Hamptons. And you hate *me*? I think you need to check your priorities."

Before I became enraged, it was time to go. I suspected they would soon stop tolerating my alpha male put-downs. Those two would still hate us because we made them feel impotent.

We drove out and down the block, then pulled off to the side. I called Stacy. "Hey, Boo, do me a solid and give my smartphone number to Babs Jaekel. I'd like to talk with her. While you're doing that, find out where she is right now so we can talk with her face to face. If she calls, we won't interrupt whatever she's doing. Did you file that lawsuit?"

"Of course. You have an invoice coming for fifty thousand dollars. Are you going to tell me what this is about?"

"Good thing you didn't take the day off and stay at the house. The terrorists may have murdered you. My suspicion is that Babs gave the bad guys our address. Whether intentionally or unintentionally is the big question and will determine if she gets to meet her Maker today."

"Damn, Ian. When can we leave for Chicago?"

"Next plane out. Maybe tonight. We'll see what Babs has to say. Quick as you can, Stacy." I clicked off.

"Maybe stage ourselves in Queens?"

"Let's get closer to where we're going to have to go. I guess if you turned on the radio, I wouldn't freak out. I have my music player on me in case you only find stations that suck. Why don't we ever get a car with a working satellite radio? The Boneyard is calling my name."

"Aha! You *do* listen to other music. Why didn't I know this before now?"

"Because you tolerated Rush. Is there anything else you're tolerating that I should know about?"

Jenny pointed at the next turn. "Nope. That's why I put up with your music, because if that's my only complaint, then life is pretty good. Except the part where three different times in two days, someone has tried to kill you."

"If someone's trying to kill you, you try to kill 'em right back!" I shouted.

"Doesn't sound like Rush."

"*Firefly*, next best thing." I tried to keep the humor train rolling, but the gravity of it all weighed me down. On the Gomez hit, the security guards and the dirty cops had come after me, but they didn't know who I was. Once the head of the cartel had been taken out, they'd lost their will to be loyal. This was different. These people would keep coming.

They held grudges for a thousand years. "Let bygones be bygones" didn't apply. No. I needed to kill the one in charge if we were to ever live free again. They would only have to get lucky once. We'd have to be lucky every day. I didn't like those odds.

I also didn't like playing defense.

We hadn't reached Queens when Stacy called. Jenny answered. Unlike her, I couldn't hear the person on the line.

Jenny asked Stacy to text an address. She ended the call and gave me the thumbs-up. "She's at the station, so Stacy asked her to meet us in Queens."

"How serendipitous." I wasn't looking forward to seeing Babs. The woman grated on my soul. I saw her as nothing more than a bloodsucking leach.

Jenny guided us to a major grocery store parking lot. We kept our firearms on the floor in front of our seats and got out. We leaned against the trunk with our arms crossed, probably looking like we were waiting for a drug deal. After two minutes of being overly obvious, we went for the loving couple look.

"I'm glad you're not upset."

"About this morning?" She snorted. "After a few years with you, that's business as usual, even though it was a hundred and eighty degrees from the usual."

I winced. That sounded like something I'd say. She was becoming me.

"Gotcha," she said. "I like the business tycoon life, but the fast-paced run-and-gun is what we train for. Still, I would prefer if we didn't do the front-line stuff. You've played the game. It's okay if you leave it to the others. We have good people. Since you've taken over, no one has left."

"Because we get good contracts, thanks to you. Good and lucrative for everyone involved."

"Purveyors of coincidence. Was the good reverend's time up, and we paid someone six million to watch a man die?"

"I don't want to know." I shook my head. "Sometimes, it's best not to know."

Five more minutes passed before a minivan pulled up next to us. The cameraman was driving. Babs hopped out but stayed well away from us.

"I have to say, I was quite surprised to get your call. After that business with the lawsuit, which the newsroom took too seriously, by the way, I'm surprised you didn't get a restraining order. Everyone else does."

I had to appreciate her candor. "How many do you have?"

She held fingers two inches apart. "What kind of scoop are you going to give me?"

"Scoop, yes. I have something a little more important than your next story. Who did you tell where we lived?" I took a casual step toward her while Jenny maneuvered to her side.

"No one. After you poached my investigator, you left me high and dry. The lawsuit was the icing on the cake."

I lowered my voice. "You told someone. In the newsroom. In casual conversation. The editor, maybe?"

"Editor doesn't care about those details. We don't talk about our stories until they're final because our own people will scoop us. It's dog eat dog in there." She tried to stare me down but seemed to understand the gravity of the situation. She turned toward the van. "He knew."

The cameraman. He had all the information.

"What's his name?"

"Sammy Baker," she replied. She squinted at me as if I were going to reveal a great secret.

"Maybe the accent is on the last syllable, and it's pronounced Bakkar."

"How did you know? He corrects us, but we're working on him. He's been here for fifteen years. Assimilate already!" She laughed.

I eased toward the sedan. "Just a lucky guess." I opened the door and tucked the weapon behind me while I returned to the reporter. At the last second, I dodged past her and shoved the barrel through the open passenger window.

"Don't move, or you'll die, and it'll hurt the whole time." He reached for the gear shift. I lunged inside, using the Vityaz as a bludgeon to drive the barrel into the back of his hand right where it would hurt the most. He jerked away from the gear shift. Jenny ran to the driver's side and stood at the window.

He cradled his hand in the other, grimacing at his own touch. Broken hands can keep even the most stalwart from taking further risks. Now we could have a real conversation.

CHAPTER TWENTY-FIVE

"Time is the school in which we learn, time is the fire in which we burn." –Delmore Schwartz

"Take his phone."

While Jenny wrestled with him, I climbed into the passenger seat. Babs watched intently. Her face twisted through a wide range of emotions.

He wouldn't give up his phone. Jenny had two hands on it but couldn't pry it from his grip. I rabbit-punched him in the side of the head, he dropped his arms for a moment, and the phone came free.

Jenny tried to access it, but the phone was keyed to facial recognition. I held his head steady so she could aim the camera at him to unlock the information. When it opened, I let go. He groaned. Jenny stepped back. I took the keys out of the ignition and handed them to Babs.

"Your cameraman is a bad guy," I stated.

"Is that how you refer to people? They're either good or bad?"

"Pretty much. And he's bad."

Jenny showed me the phone, angling it away from the reporter. Lots of calls to the same number. She kept scrolling while calling Stacy on her phone.

"Can you check some numbers and addresses for me, please?"

"I used to be somebody," Stacy complained.

"And now you're a highly paid nobody, which is the best place to be," Jenny shot back. "Get us that info. This is important."

"Closing in on the kingpin?" Stacy asked. In the background, a computer keyboard was getting worked over.

"Something like that. I'll hold the line open." Jenny jammed her phone between her shoulder and her ear to listen while she searched the phone of the man known as Sammy Bakkar.

Many of the apps were in Arabic, but only the ones off the main screen. Those, like the mapping app, were in English. The façade showed one thing while behind it, there was something else. GPS was turned on, probably because of his work with Babs. He'd forgotten to turn it off.

"Stacy, check these addresses." Jenny read off five addresses. When she read the fourth one, it was familiar.

"That last one is the station. The first one is his home. I don't know what the other ones are."

"Fourth one is Casa de Wiggins."

"Just the second and third ones, please," Jenny corrected. She handed the phone to me. I scrolled through but was ill-equipped to deal with anything in Arabic. I recognized innocuous phrases, greetings, and goodbyes.

"I can't tell you anything," I admitted. I did the next best thing. I called Rick.

"We gotta stop meeting like this," Rick answered.

"We're on the trail. I'm in possession of a cell phone

that probably has some links you want to know about. It's unlocked because we have our sympathizer right here. He might be an active player, but he's currently riding the wave of getting punched in the head."

I took his picture and texted it from my burner phone. I took shots of Bakkar's apps with my phone and sent them one after another.

"Open the messaging app."

"Which one is that?" I asked.

"Third from the left, top row."

I opened it, and a list of contacts appeared with the top line of the threads. "I'm going live. Can you stream?"

"Of course. Bring it up."

That made things go faster. I held my phone upside down with my chin and held Bakkar's phone in front of it. Rick directed me.

In the second message screen, I saw our Hamptons address.

"You see it?" Rick asked.

"All too clearly. Who is that to?"

"Some guy who calls himself Whisper if I read it correctly. We'll get someone on it. Let me dispatch someone to pick up the phone and the target. Is he still alive?"

"I can't believe you'd ask a question like that. Of course, he's still alive. Only because the reporter is here, but I think your Bureau boys will shut her down with some well-placed threats."

"These will be Agency types. This is international, so we've taken the lead."

Rick put his phone down while he made another call. He used a string of codewords that were mind-boggling. The first one was Viscous Leather. The operation was still live.

When he came back on, I asked, "Any other attacks outside the US?"

"None. Looks like those action teams went to ground as soon as the attacks were complete. Despite their lethality, the real target was right here. Now they're seeking retribution on the one who foiled their plans."

"And that's why I'm going to take care of this right now."

Jenny tapped me on the shoulder.

"The address is a strip club. There's an apartment above it. The club's name is Whispered Secrets. It's right here in Queens."

"Time to go clubbing," I suggested.

"What about me?" Babs asked, grabbing my arm.

"That violates the restraining order." I stared at her hand until she removed it.

"You said you didn't get one?"

I flicked my fingers at her to go away. She climbed into the back seat of our car. I growled deep in my throat. Under no circumstances could a reporter watch us in action.

"When the nice people from the Agency arrive, you're going to go with them and tell them everything you know about him." I pointed at the woozy man behind the wheel of the minivan.

A minute later, two vans raced toward us and blocked both vehicles. I pointed them to the side. They parked where they were and got out.

"Move the van, and take her with you." I opened the door to the sedan. She scooted to the far side, but I had had enough. I grabbed her foot and dragged her out, taking her by the arm before she fell on the pavement. "You set us up, and then they came after us. You're complicit, and men are dead because of it."

The man in a dark turtleneck and sunglasses relieved

me of my burden. He passed her off to another, who forced her into the back of the van. The first man took the phone and ran his finger gently over the screen to keep it from locking. "Good stuff," he said in a deep bass.

He gestured with his head, and a third individual moved the van.

"He's a sympathizer at the least, an active terrorist at the worst." I nodded at Sammy Bakkar.

"We'll take care of him. Now, you were never here. Go on."

"I like that. We were never here."

I hung up on Rick. Jenny and I got in and carefully backed out. No sense in drawing attention to squealing tires. We slowly rolled away, following the directions on Jenny's phone. In the rearview mirror, the agents were manhandling the individual called Sammy Bakkar while another scrolled back and forth on his phone.

A strip club. Seedy but not. It was in a decent area of town. Not upscale, but not rundown. It had a good parking area with numerous cameras visible. Maybe they deterred crime or extracurricular activities that came from too much beer and too much testosterone.

We drove by and parked on the next block over.

It was still closed. I was surprised to see that it was only two-thirty in the afternoon. Fighting for one's life slowed time. I had seen it in the Sandbox. We'd get into a vicious firefight. We'd clear the area, and on the other side, after sending the enemy packing, we'd find that thirty minutes had elapsed. Two weeks of buildup for ten minutes of intense action.

It was how things worked. In this business, it was even less. A month of quiet reconnaissance, followed by a few seconds to make the hit. Then egress and disappear. This contract was more like a military operation. I knew I didn't like it. Too many people involved.

And now Babs was getting read the third degree by the Agency.

I smiled. It couldn't have happened to a more deserving soul. I was sure she'd report about it, but how she couched it? That would determine whether she would get fired and ostracized or not.

I wondered how she'd manipulated people to give her information on us. She had paid Stacy to follow us. She must also have had a mole in the Loneham. Why not? Important people stayed there.

Jenny and I put our weapons in a couple of reusable shopping bags and strolled casually down the street. One of the terrorists' hoodies was on top to provide some bulk. The other had only the weapon. Jenny carried that. No one would suspect a woman of packing a weapon like the Vityaz.

We strolled to the steps at the side of the building and headed up a rusting but stable staircase. At the top, we knocked on the door. It was metal and opened outward. There would be no way to kick it in and breach the building.

I didn't expect there would be an answer, but it was all we had besides top cover from the FBI and the CIA, so we were far more bold than normal. A typical day would be setting up shop in a nearby building with a window from which we could see the door. We'd watch for a week to determine any patterns. We'd find his vehicle and put a tracker on it.

More pattern analysis. Then we'd find the weakness. Determine a way to make the hit. Then close the contract and disappear without a trace by leaving the city and the state. Local authorities had little reach, even with murder.

When the person making the hit had no relation to the victim, there were no threads to pull. For murders that weren't committed as part of a drug deal or a theft, nearly all of them were by people who knew the victim.

Most of these murders went unsolved. When it came to the Peace Archive, *all* of those murders went unsolved.

We retreated down the stairs. The squeak of a hinge alerted us to the door opening. A large man who looked like a bouncer came out.

I turned around and took a few steps up. His hand went inside his jacket. I stopped and held my hands where he could see them. The shopping bag dangled from my fingers. "I'm here to see Whisper. I'm bringing cash." I slowly reached into my pocket and withdrew a small wad of hundred-dollar bills, then pushed them back in.

He waved us forward.

Random people delivering cash to a code name. That confirmed we were in the right place and doing the right thing.

"The cash," he said with an accent.

"*As-salamu alaykum*," I said as I approached, putting my hand over my heart. He nodded. I started moving my hand down toward my pocket as I stepped onto the landing. I continued rotating and drove my hand upward, delivering a finger strike to his throat. I followed with a knee to the groin and moved behind him to get a grip around his head, using my body weight to leverage sufficient force to break his neck.

I pulled his body inside the small entryway and relieved him of his nine-millimeter. Jenny followed me in and closed and barred the door, then hoisted her weapon and dropped the bag. I threw the hoodie over the man's face and took my Vityaz out.

There was a small room off the short hallway leading to the living area. Soccer played on the flatscreen television on the wall. It reeked of cigarette smoke despite the small window being wide open and a fan blowing it outside.

A small screen on the desk showed a feed from a camera hidden above the door. I hadn't seen it. I unplugged the device, pulled the memory card from its front, and shoved it into my pocket. I wiped off the device with my sleeve.

Jenny waited at the door with her weapon aimed down the hallway.

I finished my quick search and left the room. I stalked toward where the corner of the living room was visible. I listened for sounds that someone was there but only heard the soccer match.

After blowing out a breath, I aimed the short barrel of the Vityaz and peeked out the door. The living room was empty. It opened to a kitchen. A second hallway led from the open area.

The furniture seemed off, scattered with too much space between. I gestured to Jenny to tell her that no one was inside. She moved forward, tiptoeing to avoid making a sound. I crept into the living room, keeping to the wall away from the second hallway. I passed the double door of an elevator that led directly into the apartment.

Convenient, as long as one had a key to the club downstairs. I wondered if the space between the overstuffed chairs allowed for private dances.

At the end of the hall, I ducked around it with my eyes down the barrel: three open doors plus a bathroom at the end. The first door to the right had the game on. I waved Jenny to where I stood. She took aim down the hall because I couldn't cover the room and watch my own back.

I couldn't tell how many people were inside if any. There were no other sounds besides the match.

Jenny took aim while I hugged the wall on the same side as the room. My heart beat too quickly. I needed to calm down. Building clearing was one of the most dangerous actions an operator could take. The instant you could see them, they could see you.

Violence was what I had learned to use to gain an advantage. Put an enemy on his heels. Take charge of a situation, then decide how to defuse it.

I lined up on the door and picked a spot on the floor where I'd plant my outer foot to turn my momentum from sideways to forward. With the semi-automatic nine-millimeter compact ready to fire, I jumped left and accelerated into the room. A man in a wheelchair sat with his back to the doorway. He worked the keyboard with a wall of screens before him. Three tower computers stood side by side under the wide table being used as a desk. Two more laptops were open on top.

He said something in Arabic without turning around. I lunged forward, yanked him away from the table, and ripped the keyboard out of his lap. He recoiled in surprise but recovered quickly.

Two shots echoed down the hallway—a double-tap. I eased to the side, my muscles as taut as a steel beam. Like he had been sitting with his back to the door, my back was to the door, and at least one hostile had been out there.

"Everything okay, honey?" I called.

"One for one," she replied.

"One here, neutralized."

"A woman?" the man asked in nearly unaccented English.

"There's a lot to be said for hiding an evil lair above a titty bar," I said.

"You make it sound like this is a joke."

"Not a joke, apprehension of a mass murderer. I should just kill you now and save everyone the grief, but your status suggests they'd make a martyr out of you. No, I think I'll turn you over to the boys who'll make you disappear and probably make it look like you embezzled the bar's funds on your way out. That would be justice." I called over my shoulder, "Can you take charge of our boy? I need to make a phone call."

Soft footsteps tracked toward me. I leaned back against the wall and kept an eye on the opening while watching our captive.

Jenny stopped when she reached the doorway.

"Out of the line of fire, please."

She hurried forward.

"Kill him if he tries anything. He's disgusted that there's a woman on the team that captured him. He may seek martyrdom instead. Grant him his wish. He'll never know that he failed everyone who believed in him."

I moved into the hallway and backed toward the living room as I dialed Rick's number.

"You're killing me, Ian," Rick answered.

"I'm pretty sure we have the mastermind behind it all. Send…" The soft ding of the elevator arriving made me stop. I dropped the phone and took aim.

The doors opened, and a man stepped out. He looked like a bodyguard, just like the others. He carried a pistol in his hand. I never hesitated. First shot in the head and second in the chest. He bounced off the doorway and fell into the living room.

A second person inside the elevator moved out of sight before sticking a pistol out and firing haphazardly around the room. Five shots. No matter what he was carrying, he had more shots remaining.

"Whispered Secrets," I shouted. "Send everyone."

The person in the elevator fired twice more, then the doors closed. I stepped in front and sprayed inside, left and right. I didn't think they'd stop the rounds. If nothing else, I got his attention so he wouldn't want to come back.

I found the doorway to the stairs. It had two deadbolts,

and they were engaged. I hurried back to the hallway. It was still clear. If someone occupied the other rooms, I suspected they would have already come forward. I picked up my phone. The screen on the burner was shattered and dark.

I put it in my pocket screen out so I didn't get glass bits where I didn't want glass bits.

I headed down the hallway to where our captive shouted an endless stream of invectives. Jenny had pulled him out of his wheelchair and deposited him face-first on the floor. She had her knee in the middle of his back.

"He was a little too incensed for me to keep looking at him," she said casually.

I gave her the thumbs-up with my non-shooting hand and continued down the hall. The final two doors faced each other. The one on the left was probably the master bedroom. It was bigger. The one on the right was probably a guest bedroom or a storeroom.

I took my chances that the master bedroom was unoccupied.

I was wrong. I charged in and ran to the side, where I wouldn't be seen by anyone in the second room. A blonde woman sat in the bed with the covers pulled up to her neck. She stared at me through eyes wide enough to see the white round the pupils. Her mouth hung open in a silent scream.

"Put some clothes on," I snarled. "The police will be here soon, and you want me to tell them that you cooperated."

She nodded and started to cry.

"Get out of bed!" I roared. She jumped up buck naked and put her hands on top of her head, fingers clasped and facing out.

A person experienced at getting arrested. I braced myself in case she was feigning her fear and grabbed her shoulder to propel her toward the door. The golden trickle that followed her suggested her fear was real. A quick glance revealed a man's robe. I snagged it off the bathroom door and followed the woman into the hallway, then ducked my head in and out of the second room, a small bedroom. If someone was under the bed, I'd leave them there for whoever Rick sent.

If he sent anyone.

I gave the robe to the naked woman. "Put it on." I pushed her forward while she pulled it over her shoulders. It was far too big. She weighed probably ninety pounds. It made me wonder if she was underage.

Probably. She had a problem stepping around the dead body as she froze and stared before shrieking.

I pushed her against the wall. "Switch," I told Jenny.

She moved into the hallway. The woman had her face in her hands, blubbering.

"Stop it. I'm sure you had nothing to do with any of this." She put her arm around the young woman's shoulders but kept her Vityaz aimed across her belly.

I was proud of Miss Jenny for maintaining control while trying to console someone who was probably distraught. I wanted to give her the benefit of the doubt but couldn't afford to.

I grabbed the man by the back of his neck and dragged him out of the room and down the hallway. I left him on the floor, away from anything he could use to pull himself upright. I couldn't find a way to lock the doors, so I ran to the kitchen and pulled drawers open until I found the silverware. I took the butter knives and returned to the elevator, where I jammed them under the doors to block them from opening.

At least without some effort by people in front of them who we could shoot through the door. Our best defense was to wait for help. We didn't need to exit.

I had gained confidence in Rick's ability to support his operation.

We moved toward the door leading to the outdoor stairs. I left the man face-down in the hallway while Jenny watched them both, plugged the outdoor camera in, and waited for it to come back to life. Without having to do anything, the screen flickered and showed the outside landing and stairs.

One man moved slowly up the stairs.

"How many thugs do you have?"

"Believers," the man corrected. "You will experience my wrath for decades to come!"

"Doubt it," I replied.

"You will die," he said in a deep and dramatic voice.

"News alert," I started while watching the man outside approach. "Everyone dies. Some sooner than others, like in the case of your believers."

When the man positioned himself in front of the door, I fired eight rounds from knee-high to head-high, then ducked back into the room to find the man was down. Bullseye.

"Phone, please," I said to Jenny. She shook her head. "Still in the car."

The same place I'd left my untraceable phone. It was irreplaceable since Vinny had never told me who'd made it for him.

I looked for a corded phone, but there wasn't one. The woman. "Where's your phone?"

She glanced from our captive to me and at the dead body leaning against the wall.

"He's sleeping," I offered.

I gestured for Jenny to take the young woman back to the bedroom and retrieve her phone.

Jenny nearly dragged her in the rush to get through the living room.

The elevator door dinged. I took my foot off our boy's back and jumped toward the end of the hallway, where I hosed down the door with everything I had left in that magazine. I leaned against the wall to pop the magazine out and put another in. A glance showed my captive trying to crawl toward the security room.

"Not so fast, buddy boy." I grabbed his foot and dragged him back down the hallway toward the living room, then picked him up and tossed him on the couch.

The door dinged again. Whoever was inside unleashed a barrage of rounds into and through the door. My captive started screaming in Arabic for them to stop. The incoming fire stopped immediately.

A round had hit his atrophied leg. I wasn't sure if he felt it. Probably not. He looked angry, not in pain.

"So, you don't want to be a martyr. No surprise there. The guy in charge never leads from the front."

He glared flaming daggers at me.

"What do you know about leading? You only know about destroying!"

"I don't care why you got into the evil overlord business. I only care that you killed Marines and innocent civilians."

"Even in your own words, your Marines are not innocent."

"War is between governments, with the people stuck in the middle. Don't be angry with the hammer for hitting the nail. Look to the one who wields the hammer. In this case, it's you. You're swinging wildly. That ends today."

I held my position behind the crippled man in case anyone fired through the door again. He was as good a candidate as any to shield me from the ones he'd sent after me.

I kept my weapon trained on him. If his people made it in before help arrived, he'd be the first to die.

Jenny reappeared with the woman, nearly dragging her. She waved the phone, her weapon slung around her back. They stepped into the living room, and the elevator door dinged. Jenny jerked the young woman backward. Jenny had a great deal of height, weight, and strength on her side. The woman flipped backward like a rag doll.

I waited, weapon raised. The doors remained jammed shut. I felt proud of my handiwork. Days like today made little victories seem so much better. And the big victory of taking out a terrorist mastermind.

If that was what he was, he'd put out the hit on Jenny and me. That was enough for him to die in my book. But if I turned him over to the Bureau or the Agency, he'd never see the light of day again.

That worked for me. He couldn't get off because of a technicality or a good lawyer or because someone had broken into his home and killed his bodyguards. That might poison the evidence well a little bit.

Someone pounded on the door to the stairs. "Police, open up!"

CHAPTER TWENTY-SIX

"When you get into a tight place and everything goes against you, till it seems as though you could not hang on a minute longer, never give up then, for that is just the place and time that the tide will turn."—Harriet Beecher Stowe

I moved closer but remained out of the line of fire. "There's no rush, so don't come in. We're not going to hurt anyone." I thought for a moment before adding, "Send a negotiator."

"How about we send a boot up your ass?" the gruff voice replied.

"Tempting. How about we don't but say we did?" I shot back.

"I'm being held against my will!" my captive shouted. I backhanded him across the face.

"He is correct. He's a terrorist, and he will be held the rest of his days against his will. Send a negotiator, and we'll talk to them to clear this up."

"What's there to clear up? We've got dead bodies all

over the place out here. We're going to give you one minute to surrender, or we're coming in."

"Check the weapons on those dead bodies. Are any of them registered? There's no rush. I'm going to call the media and let them record how you're putting this guy's life at risk by being in a hurry. He's in a wheelchair, for Pete's sake. Just sit back and relax. Don't put an artificial time on me. That tells me you might be dirty and on this guy's payroll. Are you dirty?"

"Hell, no!" he yelled.

"Then wait. No one is getting hurt. We have an innocent woman in here. She was his plaything or something. I'll send her out the back door if you keep your people away."

"Send her now. Show good faith."

"I'll send her when I get some guarantees from the negotiator. Send in the negotiator because I don't trust you. You don't have everyone's best interests at heart in here."

I looked at Jenny. "Call Rick," I whispered loudly and gave her the number. The young woman tried to pull away, so Jenny put her on the floor and held her down with a foot.

Jenny put the call on speaker and turned up the volume. "What happened, Ian?" Rick asked.

"Whispered Secrets. Send people right now. I have your man, the guy leading this parade, but we're blockaded inside his evil lair, which is above the strip club. Get here right now and call off the cops. Right now, Rick!"

"You have us scattered from coast to coast. Stay on the line. Let me see if I can break free any assets."

"Kingpin. Here. Nothing else is more important. If the police get in here, my wife and I are going to die, and your boy is going to walk free. Well, ride free because he's in a wheelchair. We have all his computers, too. You'll want those, which to keep him from spiking them, you need to take possession of before anyone else."

Rick never answered the question. He had already gone elsewhere to make the phone calls. I couldn't fault him. He wasn't a dispatcher, but he was burning up the phone lines as if he were.

"One minute," the voice called from behind the door.

"Go down a few steps and take a seat. We're working out some issues in here. Did you look at those guns yet? Unregistered or stolen, aren't they?"

He didn't answer. I moved a chair in front of the door, then stacked a second on the first. They wouldn't hold for more than a second or two, but it was the best I could do. Furniture in the room was sparse owing to the resident being in a wheelchair.

Not at present, though. He sat uncomfortably on a couch, away from anything he could grab.

He hissed at me as I returned, and I backhanded him across the head. "I can do this all day. Just sit there and accept your fate and the fact that your fortress was left undefended since you sent all your boys after me and none of them made it back."

"Ian?" The voice came from the cell phone, forgotten in Jenny's hand.

"Yes?"

"They're five minutes out. See if you can hold on."

"What if I can't?" I asked. It sounded like more feet were pounding up the stairs. The elevator door dinged.

"Then we'll hold a party in your honor. Pin a note to the asshole's chest to inform the good guys in blue not to let him out of their sight until we get there."

"I'm sure they'll abide by that." The door vibrated when something slammed into it. They were coming. "Gotta go."

I took aim.

"Get in the bedroom and lock yourself inside." Jenny

shoved the woman behind her. She ran a few steps and turned into the computer room.

"Stop her!"

Jenny bolted after her. I could hear the struggle in between the chopping on the door as if they were beating it with a fire axe.

That suggested they weren't police. I punched my captive in the side of the head. He toppled sideways.

I moved to the side of the room, away from where I had spoken before.

The young woman flew through the door and slammed into the wall. Jenny came out, bleeding from one arm. She punched the woman hard, driving her head against the wall.

"She was trying to get at the computers," Jenny said.

I gestured for her to toss her into the living room, where she'd have no cover.

Jenny obliged, but she was out cold. She lay on the floor crumpled in a ball, but Jenny was between her and the computer room in case she regained consciousness.

The elevator door dinged once more. A metallic clang suggested they were trying to pry the door open. I used a hatchet motion to fire. Jenny hit it from one angle, and I fired two rounds from my position.

The front door finally gave way, and the chairs toppled. Two men with pistols behind a balding man wearing a blue Security t-shirt fired into the room as if the death of the innocents didn't matter.

Maybe it didn't. Jenny didn't fire. She saw the blue and thought they were police. I fired one round at each man. The first spun as I moved my aim off center mass. The second man took a round in the chest, and the third bravely ducked behind the second. He sprayed the room with a black pistol. I didn't see anything more, but it sounded heavier than a nine-millimeter.

It didn't matter. At this range, anything could be deadly. I fired twice more, painfully aware that I was running low on ammunition. I wasn't sure how many rounds I had left.

"Not police," I shouted at Jenny.

She fired at the chairs, which didn't stop anything except us from seeing what was going on.

Someone started hammering on the back door. "Police! Open up."

I dashed down the hallway and checked the camera. Uniforms. "Criminals up front. Go that way!" I yelled at the door. They had a ram, but the bar across the heavy door was designed to defeat such breaching techniques.

They hit it three more times until the officer was unable to continue. He backed down the stairs, taking the tactical team with him.

Back in the living room, all was quiet. Fluff from the overstuffed chairs floated through the air. My captive stirred but stayed down. I dropped the magazine. Two rounds, plus one in the chamber. I slammed it back into place.

I looked at Jenny. She was on her second magazine too.

"Rick, we could really use a hand here."

"Police! Don't shoot."

"Don't come in, then," I called back.

"There's a lot of dead people out here. It's time to stop the killing," a calm voice replied.

"I couldn't agree more. In less than five minutes, the feds will be here and explain the situation. They'll take my prisoners into custody, and we'll be out of your hair."

He laughed.

Definitely not on Whisper's team.

"Man, if someone else is willing to do the paperwork on this one, they can have it."

"I feel you, big man. I hate this as much as you do. Bureaucrats gotta bureaucrat. The good guys won today.

Have your people check the weapons. They'll find none of them are registered. Most were probably reported stolen."

"We're already on it."

"Take a seat and have a smoke. As soon as my people get here, I'd like to shake your hand. You may have saved our lives."

"Probably not. I bet there's a lot of blood on those hands."

There was no answer I could give where I wouldn't be lying.

We waited in silence. Jenny slid down the wall and sat. I leaned over the couch so I could beat on my prisoner if he caused any trouble.

New voices sounded from the steps, familiar voices but hardly friends.

"Smith and Wesson," I said. "Glad you could join us."

"I hate that guy," the female agent remarked to her partner.

"Weapons are down," I said as I kicked mine away from the couch. Jenny slid hers down the hallway behind her. "And I'm moving the obstruction away from the door."

I pushed the chair on top to the side. A balding sergeant looked at me. I held up my hands. "No blood."

Agents Smith and Johnson climbed up the stairs and pushed the bottom chair out of the way.

"Here's your guy, but the Agency probably wants him."

Johnson produced a pair of cuffs and put them on him. "Where's his wheelchair?"

"Computer room. First door to the right. That's the prize right there. Walk softly inside. Smart people are going to be digging deep into that gold mine."

"Who's she?" Agent Johnson asked.

"Scumbag sympathizer. Played us up until she tried to get at the computers, then she got her bell rung."

Johnson stretched up to get close to my face. "I really do hate you."

"Wesson suits you better. You should consider changing your name."

She shook her head and backed away. She returned with the wheelchair and looked Agent Smith in the eye. "He wasn't kidding."

A minute later, the people who had taken away Babs and her cameraman arrived. After a brief skirmish, the Bureau left with the man who called himself Whisper.

"Can you get us some attendant shirts so we can carry a stretcher with a dead body out of here and then walk away?" I asked the police sergeant.

"Since you're with these folks, I guess it won't hurt." He motioned to a uniform behind him. She hurried down the stairs. "What'd this guy do?"

"The Marines in France, the head of the counterterrorism branch, the chapel in Annapolis. Those were all done on his orders and with dirty money. Every corpse you see? The blood is on his hands."

"Maybe it won't hurt to shake your hand. My nephew's in the Marines."

"*Semper fi.*"

We left the sedan in the airport as yet another abandoned vehicle and headed for the first-class lounge to decompress before our flight to Reagan National. Jimmy wanted to see us.

"No more of that," I said.

"I concur. Criminals, yes. Terrorists, no," Jenny agreed.

"I'm thinking we won't get a bonus."

Jenny snorted. "We're lucky to get paid at all. The government is involved."

"Maybe we can let them keep it if they stop taxing the Club."

"Do you think that's how it works?" She leaned back and made a face.

"I know that's not how it works, but a guy can dream, can't he?"

I opened my computer and started the VPN to make it look like I was connecting from South Africa. We had our backs against the wall so no one could see. I accessed our accounts in the Caymans. "Would you look at that?" I pointed at the screen. "Mark paid, too. That's twelve mil I wasn't expecting to see. Mark's and Rick's money looks good in our account."

"Happy clients all around. Kinda takes the edge off buying a house for twenty million."

"It's mind-boggling." I snapped my fingers. "I feel like the Saint. Maybe I can call myself Simon Templar and you Joan of Arc. Jenny du Arche."

"No." Jenny tapped a finger on my keyboard until everything closed out, then shut the laptop. "Enough of that. What's next, Mr. Ian Bragg?"

"I have to say that I liked our around-the-world cruise. It might be time for that again."

"But only if someone runs the company while we're gone. Do you have anyone in mind?"

I frowned and eventually shook my head.

"We need to be on the lookout for the next chief so you can get out of the game altogether. We *can* get out of the game."

I looked at the computer.

"How much more money do we need?" Jenny asked.

"I'm thinking half-million-dollar bonuses to every operator. Just because. It's only twenty-one mil. Seems like we have that in petty cash."

"If you give it away, then we'll never have enough to retire." Jenny's green eyes sparkled.

"I could give it all away, and we would still have enough to retire. I can make a mean Shirley Temple and you could deliver them to thirsty customers, but only if you wear a sexy outfit."

"You'd be fine with other men ogling me?" Jenny raised her eyebrows.

"There seems to be a flaw in my retirement plan. I guess we have to keep working, then."

"What do you think Jimmy has in store for us?"

"Dinner and another ridiculous gig. I want to tell him no."

"Then tell him no and be firm about it. This one was a total goat-rope. Did you see what they did to our rental car?"

"Not our smoothest operation. It's good I wiped my fingerprints off the smooth surfaces because heaven forbid if the authorities linked us to all that."

Jenny chuckled. "I don't know what to say to that, but you have fans! Smith and Wesson."

"If they never see us ever again, it'll probably be too soon. And Rick! That guy. He probably loved it when we called. 'Hey, Rick. More bodies, send a clean-up crew with a buffer and some touch-up paint.'"

"Do you think we'll see him again?"

"Sooner than we're both comfortable with, I expect, even though I bet he's going to have his hands full since he's got all those refugees we left for him. What is that, five or six that he's going to get to talk with?"

Jenny nodded at the flight notification board. "Looks like the flight is boarding. We better get down there. Do you think they'll have the boys in sunglasses waiting for us?" Jenny wondered. "To give us a ride, not take us to prison."

"It's good you clarified that. I can't wait to get home to Chicago. Too many bureaucrats out here, trying to out-bureaucrat each other. 'Can you sign this form?'" I laughed. "I think that will be funny for the rest of my life."

I took Jenny's hand as we walked.

"You asked what was next. More contracts. A retreat. An opportunity for our people to keep doing what they do. And expand. The New York City connection is going to pay off. We may have to expand the northeast region. I better get Lou on the hook."

"From grunt to CEO at the flip of a switch."

"I have to say that I like the view from here. But I also like to take care of things personally. I'm complicated."

"You're not," Jenny replied. "We'll stay in DC long enough to see my brother and sister."

I grimaced.

"It's not that bad."

"It's always that bad. Can't I just go back to the simple life of an operator?"

THE END OF A FATAL BRAGG
IAN BRAGG WILL RETURN...

While you're waiting for the next story, if you would be so kind as to leave a review for this book, that would be great. I appreciate the feedback and support. Reviews buoy my spirits and stoke the fires of creativity. In the interim, maybe you'll want to check out Rick Banik… **https://geni.us/RickBanik1**

If you follow me on Amazon, they'll let you know when my next book is released.

Don't stop now! Keep turning the pages as I talk about my thoughts on this book and the overall project called the *Ian Bragg Thrillers*.

https://geni.us/IanBragg

AUTHOR NOTES - CRAIG MARTELLE

Written September 1, 2021

I can't thank you enough for reading this story to the very end! I hope you liked it as much as I did.

When good people have to do bad things. I bring you Ian Bragg. And since I already brought you Rick Banik, I thought I'd tune him up in a little bit of a crossover. I hope you liked seeing him.

Rick is back, and book #2 in his thriller series is coming soon. *Loss of Power*. I hope you like it.

Of course, Rush! If you haven't already, Ian's Rush playlist is on Spotify—drop by and listen in.

https://open.spotify.com/playlist/2JdhUojL1sK8wOm76OHsfr

I like BrainyQuote—they do me right when I'm looking

for the quote that matches the chapter. https://www.brainyquote.com/

With Jimmy Tripplethorn in the picture, it moved some of the contracted work to DC, where we also have Rick Banik. I thought a crossover made sense. If you didn't know, Rick Banik has his own series of thrillers. Look for *People Raged and the Sky Was on Fire*, the first book in the Rick Banik thrillers.

And more Alaska. Always more to see and do up here. Sixty-five degrees north is an interesting place to live, a land of extremes. As I finish this book, it has finally gotten dark again after a few months of being light 24/7. It's always nice to see the stars. It rained for most of August, so I didn't see the sky until a few nights ago.

This is a great place to live to see the wonders of nature. There are a certain number of compromises that have to take place to stay here, but once those are settled, the beauty is nearly unrivaled.

Peace, fellow humans.

If you liked this story, you might like some of my other books. You can join my mailing list by dropping by my website craigmartelle.com or if you have any comments, shoot me a note at craig@craigmartelle.com. I am always happy to hear from people who've read my work. I try to answer every email I receive.

If you liked the story, please write a short review for me on Amazon. I greatly appreciate any kind words; even one or two sentences go a long way. The number of reviews an ebook receives greatly improves how well it does on Amazon.

Amazon—www.amazon.com/author/craigmartelle

Facebook—www.facebook.com/authorcraigmartelle
BookBub—https://www.bookbub.com/authors/craig-martelle
My web page—https://craigmartelle.com

Thank you for joining me on this incredible journey.

OTHER SERIES BY CRAIG MARTELLE
- AVAILABLE IN AUDIO, TOO

Terry Henry Walton Chronicles (#) (co-written with Michael Anderle)—a post-apocalyptic paranormal adventure
Gateway to the Universe (#) (co-written with Justin Sloan & Michael Anderle)—this book transitions the characters from the Terry Henry Walton Chronicles to The Bad Company
The Bad Company (#) (co-written with Michael Anderle)—a military science fiction space opera
Judge, Jury, & Executioner (#)—a space opera adventure legal thriller
Shadow Vanguard—a Tom Dublin space adventure series
Superdreadnought (#)—an AI military space opera
Metal Legion (#)—a military space opera
The Free Trader (#)—a young adult science fiction action-adventure
Cygnus Space Opera (#)—a young adult space opera (set in the Free Trader universe)
Darklanding (#) (co-written with Scott Moon)—a space western

Mystically Engineered (co-written with Valerie Emerson)—mystics, dragons, & spaceships
Metamorphosis Alpha—stories from the world's first science fiction RPG
The Expanding Universe—science fiction anthologies
Krimson Empire (co-written with Julia Huni)—a galactic race for justice
Zenophobia (#) (co-written with Brad Torgersen)—a space archaeological adventure
Battleship Leviathan (#)– a military sci-fi spectacle published by Aethon Books
Glory (co-written with Ira Heinichen) – hard-hitting military sci-fi
Black Heart of the Dragon God (co-written with Jean Rabe) - a sword & sorcery novel
End Times Alaska (#)—a post-apocalyptic survivalist adventure published by Permuted Press
Nightwalker (a Frank Roderus series)—A post-apocalyptic western adventure
End Days (#) (co-written with E.E. Isherwood)—a post-apocalyptic adventure
Successful Indie Author (#)—a non-fiction series to help self-published authors
Monster Case Files (co-written with Kathryn Hearst)—A Warner twins mystery adventure
Rick Banik (#)—Spy & terrorism action adventure
Ian Bragg Thrillers (#)—a hitman with a conscience
Not Enough (co-written with Eden Wolfe) – A coming of age contemporary fantasy

Published exclusively by Craig Martelle, Inc
The Dragon's Call by Angelique Anderson & Craig A. Price, Jr.—an epic fantasy quest
A Couples Travels—a non-fiction travel series
Love-Haight Case Files by Jean Rabe & Donald J. Bingle –

the dead/undead have rights, too, a supernatural legal thriller

Mischief Maker by Bruce Nesmith – the creator of Elder Scrolls V: Skyrim brings you Loki in the modern day, staying true to Norse Mythology (not a superhero version)

For a complete list of Craig's books, stop by his website —https://craigmartelle.com

Made in United States
North Haven, CT
01 August 2022

22123615R00165